by Jane Duncan
My Friends the Miss Boyds
My Friend Muriel
My Friend Monica
My Friend Annie
My Friend Sandy
My Friend Martha's Aunt
My Friend Flora
My Friend Madame Zora
My Friend Rose
My Friend Cousin Emmie
My Friends the Mrs Millers
My Friends from Cairnton
My Friend My Father
My Friend the Macleans
My Friends the Hungry Generation
My Friend the Swallow
My Friend Sashie
My Friends the Misses Kindness
My Friends George and Tom

My

My Friend the Swallow

Jane Duncan

Macmillan London

ISBN 0 333 11301 2

First published 1970 by
MACMILLAN LONDON LIMITED
London and Basingstoke
Associated companies in Auckland, Dallas, Delhi,
Dublin, Hong Kong, Johannesburg, Lagos, Manzini, Melbourne,
Nairobi, New York, Singapore, Tokyo,
Washington and Zaria

Reprinted 1983

Printed in Hong Kong

For George

PART ONE

'Speak of the spring and foison of the year'

from a sonnet by SHAKESPEARE

EARLY in September of 1956 I returned to St. Jago from a holiday spent in Scotland and my husband and our friend Sashie de Marnay met me at St. Jago Bay airport. The first words that my husband spoke to me were: 'You look ten years younger' and when we went out of the air terminal to the car, where Sashie was waiting, he struck an attitude of amazement and then said: 'Speak of the spring and foison of the year! She has called back the lovely April of her prime.'

'Thank you both very kindly,' I said, 'but time does not go backwards and spring, foison and April apart, this is September and autumn of the year and I am forty-six.'

I was so happy that I was almost drunk with it and I was trying to anchor their feet and my own to the ground. My holiday had been spent with my family and mainly in the company of my brother's four young children and I felt that they had given me some of their own plentiful venturesome ebullience, so that this moment might have been that other moment six years ago when I first met Sashie at this same airport, when a new life, bright with

7

promise was opening out before my husband and myself. But under the happiness was the knowledge that this was not that other moment of six years ago, for much had happened in the six years and not all of it was happy. Anxiously, I looked at my husband, trying to see him truly and not through the shimmer of joy at being back beside him.

He had been nicknamed 'Twice' because of his repetitive Christian and surnames, Alexander Alexander but the nickname had an accidental aptness of application to his character. He did things, big things and little things, like putting my luggage into the boot of the car as he was doing now, in a way that brought to mind phrases like 'neat and tidy', 'sure and certain' or 'once and for all', repetitive phrases that suggested firmness and finality.

In 1953, he had become ill with heart disease and he had done this with characteristic firmness and almost with finality, for he had nearly died and since that time there had always been a shadow of anxiety in a corner of my mind. Our doctor had advised him not to risk the British climate and I had been persuaded to leave him and go to Scotland by myself only with the greatest difficulty, so it was disconcerting, although happy, to discover that my absence of some six weeks had done him good rather than harm. I had thought he needed my constant care but this had not been so. Even in these first moments, it was obvious to me that he had come up over the shoulder of a hill, leaving the valley of his illness behind at last, out of sight and out of mind.

I do not mean to imply that a physical miracle had occurred. His heart was permanently damaged and would never return to normal, I knew, but in my absence his mind seemed to have shed the consciousness of illness which had hung over and between us during the last three years. The change in him was a subtle one, yet it showed in his bearing, his attitude to Sashie and me and the situation of my return as if this little event were his affair, under his control and to be carried through in his way. This was how he had been

8

before the illness, the illness which had taught him to bow before it, to defer to the opinions and instructions of the doctors and the rest of us, to allow himself to be managed. His eyes and chin now reminded me of the first moment I had seen him at a small engineering works in south Scotland, when I had been made aware that this Works Manager, Mr. Alexander Alexander, was one of the most managing and unmanageable of men.

'Get in,' he said to me now, opening the door of the car, 'and don't stand there staring and letting the sun burn your hide off' and I felt rise in me the impulse of those stormy early days of ours to say: 'Don't you boss me around. I'll stand and stare if I choose.'

As he turned the car out of the airport park and on to the road that would take us to the town of St. Jago Bay, he said: 'You picked a rotten day to come back. The Sugar Congress is in full swing. I shall have to dump you with Sashie until lunch-time and I have another meeting in the afternoon but one of Sashie's drivers can run you home if you like.'

'Since when have you taken to sitting on your backside at sugar meetings?' I asked, using his own phrase for such activity while Sashie, in the back of the car, giggled mischievously.

'Since the Congress started last week,' Twice told me. 'Mackie is reading a paper on the final day and I want to hear the other papers for comparison. I am prepared to admit that I think I am getting corns on my tail, though. Here we are. You go with Sashie, darling. I shall see you at lunch.'

'Not even a tiny speech assuring her of your love, Twice, darling?' Sashie enquired. 'Even something clumsy like: I am glad you are back but I have this meeting to attend?'

'I am glad –' Twice began obediently, his mind engaged on something else until, realising what he was saying, he barked: 'Get the hell out of the car, the two of you! I am late as it is.' Sashie and I got out of the car, which swung

9

away with a spurt of gravel, leaving us staring at one another.

'What has happened to him?' I asked.

'Are you pleased with it, darling?'

'It is a sort of miracle. I can hardly believe it. But what has caused it? My going away and leaving him to stand on his own feet, to find himself?'

If this were so, I would feel hurt and foolish because all my care had gone for naught, had indeed been doing more harm than good.

'That perhaps, but that is only a very little part of it. It is all very complicated, as everything else is,' Sashie told me. 'Let's go inside, darling, out of this brouhaha.'

Brouhaha was a mild word to describe the noise of chatter and tinkle of ice in glasses that rose into the hot sunlight above the crowd that was gathered in the Peak Hotel that day. St. Jago had a large and profitable tourist industry, of which the Peak Hotel, owned by Sashie and his partner Don Candlesham, was fashionable and expensive peak, but the tourist season proper did not begin until October. To-day, it was crowded with the residents of the island, an island whose main crop was sugar and the air was shrill with many voices as they exchanged greetings and gossip over glasses of iced gin.

There were the wives of the sugar men who were attending the Congress, there were the representatives of oil and machinery firms, there were the owners of the town's larger stores, there was an air of all the world and his wife being present and present for the one simple reason, the hope that, by the end of the day, they might have achieved some material benefit. A husband who was third engineer at one sugar factory might have attained the post of second at another, a contract for the supply of oil or equipment might have been obtained or Mrs. A. and Mrs. B. might have been lured down to the department stores to see the new stocks of dresses. I had seen it all before, down the years we had spent in the island but now, fresh from my brother's small country home in Aberdeenshire, I saw it differently and did not much like what I saw, as we paused in the doorway of the crowded hall that led to the equally crowded patio bars and the lawns beyond.

It was only when we began to make our way forward, however, that I became aware of something that was different from the atmosphere of former years. The chattering crowd parted to allow us to pass and suddenly a woman I hardly knew and whose name I could not remember said: 'Janet, how nice to see you back. Did you have a good time?' and other voices, voices of people I knew only vaguely, echoed her: '– you back. Nice! Good time?' And among the effusive greetings, the ranks parted before us, making an avenue for our passage, until I was invaded by a feverish notion that, at any moment, a royal red carpet would appear on the floor before my feet. This notion was made more pronounced by Sashie taking my hand and laying it on his upheld forearm while he strutted beside me through the ranks which looked as if, at any moment, they would sink in a wave of bows and curtseys and I was much relieved but still puzzled when we had attained the privacy of Sashie's suite in the main building. Sashie's face now wore a mischievous smile and before asking him what was happening, I looked hard at him for a moment. The most remarkable feature of the human race, in my opinion, is that every member of it, although made up of similar parts and features, is so different but most of us try to conform, in surface ways at least, try to sink our differences and to resemble some imaginary norm. Most of us try to find common ground with the other members of the race but Sashie did not subscribe to this idea. Sashie specialised in emphasising his differentness and life had conspired with him by making him strikingly different from other people. He was half-Russian, half-French and had British nationality. He was only about five feet six inches tall and very slightly built but when he appeared in the midst of a crowd, such as the crowd that filled the hotel at this moment, he could if he wished become its centre and dominate it. It was not commonly known that he walked on two artificial legs, the result of being shot down in his fighter aircraft by the Japanese in 1945 and Sashie had turned this difference from other men into a further asset of his own kind. He danced and minced about on his artificial legs, wore brilliantly coloured clothes and could adopt absurd affectations of speech and manner, all of which, in the tight little white society which was about three per centum of a coloured island, made of him a small waspish outrage. The coloured people liked him because, in his dealings with them, he dropped his affectations and was scrupulously forthright and honest but although the whites tried to regard him as a figure of fun, many of them were uncomfortable in his presence, as if they were vaguely aware that he was a sinister deriding comment on their petty ambitions, pettier intrigues and defensive conventions.

On this forenoon he was dressed in slacks and silk shirt of a brilliant blue that was almost iridescent, as if floodlights were shining upon him and now he made me a deep obeisance reminiscent of the court of the first Elizabeth and raised my hand to his lips. Aware that this was a satirical comment on our progress through the crowd beyond the closed door of his sitting-room, discomfited by what I could not understand, I felt my temper rising, for I have a tendency to take refuge in rage from any situation that I find uncomfortable.

'Look here, what is going on around this place?' I asked sharply. Sashie was unperturbed. He was an excellent mimic and now turned himself into the bluff hearty Sir Ian Dulac who owned Paradise sugar estate where Twice worked and where we lived.

'By Jove,' said the voice of Sir Ian, 'nothin' like a week or two in the old country for bringin' back the old thunder, what?'

'There will be more than thunder if you don't explain this carry-on,' I threatened.

'Darling, do sit down and stop being so exhausting.' I sat

down and glared at him. 'A double slug of whisky?' he enquired. 'You look like a thwarted gun-moll.'

'Stop being stupid, Sashie. Tonic water and a slice of lime, please and give with a short explanation that I can understand.'

He put his small hands on his hips, his head on one side and studied my face. 'So intelligent,' he said, 'and so politically stupid. Remarkable and so very refreshing, my sweet.' He turned away and came back after a moment to hand me a tall glass that tinkled with ice. 'Long long ago,' he said, 'before you went away to Scotland, we had an earthquake here in the island, remember?'

He had drawled out the words 'long long ago' and they seemed to lie upon the shaded air of the room like a skein of mist. Across this skein, I looked into his bright dark eyes while I marvelled, not for the first time, at Sashie's capacity to understand things that I felt and could seldom express. The earthquake had happened only about seven weeks ago, but during those seven weeks I had been to Scotland to visit my family and so much had happened to me in an emotional sense that the short period seemed like a lifetime. Sashie understood that it was like this for me and with the words 'long long ago' he told me that he understood.

'I remember,' I told him.

'And Rob Maclean, the manager of Paradise, was killed, remember?'

'I remember,' I repeated bleakly. My friends, Rob and Marion Maclean had been crushed to death by a stone pillar that fell a few yards from Twice and myself.

Sashie shrugged his slim shoulders and by a slight gesture of his head indicated the crowd of people drinking and chattering beyond the jalousies that screened the windows. 'Le roi est mort, vive le roi,' he said.

The ice in my glass clinked as my hand jerked. 'Twice, you mean?'

'Who else?'

13

I nodded my head. 'Stupid of me,' I said, 'but I hadn't thought of it.'

'Standing in your relation to Twice and with your knowledge of his health, you would not think of it,' Sashie told me.

'Twice looks remarkably well but he could never live the life that Rob Maclean lived,' I said after a moment, 'flying from island to island all round the Caribbean – all those meetings and sugar jamborees. Twice loathes meetings and—'

'I don't think it is a case of *could* live,' Sashie broke in on me. 'Twice *would* not live the life Rob Maclean lived no matter how physically fit he was. The role of manager of Paradise does not necessarily entail flying from island to island and being big noise at sugar jamborees. Rob Maclean made the job into a certain thing that suited Rob Maclean. Twice, I am certain, would stamp the job with the mark of Twice Alexander.' Repeating that slight movement of his head, he again indicated the crowd beyond the windows. 'That lot out there expect another Rob Maclean, a man who enjoyed being able to make or break the career of any sugar engineer, chemist or agronomist in the islands but you ought to know better than anybody that Twice is not another Rob Maclean. Twice is a person and not a position and if Twice took the position of manager of Paradise, he would be, quite simply and directly, Twice Alexander, Manager of Paradise and no more interested in sugar politics and the careers of other men than he has ever been.'

'There is no need to get up such a head of steam and go on as if I were half-witted,' I said. 'All right, I was wrong about the nature of the job but let us get down to facts. Has Twice been offered the appointment? Has he told you so?'

'No but I am sure that Madame and Sir Ian would like him to take it.'

Paradise, unlike most of the other sugar plantations in the island, was not part of a large combine but was privately owned by the Dulac family, Madame Dulac who was nearly ninety, Sir Ian, her son who was in his late sixties and Sir Ian's son, Edward, a man of about thirty.

'Is Edward still here?' I asked now.

'No. Back in London, the faithless brute. He should have stayed here eating his heart out like the rest of your lovers.'

'I wish you would stop being silly. What do *you* think about Twice and this appointment?'

'I think Twice has been waiting for you to come back before making a decision.'

'I know that. I noticed something on the way back from the airport but I didn't know what it was. This explains it. But you haven't as you well know answered my question. When you threw that fit of passion about Twice being different from Rob Maclean, were you not telling me not to discourage him from taking on this job?'

'I would not presume to *tell* you anything, my sweet.'

'Oh yes, you would,' I contradicted him. 'You are very good at telling me things for my own good and I am very grateful. Sashie, tell me honestly what you think.'

He looked down at the toes of his small shoes. 'If I were you,' he said, 'I would encourage him to take the appointment but I am not you. This is a decision which you and Twice have to make, Janet. All I can do to help is to make a few observations.'

'All right. Observe.'

'Twice would like to take this job,' he said positively. 'If you did not exist, he would have taken it already but if you did not exist, Twice would not be here to take it. He would be dead. Complicated, isn't it?'

'Not very. All I want is for Twice to have what he wants.'

'I know, my sweet, but there is no use in your letting Twice take the job and then fretting yourself to death with anxiety. If you go along with this at all, you have to go along with what the poet Milton called a gladsome mind.'

'I see.' Now that I knew Sashie's opinion, I shelved the

problem until later. 'You have been seeing a lot of Twice while I have been away, Sashie?'

Before I went, he had promised to 'look after' Twice for me.

'Your going left a vacuum, darling. It was natural that your two lovers should coalesce to comfort one another.'

I ignored this. 'You have helped him, Sashie, and I am grateful.' I laughed suddenly. 'You are the most unlikely pair. You must have looked very comical sitting round Guinea Corner together.'

'I always wore my dark grey suit, of course,' said Sashie wickedly. 'One did not wish to give rise to any strange suspicions. And much of the time, too, we were à trois.'

'Oh? Who was the third member?'

'A little girl, a newcomer to the island who has attached herself to Twice, darling. You know how they do.'

I knew how young people, male and female, attached themselves to Twice.

'She is a clear-headed independent little thing,' Sashie continued, 'and won't be a nuisance or create scenes. And Twice and I are not really such an unlikely pair, darling. We are deeply alike in that we have both been stopped in mid-career.' It was very seldom that Sashie spoke of his disability and I waited in silence until he spoke again. 'Of course, I am *much* better than Twice at being a physical wreck. It happened to me when I was much younger so that I have had much more practice at it. And it is much easier for me in any case because I never wanted to do madly energetic things like building sugar factories or to climb up and down and around them as Twice likes to do. But people like you and me, darling, who have no ambitions except to go on from day to day have to understand that people who build sugar factories naturally have an ambition to go higher and higher in the sugar business and to be manager of Paradise Estate and factory is really quite high in this way and of course Twice would enjoy being up there.' He nodded in the direction of the chatter beyond the jalousies again. 'Those people out there see in him another Rob Maclean but that is merely a habit of thought that the manager of Paradise must be a bombastic tycoon. And you and I have a habit of thought that Twice is an invalid. Twice is neither a tycoon nor an invalid but a sensible man with an opportunity to top off his career in a satisfying way and he should be allowed to do it without being beset by your and my anxious un-glad minds nagging at him. Have I made myself clear and shall we now chat of something else? How was your holiday? You had a good time, obviously.'

'I had a splendid time and yet there is nothing to tell about,' I said. 'When I look back on it it was nothing but cooking food for the children to eat, seeing that they were clean and settling the rows between them but it was all marvellous. What else has happened since I have been away?'

'Nothing, darling. Everybody is a little older but none are any the wiser, except myself of course.'

'In what way have you grown more wise?'

'I have decided that I have arrived as a hotelier. This place—' he waved a hand that seemed to sketch in the air the old plantation house, the new additions, the bungalows, the boat-houses, the bars and patios, the beach, the lawns, the gardens, the arbours that formed the luxurious complex of the Peak Hotel on the site of the former Peak Plantation – 'is now complete. It is reliably organised and staffed and Don has his women and his motor cruiser. It no longer needs me.'

'What you mean is,' I said, 'that you have coined a packet out of this place already and that it will go on coining packets of its own momentum now.'

'There is no need to put it so crudely, darling, but if be crude we must, you are quite right. And there is also the fact that I am sick to death of the bloody place. Also, I feel a new foison rising in me, the need to make a new departure. Don't you like that word foison? I am mad about it just now and use it all the time.'

'So I notice. In south Scotland, it is pronounced fooshion

to rhyme with pooshion, which is poison. Old Mattha who helped us in the garden at Crookmill had a lovely word – fooshionlessness. We had two silly women who helped us in the house who we called Loose-an'-Daze and Mattha said they were fooshionless and that the way they carried on was pure fooshionlessness. In what direction is this upsurge of foison leading you?'

Sashie listened for a moment to the noise from beyond the windows before he said: 'It is so very dull to arrive, even as a minor hotelier. Every arrival, every mission completed is a little death, a foretaste of the death that lies at the end, one supposes. Tout lasse, tout casse, tout passe. But let us be more cheerful.'

'I should think so, too. You are being very middle-aged suddenly. Of course, you *are* middle-aged – thirty-nine, now, aren't you?'

'I am still seven years younger than you,' he said spitefully.

'I am not beefing about my age. What are these plans for cheering your grey hairs on their way to the grave?'

'You know Silver Beach?'

'That little coconut property along the coast?'

'I bought it the other day.'

'You will be a riot in the coconut business,' I said.

'I do not propose to take the coconuts seriously. There is a good little Georgian house along there, falling down with neglect but basically good. I have some decent furniture lying in a warehouse in London. It has been there since 1939, costing me a fortune. I thought I would repair Silver Beach, have the furniture shipped out and spend my declining years contemplating the waters of the Caribbean.'

I shook my head. 'It won't do, Sashie. You will turn Silver Beach into another Peak Hotel before you know it. Like my grandmother, you have got to be *at* something.'

'But not hotels any more, darling. I am not the hotel sort in any case. I only set this place up because of Don, because it seemed to be a quick way of making some money for him. After all, he kept me alive in that Jap holiday camp as I told you once and naturally I felt that I had to do some tiny thing for him in return. When we got back to England, I discovered that Don had the most extraordinary ambition.'

'Is running a hotel so extraordinary then?'

'Darling, Don didn't want to run *anything*! All Don wanted was to be rather rich.'

'And is that so extraordinary?'

'Don't you think so? Isn't it odd not to want to do anything or be anything except rather rich? Although I must say that now that Don is as rich as he wants to be, he is very good at it. He never tires of his absurd canoes, his skin-diving, his smelly motor cruiser and his cars. I have never seen a child more contented among his toys. He never gets bored and he never overdoes the drink or the food or the women or *any*thing, as I should do in his place. He is madly moderate about everything, including being rich. He does not want to be a multimillionaire or anything.'

'Maybe he is very wise. At least he has arrived without dying of it as some seem to feel on arriving.'

'Darling, how very nicely put,' said Sashie and added sombrely: 'but I wish that one were sure that he wasn't *born* dead. However, let that pass. The point is that my responsibility to Don is now discharged. I shall continue to keep an eye on him and on this place of course but in a dilettante sort of way. Indeed, perhaps I intend to be just that, a dilettante.'

'What Twice calls a fiddler-about. Yes. I should think you might be quite a success at that. What in particular will you fiddle with – the coconuts?'

'I doubt whether even I could be lightsome with a coconut but I am sure that some suitable material will turn up. In the meantime, you and Twice will visit me at my new residence?'

'Frequently,' I assured him.

At that moment, the shaded light of the room became dimmer as a group of people came close to the outside of the windows and two of them propped their shoulders against the wooden jalousies to derive benefit, no doubt, from the cooled air from the conditioner that escaped between the slightly open slats.

The main nucleus of the hotel was the old plantation house with thick stone walls and these jalousied windows which were becoming a rarity in the island for, in modern times, there were few joiners skilled enough to make them. Sashie had preserved the jalousies of the Peak and the wooden slats turned silently and smoothly on their pivots, allowing those inside the room to see out but preventing those outside from seeing in, other than by coming close to the woodwork and peering through between two angled slats. The people outside were a group of women and one of the backs against the woodwork I could identify as that of Miranda Beaumont, from the ill fit of her garish cotton dress and the multiple strings of red beads that spanned the back of her neck.

Miranda and her husband Hugo owned a shop in the town called 'Milady's Bandbox' which catered to the tourist trade with cheap native basket-work, costume jewellery and clothing. Miranda advertised their wares by wearing them herself and was always dressed in ill-made, garishly-coloured cotton dresses, while her scrawny neck and arms were invariably hung with necklaces and bracelets made from brightly-coloured island seeds or shells. Today, she was wearing a tight sleeveless dress of brilliant poison green, the sort of dress that depended entirely on cut for its success but Miranda's was not a success. It was too narrow round the chest and too wide at the neck so that, between her shoulder-blades, there was a gaping pocket of material standing out from her knobbly spine as she leaned her hips against the window-sill.

'She is back,' her voice said, 'but the boy-friend didn't come back with her.'

Sashie caught me by the wrist and drew me in silence into a corner beside the window.

Like all societies, the small white society of the island

had its leading personalities and Miranda had long since established herself as the leading gossip. She was extraordinarily malicious and never at a loss for an audience, although the members of that audience, later, would assure each other that they did not believe a word that she had said. Miranda's position in relation to the other women reminded me of the position of a girl called Jean Stewart who attended the village school I went to as a child. Jean knew every 'bad word' in the language. The rest of us knew them too but Jean was different in that she was not afraid to say them out loud, had no fears that God or our headmaster, Dominie Stevenson, might hear her and punish her. Like Miranda, Jean never lacked an audience and I have come to think that both served an obscure but useful purpose in their societies. They provided an outlet for the frustrated malice or 'badness' of their fellows who, having listened only passively, felt free of the guilt of malice or badness. The children, later, would assure one another that the Dominie would catch Jean some day, just as the women, later, would assure their husbands that, some day, somebody would sue Miranda for slander.

Preceded by a shrill giggle, her voice came again : 'When she arrived, she disappeared as usual with de Marnay. I wonder how she will take to the new manager's new girl-friend?'

As I realised that I myself was the subject of Miranda's discourse, I saw Sashie silently lift the lid from the thermos bucket, pick up the ice tongs and lift out two large blocks of ice. The tongs moved forward and the ice dropped into the pocket of green material between two slats of the jalousies before Sashie touched the lever and all the slats swung silently shut into a green wooden wall. From outside, there was a shrill scream and a tinkle of breaking glass as Miranda's drink, no doubt, fell from her startled hand and Sashie and I fled into his bedroom behind the sitting-room where we collapsed in a ridiculous giggling heap upon the bed.

'Darling, what a *jape*!' he said. 'There has *never* been such a merry prank since I was at prep school.'

We were still giggling when Twice appeared in the doorway between sitting-room and bedroom and when we had told him what had happened, I said: 'I don't know where people get their ideas from. Just because I travelled to London on the same plane as Roddy Maclean, he is my boy-friend.'

Twice cocked a malicious eye at Sashie and myself, side by side on the bed which we had rumpled not a little in our paroxysm of glee.

'Ideas are never born out of a vacuum,' he said. 'If Miranda could see you two now, she might get yet another idea.'

Sashie rose with dignity to his feet. 'You are quite right, Twice,' he said. 'Janet, you and I must remember that we are growing elderly and must behave more fittingly. Let us go and have some lunch.'

We had lunch at a small table that seated only Sashie, his partner Don, Twice and myself, which was the target of covert glances from all corners of the large crowded dining-room and I felt disoriented, as if an identity not my own were being thrust upon me by all the speculative eyes, behind which conniving minds were at work. Rob Maclean, the former manager of Paradise, and his wife Marion had created for themselves a position in the island that was almost mythical and although Rob Maclean had retired officially before the disaster of the earthquake, I realised now that everybody, including myself, had failed to imagine the island sugar trade without a Rob Maclean at its head. The people in this room now saw Twice as his successor, as a position and not an individual, a position of power that had to be propitiated, as Rob Maclean had demanded propitiation and they saw me, as they had seen Marion, as the consort of this petty power.

Their attitude filled me with resentment, resentment that they were foisting upon me an identity not my own, resentment of their own pettiness and resentment against the dead Rob and Marion Maclean who had left behind them this image that shed a falsifying light on these people, Twice and myself. I suppose too that I was tired after my long journey. In 1956, a feature of air travel that had not as yet been recognised was the disorienting effect psychologically of sudden transition from one side of the globe to the other. My journey had begun on a Tuesday evening by train from Aberdeen to London and it was now midday on a Thursday. In that period, I had travelled four thousand miles into a world as different as could be from my brother's country home and it was not even a return to the world I had known a few weeks ago, it was not the world I had remembered while I had been away. In the few weeks, much had happened, notably the extraordinary improvement in Twice's health which amounted to a change or renewal of personality and I was beginning to discover that, in the course of the short period, a change had taken place in myself as well. Feeling almost tangibly, like pin-pricks, the speculative glances, hearing almost in words the envious thoughts, I had an acute awareness that this was not for me, that this was not my relationship to the world about me, that I did not want to live in the cocoon of this artificial identity.

By the time the coffee arrived, a negative sort of determination had formed in my mind: 'I am forty-six and I am not anybody in my own right. For forty-six years I have been nothing but a reflection of other people but this petty-power image of the wife of the manager of Paradise is one which I will not accept. It is time I discovered who and what I really am.'

'You are very silent, darling,' Sashie said.

'You ought to be grateful that one person in this parrot-house is not screeching her head off,' I told him.

'You are tired,' Twice said. 'Would you like one of Sashie's chaps to run you home now or will you stay until after the afternoon meeting? I should be free about four.'

'I'll stay, thank you. If Sashie will lend me his bed, I shall have a flap with my book.'

'With pleasure, my sweet,' said Sashie. 'Let us instal you right away.'

It was cool and quiet inside the thick-walled core of the old house but I did not sleep and I did not read much either. I had a curious sense of making a new departure and of making it alone, as if all the rest of the world, including Twice, had withdrawn to a distance so that I saw the world and everybody in it from a point of detachment where I was no longer personally involved. And I was aware of a strange new contentment in this detachment, happy that I was freed from commitment for, I told myself, what I did or did not do was unimportant. For a number of years, I had devoted all my time and thought to Twice's health and now, after a few weeks of my absence, he was better than he had ever been since the first onset of his illness. The time had come to stop being the devoted wife, the anxious nurse or any of the other identities that life had thrust upon me and begin to be someone in my own right, thrusting myself upon life. How this was to be accomplished I was not sure but this was less important than that the break through the bonds imposed by life had been made. There was a deep satisfaction in having found this place apart where I could stand still and look around me, as I had physically stood and looked around me as a child, on the hill of Reachfar with its views over the vast distances of the surrounding sea and hills.

About four o'clock, Sashie came into the room, followed by a waiter with a tea tray, and as he poured out the tea, he said: 'Twice should be here before long, darling, but before he comes I wanted to ask if I may continue my frequent visits to Guinea Corner. They have become rather a habit.'

'But of course you may. Come any time you like. Come to stay if you like, Sashie. There is lots of room.'

'I do thank you. One gets so very bored here, you see. When work begins on the house at Silver Beach, of course, things will be better.' He made a prissy fluttering movement of his hands and body. 'Dear me, I feel quite strange and peculiar. I suppose it is your going away and now coming back. Such an unlikely thing to happen – your going away, I mean.'

'It was you who persuaded me to go,' I reminded him.

'But that does not make it less unlikely,' he pointed out. 'And when you had gone, everything was so strange that I began to look at myself – really *look* don't you know – for the first time in a long time and what I saw was poor little me who was utterly tired of being the comic little pansy boy who runs the Peak and that is how everything began.'

'Silver Beach, you mean?'

'That is the mere outward manifestation of an inner regeneration,' he said sententiously. 'I feel most peculiar, as I said but in a very pleasant way as if I had a touch of spring fever or something equally delicious.'

'You are a bit old for that,' I commented.

'You must not think that you have a monopoly in regeneration, darling,' he told me, putting his head on one side and regarding me solemnly. 'But it is really remarkable, the change in you, quite remarkable.'

'Not as remarkable as the change I see in Twice,' I told him, 'and thank you again for your part in that.'

'We are all going to have an Illyrian spring or an Indian summer or something. Isn't it *fun*?' Twice came into the room. 'Oh, there you are, my pet.'

'Are you two still gabbing?' Twice asked. 'You ought to join the sugar trade and come to the Congress. I have never heard so many men talking so much pointless rubbish in my life. Any tea left? I am as dry as a wooden god.'

'Here you are, dear, and then you must take Janet home. She does not like being the consort of the local sugar boss.'

'Sugar boss my backside,' said Twice.

'Cor,' said Sashie, suddenly Cockney, 'i'n't 'e *rude*?'

'A waste of time this whole business,' Twice continued. 'They could have said all that needed saying in a single afternoon. However, if Mackie comes out of it with some self-confidence after reading his paper tomorrow, it will have been worthwhile.'

'You have still got to get Mackie on to that rostrum, dear,' said Sashie.

'I'll get him there if I have to carry him,' Twice assured us.

'Wouldn't it be less tiring to read the paper yourself?' Sashie asked. 'After all, it was based on an idea of yours in the first place, Mackie told me.'

'I don't need to read papers to congresses to convince myself that I know about sugar engineering,' Twice said crushingly. 'Mackie does. I have never seen a clever bloke with less self-confidence.'

'Except me, angel,' said Sashie, uncrushed. 'I am a modest self-effacing violet, just like Mackie, only my feet are not quite so large.'

Twice simply stared blankly at Sashie but I giggled, for I could think of no two people more unlike than Sashie and Mackie, the senior of the three young shift engineers at Paradise.

'Come, Janet,' Twice said after a moment. 'I'll take you home.'

When we drove up to the door of our home, Guinea Corner, it was after six in the evening and already dark. Fleetingly, I thought of the long twilight around my brother's home in Scotland, of the children laughing and quarrelling in the overgrown shrubbery which was their kingdom, before the memory was blotted out by the reality of this little kingdom of my own. Old Cookie, old Minna, young Clorinda and young Caleb, the yard boy, crowded round the car, white teeth and white eye-balls shining in their black faces, while Dram, my mastiff dog, placed his forepaws on my shoulders and began to lick my face. Even Charlie the cat, lazy and stand-offish as he was, had bestirred himself to welcome me by rubbing himself round my ankles.

When the fuss had died down, I crossed the veranda and

went into the drawing-room with a consciousness of rediscovery, seeing the room afresh and yet in all its familiarity until my attention was suddenly arrested to the particular in the form of an arrangement of hibiscus flowers in a shallow glass bowl.

When I was a child, I had spent much time picking bunches of wild flowers on the moor at my home, Reachfar in the north of Scotland. These bunches were 'presents' for my mother and when I brought them to her, she would take the bunch from my hand carefully and place it in a little straight-sided crystal vase so that the flowers remained in the accidental arrangement that they had fallen into as I picked them. She liked them to stay like this, she said and because of this, probably, I have never 'arranged' flowers and do not like 'floral arrangements'. I like bunches of flowers in simple vases that hold plenty of water and I narrowed my eyes at this curiously airy arrangement of hibiscus, cunningly balanced in half an inch of water and a tangle of wire net. The flower heads, on their slender branches from which all the leaves had been stripped, looked as if they were in flight. This was no copy of an arrangement from some manual of floral decoration but the work of someone with an individual touch and that someone had been in my drawing-room that day, for the hibiscus flowers of St. Jago open in the morning and die away into colourless tissue the same evening.

I walked away from the flowers and looked out of the window, across the veranda and out to the grassland of the park where the trunks of the palms were now being picked out in silver by the light of the rising moon.

'Goodness,' I said, 'Olympus is like the sultan's turret. It is caught in a noose of light. Is somebody living up there?'

Olympus, the house on the wooded hill on the other side of the park, had been the home of Rob and Marion Maclean and I gazed up at the distant blaze of lights with something akin to fear. Olympus was, architecturally, the most beautiful house on Paradise estate but I had never liked it. Seen from our own house, Guinea Corner, it had always seemed so secretive, away on its hill among its thick trees and tangled underbrush and when I went up its hill and went close to it, it had always seemed to tower over me with a crushing arrogance. But now it looked different. Before, only a dimmed light here and there among the trees had betrayed its secretive presence; now, it was ablaze with lights and its outline exposed by the rising moon. Marion Maclean, I thought with a shiver, would not have liked this and I had a momentary terror that the ghost of that strong arrogant woman might return to take vengeance on us all for this desecrating exposure of the place where she had planned and plotted for a lifetime.

From behind my shoulder came the laughing voice of Twice, dispelling the haunted terror. 'These are the Teeth and Feet Lot as Sir Ian calls them.'

'Who?'

'The Child Health Mission that has come out from home. The new clinic is working now but half the quarters they were building for the staff fell down in the earthquake so when they arrived at the beginning of August, Sir Ian offered them Olympus.'

I went on staring at the distant lights. 'How many of them are up there?'

'Fifteen or so, mostly young but with one old chap in charge of them. Their chief and his wife and family are in a house in the hospital compound down in the Bay and some nurses are quartered in the Nurses' Home down there but there are two or three dentists, a few young doctors, a psychologist and a few clerical types up there at Olympus. They are a lively lot. Brighten the place up, as Sir Ian says.'

'He would,' I commented. 'Why feet though? Are there chiropodists among them too?'

'No, I don't think so. Somebody used the word paediatrician in relation to the doctors and Sir Ian decided they dealt with feet.'

'Why?'

'Because of pedestrians, he said.'

I turned my back on the lights and on the through-the-looking-glass feeling that Sir Ian's reasoning could induce. I was aware that Twice and I were chatting like this because there were so many important things to say but for which, as yet, we could not find words.

'I am so very glad that you are back,' he said suddenly, cutting through the trivia of the Teeth and Feet Lot. 'I didn't notice it while you were away – there has been a lot going on, what with the earthquake damage at the factory and now the Congress, but now it seems like centuries since I saw you last. Sometimes, at night, I thought that you might never come back at all.'

'You silly ass, but suddenly it seems like centuries to me too,' I agreed. 'So much can happen in a few weeks. One becomes different. Twice, I suddenly know that I am middle-aged, that soon I will be old.'

He looked at me, his blue eyes wide and began to laugh. 'But you look ten years younger, as I told you. Sashie saw it too.'

'Maybe, but I am a lot older inside. Maybe Jock's children had something to do with it. They made my own childhood seem so very far away. Yet, that is not the whole truth. In one sense, they made it seem far in the past, yet in another sense they brought it back, made me live it over again. I am calling it middle-age but I feel that I am beginning a new cycle.' I found it difficult to say what I meant and let the matter drop. 'I found the children fascinating, Twice.'

'Yes, the children,' he said quietly, thoughtfully. 'You will miss them.'

He seemed sad, as if he regretted for my sake that we had no children in this big quiet house of ours.

'But I wouldn't be Jock or Shona for anything,' I said hastily. 'I don't think I was designed to be a parent. Their responsibility for those four newly-minted people that they have created makes my mind turn pale but they seem to take it all in their stride.'

'Probably the ability to cope comes with having the children,' Twice said, 'built in in the package.'

'I suppose so.'

He paced slowly down the long room that ran from the front to the back of the house, then came to a standstill, facing me.

'When I got Sashie to help me to persuade you to make that trip to Scotland,' he said, 'I did it purely for the sake of your health. I had no idea that it would lead to so much complexity.' His eyes moved from my face to the bowl of flowers on the table by the wall and I stood quite still.

'Your letters were almost entirely about the children,' he said.

'There was nothing else to write about,' I said as lightly as I could. 'I spent all my days with them and quite a part of my nights, come to that.'

'You were not here,' he continued. 'The house was very different.' He flashed a sudden smile. 'I am not playing the Pathétique, darling. I wasn't lonely. I had plenty of company but the place was just different and your letters told of things that were new and different, especially the children.' He paused. 'One night, I suddenly remembered that I have a son,' he said suddenly. 'Does this shock you? Hurt you? It was as sudden as that. The thought came roaring out of the past like an aircraft breaking the sound barrier: I have a son.'

His eyes wide and startled, as they must have been when the memory first struck him, stared at me. 'Would you prefer that I didn't talk about this?' he asked in a curious formal way.

'Of course not, Twice.'

'It is difficult to talk about it in a way that makes any sense.'

The phrase 'talk about *it*' seemed to indicate that he was not talking of the boy as a person but struggling in his mind with a situation, the fact of the existence of this child of his and I had a sudden need to personalise the child.

'The boy must be a young man by now,' I said, 'and not a child any more.'

'He will be twenty-three years old,' he said quietly.

Twenty-three years was a long time. I looked back down that stretch of time that lay behind me and saw, as if in a distant mirror, myself in the home of Mrs. Whitely-Rollin, to whom my friend Muriel and I were joint secretaries. I saw the recklessness of my approach to life, the confidence that the world was created for my enjoyment, the cruelty with which I badgered my hypocritical old employer whom I heartily disliked. 'Twenty-three years is a long time,' I said. 'It is difficult to believe that one could ever have been so painfully *young*, so over-confident and reckless—'

'And in my case so bloody stupid,' Twice broke in. 'Looking back on it, I knew all the time that Dinah was such a spoilt darling that she was barely human. I knew that she was scared of life, of me, of everything and didn't want to come out of her cellophane box but I was mad about her, quite literally mad, you know and there it was.'

Twice's marriage to Dinah had lasted for three days only, it had happened thirteen years before I met him and in the eleven years we had known one another, we had discussed it only once before. At that time, we had decided to make a life together in spite of this legal impediment and in a peculiar way, Dinah and the child had ceased to be persons in my mind and had turned into a rigid stumbling-block, a literal impediment that it was pointless to discuss. Also, at the time that Twice had told me of the existence of Dinah and the child, it had obviously been a matter of great pain and shame to him, a wound for which there seemed to be no betterment and which it was best to try to ignore. Our life together had been happy enough, full enough to make forgetfulness easy until now when, by a chance turn of the wheel of circumstance, that reckless youthful mistake that Twice had made had come to the forefront in a new dimension, but now the pain had been extracted from it by time.

In the time of his illness, we could not have discussed this thing so charged with emotion but now, in the new strength and calm that he had achieved, he showed no sign of the physical disturbance which, formerly, had accompanied any discussion of the slightest emotional content.

'It is still strange to be able to think about Dinah and stranger still to be able to talk about her in open words,' he said now. 'I am not good at explaining feelings, as you know. Anyway, I don't think anyone can ever understand precisely what another person feels and if I talked till all was blue, I would never make you understand about Dinah. You and she are too different in yourselves. You could never conceive of the cold sullen chill that developed in Dinah, not hatred but a leaden sort of deadness.' He moved his shoulders as if to throw off a shiver and his thought took a new direction. 'It was not only you writing about Jock's children that made me begin to think about the boy, you know. There are a lot of factors. When you went away, the house was different, as I said. There was a big gap in it. Then there has been a lot to do at the factory and Mackie and Vickers and Christie have been around here a lot, for meals and so on. We could go on discussing things while we ate, you see.' He smiled at me, smiling at himself too. 'I suddenly found myself at the head of the table with these three youngsters around me as if I were a Victorian papa. Then the Teeth and Feet lot took to popping in and out, especially—' he glanced at the flower arrangement on the table '—this little girl.'

'Oh, yes,' I said. 'Before Sashie put the ice down her back, Miranda was wondering what I would think of your girl-friend.'

'That woman will come to a sticky end.'

'I hope so. Tell me about this girl.'

'I don't know much about her actually except one thing. Her father ran away and left her and her mother. That makes me like her. Is that peculiar?'

'I don't see why it should be.'

'The thing is that she doesn't mind her father having

run away. I always had the idea that children would hate fathers who ran away but she doesn't. I don't blame him, Percy said, quite airily. Women like my mother aren't easy to live with, she said.'

'Percy? A boyish sort of name,' I commented.

'She isn't boyish, though. She is a very feminine little number, very small and fair and wears glasses, not my type of woman at all in the woman sense.'

'But adoptable as a daughter?'

'Actually it was she who adopted me, or not me, exactly. It was rather that she adopted this house at first.'

'How did she first start coming to the house?'

'Well, you know Sir Ian,' Twice replied with seeming irrelevance, 'and you know Edward. When the Teeth and Feet lot arrived, Sir Ian was down in the Bay and heard that the medical people had no quarters for them so he romped in and said to send them up to Olympus. Then the next day, he gets hold of me and says that Edward is going on a bit about this bunch of strangers on the estate. They might set the house on fire or something, Edward said. Edward is turning into a proper scary old maid,' he said impatiently. 'I have never seen a son who was less like his father.'

'Oh, Edward is all right. After all, Sir Ian is inclined to go off at half cock a lot of the time,' I said.

Twice looked at me, seemed to decide not to argue with me about Edward on my first evening home and continued: 'Anyway, Sir Ian asked me to invite them all over here for a drink one evening so that he and I could size 'em up as he put it. After that, they all got the habit of popping in in the evenings but especially this little girl. She started coming over at any sort of time, just appearing, sitting there—' he pointed to a chair in a corner— 'sketching. She sketches a lot.'

I looked at the chair in the corner. It was an old wicker arm-chair, with a high fan-shaped back and tall sides that formed a cave and there was a wicker stool in front of it which turned it into a sort of chaise-longue. When Twice and I came to Paradise, Guinea Corner had been furnished for us out of the capacious crowded cellars of the Great House of Paradise, which contained a vast amount of very good furniture that the acquisitive Madame Dulac had bought when various of the island's other great houses had been displenished on changing hands. Most of the furniture in Guinea Corner was Georgian but I had been allowed to choose what I wished from the cellars and I had chosen the wicker arm-chair because there had been one exactly similar, but without the stool, in my mother's bedroom at Reachfar.

'If that is where she likes to sketch,' I said now, looking at the chair, 'she is welcome but she may not come any more now that I am here. Will you mind, Twice?'

'Of course not!' he said forcefully but then became thoughtful and frowned again. 'Yet I don't know that that is true.' He held out his left hand, palm upwards and looked down at it before beginning to speak as if he were reading something written on his palm. It was a mannerism that he had when he was trying to express something that he found difficult. 'When I was a kid,' he said, 'the swallows used to nest under the eaves of our house every spring. I used to forget about them for most of the time but when they came, I was always pleased to see them and I would remember that if they had not come, I would have been disappointed.' He paused and then: 'Once they were there, I didn't pay any attention to them and when they went away in the autumn, I didn't mind. I would tell myself they would be back in the spring and forget about them again. This girl is a bit like that, like the swallows. Sort of silly, isn't it?'

'No, Twice. No, it isn't,' I said hastily. 'I hope that Percy the swallow keeps on arriving. By the way, is she Teeth or Feet?'

'Neither, as it happens. She is not a member of the Mission at all. It seems that she came out here on her own—she seems to be financially independent. Then she made the acquaintance of the Teeth and Feet Lot and now she is acting as housekeeper at Olympus, arranges the meals, controls the staff and so on.'

'She sounds like a capable little party.'

'She is.' He frowned. 'They are so different from what we were, the young, I mean. They are so much more independent of mind, so much more responsible.'

'That is not the common view of the young,' I told him. 'They are mostly accused of a total lack of responsibility.'

'That is not how I see them. Percy, Mackie and the rest have a bloody sight more real sense than I had when I was their age. Look, you must be exhausted, darling. That's dinner going in. Then you must go to bed. Mackie is coming round later to go over his paper for tomorrow.'

'I felt tired at lunch but not now,' I said as we crossed the hall to the dining-room. 'That is something I have discovered during my holiday. Even to talk about young people energises one. Some of their youth rubs off on to old crocks like us.'

'That is true. There is something rejuvenating in thinking about that boy.'

Suddenly, there was with us not a dead situation out of the past but 'that boy', a personality of the present and going forward towards the future. After a short silence, I said slowly and carefully: 'Twice, have you thought of trying to get in touch with him?' and after another short silence, he replied just as slowly and carefully: 'I have got as far as wondering if I have the right to try to get in touch with him. It seems presumptuous when, for all these years, he has meant literally nothing to me.'

He looked at me from under lowered brows. 'As a woman, I suppose that this strikes you as horrifying, but there it is. I didn't know of his existence until he was about four years old and then I saw him only for an instant, being hustled from the door to the stairs by a maid. I had gone to Belfast to try to persuade Dinah to divorce me. She didn't want me and I don't think she had much use for the child either but divorce – no. From my point of view, the boy's existence only made the situa-

tion more sickening still and I came away, put the whole
thing behind me, for good, as I thought at the time. There
was no point in thinking of two people who hated my
guts, it seemed. Then Percy comes along and mentions
that her father had run away from her mother when she
was quite small. She literally mentioned it, airily and with
no emotional charge of any kind, as I said. It made me
start to think.' He paused and added: 'Of course, the boy
may be different from Percy. If he has been influenced
by Dinah, he will be a sight less reasonable and balanced
than little Percy.'

'It should be possible to trace him and find out what
he is like,' I said.

'It has been a long time. I last saw Dinah in 1946 – ten
years ago.'

'It seems longer than that since you first told me about her.
So much has happened since then and she has never been
part of any of it. I remember you said you had seen her only
that once in fifteen years. It made her unreal, far away—'

'Did I say at that time that I hadn't seen her for fifteen
years?' he asked me.

'Yes. You did. I am sure you did.'

'Then it wasn't true. In 1946, it was about fifteen years
since I had married Dinah but I saw her again in 1936.
That was when I found out about the boy. I wonder why I
lied to you about that?' he asked thoughtfully and then
answered himself: 'I suppose I wanted to put Dinah as
far into the distance as possible, give her as little relevance
to you and myself as I could. It is frightening how easily
one can lie even without meaning to.'

'I don't see that it has any importance,' I said. 'The boy
will be twenty-three now, you said?'

'Yes. He must have been born in 1933.'

'That makes him not a boy but a young man, a young
man with a mind of his own. I think you should try to
get in touch with him, Twice. He may be like this Percy
girl. He may even wonder about you, what you are like –
he must I think. And if he doesn't want any part of you –

or me, especially me – there would be no harm done. We would both be a little hurt, I suppose but maybe we deserve that for never sparing him a thought for so long.'

'I have to think about it a bit more,' Twice said. 'It is less simple than you think. You don't know Dinah.' There were footsteps on the veranda and he called: 'Come in, Mackie.' Mackie, gangling and awkward, dark, rangy, gipsy-like, appeared in the door, an untidy sheaf of papers in his hand.

'Hello, Missis Janet,' he said. 'Glad to see you back' and to Twice: 'I shouldn't be bothering you tonight, sir. I'll—' Twice rose to his feet, put a hand on Mackie's shoulder. 'We'll go through to the study,' he said and turned to me. 'Mackie is reading a paper to the Congress tomorrow,' he told me as if I did not already know of this.

'Really? Congratulations, Mackie.'

Mackie's Adam's apple jerked convulsively in his long scrawny throat before he said, waving his handful of papers wildly at Twice: 'He helped me with it. If it hadn't been for him— You see, we thought of this way of— Well, anyway, *he* said—' 'I have to go upstairs to attend to a few things,' I broke in on Mackie's incoherence. 'You two had better go through to the study and get on with it.'

In the rediscovered familiarity of my bedroom, I began to unpack my bags but soon found myself sitting at my dressing-table, my silver hairbrush with the dent in it between my hands, while I thought of Percy the swallow. The dent in the silver back of the hairbrush had been made long ago when I threw it at Twice in the course of a quarrel about a young girl, Dee Andrews, who had attached herself to him. In those days, before Twice was ill, we had quarrelled frequently and violently but those days had passed. Nowadays we were a little wiser, perhaps and considerably less impassioned. To remember, now, the energy and emotion expended in these quarrels made me feel mentally and physically tired.

My mind moved now from memories of Twice, Dee

and myself to my brother, my sister-in-law and myself in their home in Scotland and out of this came knowledge of a difference between these two and Twice on one side and myself on the other. Jock, my brother, and Shona, my sister-in-law, were the parents of four children and in their relationship with those children they were endowed with a confidence that I did not have. Jock and Shona could take decisions for the welfare of those four children without conscious thought, guided by an instinct that I now saw was part of parenthood – part of the parenthood package, as Twice had put it – an instinct with which I, having no children, was not endowed. To me, the children were entirely separate 'other' people and I had no confidence in my ability or even my right to interfere in their lives. In this, I now realised, Twice differed from me and was more like Jock and Shona. There was in him something parental, something that attached him to young people such as Dee Andrews, Mackie, Vickers, Christie, the junior engineers, even my niece Liz when she had first seen him at the age of three and now there was Percy the swallow. They became attached to him in the trusting confidence that he would help and not harm them while I, in their eyes, was simply one more person with a potential perhaps for good but also, perhaps, for ill.

I looked into the glass at my own face, undistinguished under slightly greying hair and as if out of the shadowed corners of the room behind me came the thought: 'But of course, Twice *is* a parent. He is the father of this boy.' Out of the shadows too came memories of the wide eyes of my small niece and nephews, with the moment-ago memory of the dark eyes of Mackie, full of trust that if Twice was satisfied with his paper, it was fit to present to the Congress on the morrow.

My eyes reflected in the looking-glass widened while I felt as if my mind were widening, reaching out, searching for the child that was the outcome of a three-day marriage, the marriage of a reckless young man of twenty-two. The world seemed suddenly enormous, full of the ebb and flow of countless people, among whom wandered a young man, the son of Twice, whose name, even, I did not know.

As I unpacked my bags, the bedroom, so long familiar, seemed to have changed in the subtle way that the texture of my life had changed since this homecoming. In one sense, Twice and I were now people more separate than we had been before, more aware of the differences between us than we had hitherto been and yet these differences had come to the forefront because Twice had brought out of a mental limbo and into the light an intimacy of his life which he had never before wished to discuss or even remember. Paradoxically, his sharing of this intimacy with me made me see him in a way more detached and dispassionate than I had ever seen him before. He was no longer an extension of myself in my mind, but a separate identity who might be moving forward into a relationship in which I had no share but I did not find this a matter of grief as I would have done a short time ago. Tout lasse, tout casse, tout passe, Sashie had said that morning. Had this happened to the bond between Twice and myself? Had it grown tired? Was it about to break and pass away for good?

I sat down on the bed, holding between my hands a little white porcelain box, decorated with gilt and blue harebells that had been given to me as a parting gift by my brother's children. It was a Victorian money-box, with a slot for coins in the lid which I was raising and lowering as I looked down at it but the children had not given it to me as a money-box.

Each evening, while I had stayed at my brother's house, I had told the children a story at bed-time, stories drawn from my own childhood at Reachfar, our family home, which had long since been sold and one of the stories had been about a sandy stony bank where the harebells grew in summer. This little box was, according to the children, 'a symbol of Bluebell Bank'. This, by a curious alchemy, was what their imaginations and their love for my stories and me had made out of a shallow strip of rocky land where only harebells grew to dance and tinkle on the wind. They had not rendered my memory of that place void by symbolising it in this concrete form that I could hold and examine between my hands. On the contrary, they had made the memory more rich and precious.

I discovered that, in a similar way, my new detachment from Twice did not mean that I loved him less but that it was making me see him more clearly than I had ever seen him before and was making me find in him more to admire. The passion and the possessiveness had gone out of what I felt for him and I recognised this with relief but the bond was not broken. We were simply moving into a new phase of relationship, in one way more distinct from one another than we were before, in another way recognising one another more clearly than we had before and through this drawing even more closely together. The sandy harebell-bedecked strip of ground, at the mercy of wind, rain and winter frost, had solidified into the security of the porcelain box, the symbol of more impassioned but shallower times.

As I continued with my unpacking, I noted that the one matter which had been uppermost in the minds of all the people at the Peak Hotel, the managership of Paradise, had not been mentioned by Twice. There had been a time when the possibility that this post might be offered to him would have swamped all other considerations and the fact that it seemed to have been relegated to a lower place in his scale of values marked more clearly still the change in his focus. Formerly, Twice had been perhaps a little more than normally ambitious in his profession and willing to work more than hard to achieve a place in the competitive field of plant engineering until his ambition and fitness to work had been curbed by his illness. He had hitherto had the attitude of the scientist rather than the humanist, an attitude summed up in dicta like: 'People! Give me a good machine any day. When you press a switch on a machine, you know what will happen.' His relationship with myself had been the only one in his life that was of any depth and from my new standpoint I saw that I had been as predictable to him as one of his machines. He knew precisely how to please me, how to annoy me and he knew also, with security, that in any crisis he would lead and I would follow. If his firm sent him to the West Indies, I would come with him to the West Indies, when his health did not permit of his returning to Britain, I gave up all thought of returning to Britain and in a similar way I had tried to follow the strange journeyings of his mind, during his long convalescence on his way back to life from death.

His experience with Dinah had destroyed his faith in human relationships but it seemed to me now that, in the course of some ten years, I had inadvertently rebuilt what had been destroyed. This was no matter for pride or for the taking of credit unto myself, for this rebuilding was a mere by-product of the relationship between him and myself and partly, too, a product of his maturity. There had come a change in his priorities, as commercial circles would put it and a far-reaching human predicament of over twenty years ago had come to the forefront, relegating material ambition to second place or, perhaps, as I listened to the resonance of his voice addressing Mackie in the study down below, to a place much further down the line of priority in his mind.

I took out of the bottom of the case the books I had brought back for him, put them in a pile on top of the chest of drawers. Later, at some opportunity before he went to bed, I would take them down to his study-bedroom and put them on his pillow. Twice had not been upstairs since his illness.

As I carried the empty cases across the landing to put them away in the linen cupboard which was also a storeroom, the door of the study below opened and Twice's voice rang out: 'Now, listen, Mackie, so far at this Congress there has been nothing but a lot of luke-warm air. This technique that we have dreamed up is a real contribution. *I* believe it and *you* believe it and while you are speaking tomorrow *remember* that you believe it. If you do that, you can't miss.'

This was the voice of Twice Alexander of more than ten years ago, as he blasted his way around the small plant that was Slater's Works at Ballydendran in Scotland and as they came through the front hall, Twice saw me at the top of the stairs. 'Are you not in bed yet?' he called. 'Well, come down here and have a drink and see if *you* can put some backbone into this two yards of limp seaweed.'

The description of Mackie was so apt that I had to laugh, cruel as it was, at the long gangling dark-brown tangle of drooping face, dangling arms and sprawling legs with its limp sheets of paper slipping from a nerveless hand to drift across the floor. It was I who picked up the sheets and put them back in Mackie's hand. And we gave him a drink and we talked to him for perhaps half-an-hour but it was a little like hitting one's head against a soft rubbery wall. There was no resistance but neither did one make any impression and at last he gathered his long legs, rose on to his large feet and stumbled out of the house as if in a dream. Twice watched him go, his face showing mingled feelings of pride, exasperation and also an indulgent affection.

'Twice,' I said, 'Mackie will be all right when it comes to the crunch.'

'You think so?'

'I am sure of it. He has too much imagination and at the moment it is all out of control but tomorrow, when it comes to it, he will harness it and it will work for him. He reminds me of Hugh Reid before the bursary examination.'

'Maybe you are right.'

'Why are you so anxious about this, Twice?'

He turned his head to look at me, then frowned as if this were a question that he had not asked himself and did not know the answer.

'He is a first-class engineer,' he said then, 'but he has no confidence in himself. I want him to find his level among that lot at the Congress, prove himself to himself.' He paused, continued: 'More than that. I like him, admire him. He came up the hard way.'

When we first came to Paradise, the three shift engineers, Mackie, Christie and Vickers, were already installed in what was known as Bachelor's Bungalow, where they lived amid unbelievable squalor and an amazing technical ingenuity of devices of ropes and pulleys by which they could obtain bottles of beer from the refrigerator without rising from their beds or arm-chairs. They were all three, in our early days, in their early twenties and regarded less as people than as social conveniences. In former times, much entertaining was done at Paradise, at the Great House by Madame Dulac, at Olympus by Rob and Marion Maclean and in a less formal way by Twice and myself at Guinea Corner and it had been our habit, if males were needed to balance a dinner table, to call upon the denizens of Bachelors' Bungalow who were always glad of a decently served meal. When not required in this way or to make up a sailing crew, a tennis four or a cricket eleven or if Mackie was not in demand to entertain with his bagpipes, we forgot their existence, comfortable in the certainty that they would take no offence and appear obligingly on the next occasion that required their presence.

'I know nothing about Mackie except that he is an engineer who plays the bagpipes,' I said now.

'I didn't know anything much more than that about him either, except that he was an unusually gifted engineer until one day little Percy said something. Percy is very interested in ships,' he told me with seeming irrelevance. 'She is always hanging around the wharves down in the Bay in her spare time.'

'Yes?'

'She told me one evening, all excited, that Mackie's father had helped to build the *Queen Mary*. He was a Clydeside riveter. You know what they called her? Percy asked me. The Five-three-fower.' Twice smiled. 'It made me think of you, you remembering the days when the *Queen Mary* was Number 534 in John Brown's yard at Clydebank. The next day I talked to Mackie about Clydebank. Queer how things connect up, isn't it?'

'What age is Mackie?' I asked.

'Thirty last August.'

I made a quick calculation. 'As a riveter's son in Clydebank in the late '20's and early '30's Mackie remembers more than the Five-three-fower,' I said.

'That is just the point. He remembers the trade depression, his father on the dole. He remembers his father being killed in the Clydebank raids during the war and having to leave school, give up all ideas of university. Mackie hasn't had it easy. And he has been making a monthly allowance to his mother ever since he came out here. You have to hand it to a chap like that.'

'Especially if he is a good engineer,' I amended.

'He is good.'

'And you are fond of him and want to help him.' I rose to my feet. 'You and your adopted children. Listen, I must really go to bed.'

'My adopted children are all mixed up with you and the Five-three-fower and God knows what else. You don't mind about them, do you?'

'Don't be silly. I am glad about them, glad, you hear? And Mackie will be all right tomorrow. You wait and see.' I said goodnight and went upstairs while Twice called Dram in from the garden to his basket in a corner of the veranda and noticing the pile of books I had brought, I picked them up to carry them down to the study. On the landing, I stopped dead with the bundle in my arms, while all my bones seemed to turn rigid with shock which might have been joy, might have been fear. I stood staring at Twice on the landing while he looked from my face to the books in my arms.

'Anything the matter, darling?' he asked.

44

The rigidity left me, changed to limpness so that the books began to slip from my hold. He caught the volume that fell from the top of the pile as I said: 'Twice, you are upstairs!' my giddy brain clutching at miraculous fact.

'Yes and I can go down them too,' he assured me solemnly.

I was stupefied. The years of his illness seemed to go cascading down the staircase to be lost in the shadows of the panelled hall below and to my chagrin I felt my eyes filling with tears while a sob was bulging in my throat. The long habit of no bursts of emotion, no scenes that might upset the 'patient', the control imposed by years of caring for him came to my aid. 'I brought you some books,' I said. 'I was going down to put them on your pillow.'

He pointed through the doorway behind me to the bed. 'That is my pillow in there,' he said.

This was too much. I turned about, dropped the books on to the bed, myself on top of them and began to cry as I had never cried throughout the long anxious years since he first became ill. When I sat up and looked at him again, he was sitting at my dressing-table, his back to the glass, with my hairbrush in his hands, his fore-finger rubbing the dent in the silver. 'I must take this up to the workshop and take this dent out,' he said. 'I have been meaning to do it for years.'

'You let that alone,' I told him. 'I like that dent there.' He put the brush down on the table. 'I like all the dents in my things and in me and in us,' I added confusedly, asserting myself against all odds in a world that was threatening to become too full of joy for me. 'Twice, what has happened?'

'I have come upstairs, that's all.'

'I don't understand. I just don't understand. I go away and when I come back you are better than you were when I was doing everything for you that Doctor Mark said for three whole years. Doctor Mark must have been all wrong. I must have been all wrong—'

'Nobody was all wrong, darling,' Twice stopped me quietly. 'Mark was right and so were you and the three years you devoted to me have paid off. But I had accepted too much, I think, too much from you and everybody and I had accepted that I was somebody who – who couldn't come upstairs. I'd got a habit of semi-invalidism but there has been no miracle. I am still a bloke with a faulty heart and I have no intention of pushing it too far. But I have got the fault into truer perspective. I think I have got a lot of things into truer perspective recently.' He watched me mop my face and began to pull the pins from my hair while I sat limp on the bed. 'Look,' he said, 'for pity's sake get undressed and into bed. In the words of old Mattha, your eyes look like piss-holes in the snow.'

At this reminder of our early days together, I began to laugh and laughter was still with me when I fell asleep, but laughter tinged with amazement at what, in my childhood, I would have called the 'same only different' quality of Twice and myself as we were in those early days and Twice and myself as we were now at this point of new departure.

The next day I spent alone until the later afternoon when Twice and Mackie returned from the final meeting of the Congress and I spent it in rediscovering my territory, which was the garden. I have always been an inveterate grubber-about in the earth and although I was not enamoured of all aspects of St. Jagoan life, one feature of it that pleased me was the availability of people willing to undertake domestic work which relieved me of duties inside the house. The only features of housekeeping that I enjoy are cooking, needlework and mending and I was happy to pay Clorinda to make beds, sweep and dust, old Minna to do the laundry and Cookie to do the staple cookery of day to day which left my time and energy free to devote to the garden.

When we had first been installed at Guinea Corner, the house had lain empty for a number of years and the garden, inside its grey stone wall, had been a jungle. Jungle, in St. Jago, can overtake cultivated land in a few months; in the course of years it can attain to tropical forest and it was from such a forest that Caleb, my yard boy, and I had reclaimed the garden. Human affection is called out by what has been created by hard work and I had a deep affection for this garden and a deeper affection for Caleb who had helped to create it, for in its creation he had developed from puny underfed youth to virile well-nourished manhood. Nor was the garden the only bond between Caleb and myself. I had nursed him through an attack of measles of which he had nearly died and on the morning when I was sure of his recovery, the news came from Scotland of the sudden death of my father. Caleb's recovery and the loss of my father were inextricably bound together in my mind and the boy by some inexplicable empathy knew of this perhaps because, in the garden, I spoke to him a great deal about my father who had been a gifted gardener. When Caleb and I were planting a shrub, for instance, we would pool our knowledge, I deferring to Caleb's inborn understanding of his own earth and climate, Caleb deferring to what he called my 'educatedness'.

'My father would have done it like this, Caleb,' I would say.

'But not there, ma'am,' Caleb would answer. 'All water going to drain down to here. Mars D. Sandison woulda done it like you say but not there but here' and we would plant the shrub as Mars D. Sandison would have planted it but not there but here.

When Caleb first came to us, he had had the minimum of schooling. He knew his letters and figures and very little more but he had an instinctive peasant knowledge of the earth which had bred him which made him infallible as a cultivator of the native fruits and vegetables. It was when we became more ambitious and began to grow

47

produce native to more temperate zones that Mars D. Sandison had to be invoked. Caleb, however, had an ambition to become literate and in the heat of the day would copy headlines from the newspaper on to the kitchen slate and then went on to copy my father's copper-plate handwriting from discarded envelopes which he rescued from the wastebasket. After my father died, I allowed Caleb to read a page from one of the last letters in which he was enquiring about the boy's progress, adjuring me to do my best for him and hoping for his recovery and after Caleb read the signature, my father changed in his parlance from 'yo' father, ma'am' to 'Mars D. Sandison', as if Caleb were claiming a kinship with him that was separate from his position as my father.

Caleb, although he was still referred to as 'the yard boy', was now about six feet two inches tall, black as ebony and a magnificent specimen of his race. In age, he would be about twenty now, I thought, but there was no certainty as to this for, in the fecund hollow by the river where he had been born, it was no easy matter to remember which child of Missy Rosie's and which children of her many daughters had been born when. And by this time, Caleb himself had fathered an illegitimate child or two by the wayside in a traditional way, as a preamble to marrying at a later date and rearing a family which, he told me, would be 'legit'mate and not sprinkle, ma'am.'

In addition to his gifts as a cultivator, as he called himself, Cabel was musical. All the islanders were musical to some degree but Caleb was unusually endowed in this way and had inherited a guitar from Rob and Marion Maclean's youngest son on his departure to Scotland and school. And Twice, like many engineers, was fond of music, could sing well in an untrained baritone and possessed a record-player and a vast collection of records, many of them of the great singers of the century.

Caleb played his guitar by ear, at first the island songs which were born in him but, as time went on, he began to play and sing from the records so that, in the heat of midday, it was not uncommon to hear from the shade of a tree in the garden a concert that might begin with a calypso and continue through the metrical version of the twenty-third psalm to an operatic aria and on to a few ballads before ending with a love song sung in Gaelic. And Caleb was not a barren copyist. His Italian aria or his Gaelic love song was accompanied on the guitar by the strange chords which were the music of his race.

While Twice had been ill and during most of his long convalescence, the record-player had been silent. Caleb's guitar had been silent too and it was only on this first day home, when the sun climbed to the zenith and I took to the house while Caleb took to the shade of a tree and the cool liquid notes of the guitar made themselves heard, that I discovered how I had missed the music of Guinea Corner. With the music, life came back to the house but life of a new kind, life in a quieter, more contemplative, more contented tempo than the feverish stormy life that we had generated around us in former days.

In the sullen heavy heat of the early afternoon, I went up to the bedroom at the back of the house which was my secret place. From my childhood onwards, I have had secret places, the first being my Thinking Place in a thicket of tall fir trees above the well at Reachfar but it was on this afternoon that I learned the real meaning of my need for these places where I could be quite alone. At some time between the ages of fourteen and twenty – and perhaps earlier than that although I did not recognise it – I had vaguely formulated a desire to be a writer one day but although, down the years I had instinctively found secret places where I could move mentally into the dimension of fiction, the world had always called me out of them for the world's own very valid reasons. My grandmother called me out of the Thinking Place above the well to go on an errand for her, later, the need to earn my living had called me from the secret place to perform other duties and later still, the exigencies of Twice's health had made retirement to this Guinea Corner secret place sporadic and unproductive. Now, however, I could feel the wind of change. Twice was better and making a new departure into a new and responsible post of wide interest which would leave me free as I had never been before.

From a drawer, I took a helmet made of thin bronze, a souvenir of the early days of our courtship, one of those relics which lumber households but which one can never decide to throw away. I set it on the table and took out a sheaf of papers that it had weighed down in the drawer. This sheaf was the manuscript of a novel. I read a page here, half a page there, shook my head and sighed. 'This is sad stuff,' I quoted to myself. I took the large bottle of ink and the fountain pen out of another drawer, and stared at the bogus medieval helmet and thought of my brother's children, their passion for dressing-up and enacting plays. They would love this helmet to add to their collection of properties. I ought to pack it up and send it to them. And then I remembered the stories of Reachfar that I had told them at bed-time and how, out of these stories, they had constructed a dream world. The world that they had made was not the Reachfar that I had known or told about but a new world that they had carried forward into another dimension by playing the light of their minds on what I had told them. The stories had been my memories but the children, by listening, had made of them something different, something that was no longer entirely mine but in a large part their own. With a sudden thrill of discovery, I realised that story-telling was a two-way process. No story could exist without a listener but, given the listener, it became something greater than itself, grew in stature through mental contribution made by the listener.

I took some clean white paper from a drawer and took up my pen. Reachfar had been a beautiful place, the children had never tired of hearing of it. Was it possible to tell a wider audience about Reachfar, interest that audience to the degree that, in the light of their own minds, they would develop their own vision of it, come to love it and derive from it some of the joy that I had derived?

There was no harm in trying. I filled the fountain pen from the ink bottle. But where to begin? There was so much of Reachfar, the place that was the mainspring of my life, even now, after the passage of so many varied years, years during which the winds of the world had blotted out its identity so that it no longer existed, its fields and moors now no more than an anonymous corner of a larger estate. But I was the custodian of that lost identity and it might be that I could perpetuate something of it in the written word, as people perpetuate some of their own physical features in their children. There was no harm in trying.

About six in the evening, Twice arrived home, bringing Mackie with him and as they got out of the car, it was obvious to me from their bearing that Mackie's speech had gone well, but I made my enquiry none the less. 'Well, Mackie, how did it go?' Mackie's wild dark eyes swept over me and the length of the veranda before fixing themselves on the leg of a table.

'Great!' said Twice with enthusiasm. 'He had them glued to the walls. Spoke as if he had spent his life speaking a blue streak at Westminster.'

I nodded my head. 'I thought so. Congratulations, Mackie. What will you drink? Whisky?'

Very carefully, Mackie sat down. In company, he always moved carefully, as one unaccustomed to his own long bony legs and arms which seemed to have three elbows each, making movements that were beyond his control, movements which knocked over vases or other bric-a-brac.

'Did you have a good time in Scotland?' he asked me as I handed him his drink.

'Very good, thank you.'

'I should have asked you that last night,' he apologised, 'I meant to but then, one way and another and what with everything—' His voice came breathily to a halt.

'Now that all the speechifying is over for the moment, Mackie,' Twice said, 'we have to get on with that conveyor lay-out.'

Mackie's entire demeanour changed. Suddenly, his feet seemed to shrink and the preponderance of elbows disappeared. His bright dark eyes stopped trying to hide in corners and looked with direct intelligence at Twice.

'I have been thinking about that, sir. Listen, I was wondering if—'

He set his glass down, gathered a few ashtrays and other objects on to the table beside him.

'This is the vapourising floor, sir—' he began, putting a book into position, his long thin fingers moving with delicate precision but after half-an-hour of precise explanation of his ideas, he suddenly became covered in bony protuberances again as he rose to his feet and said: 'It must be your dinner-time. Sorry, Missis Janet. Thank you for the drink.'

'Stay and have some dinner, Mackie, won't you?' I said.

He looked startled, almost as if I had suggested something obscene.

'Yes, do that,' Twice said. 'There will be nothing but bully beef at Bachelors' anyway. Christie and Vickers are still down in the Bay. Mackie—' he pointed to the row of cigarettes that represented the conveyor '—that is going to lead to a lot of re-positioning inside the bagging house.'

Mackie did not say in words that he would stay for dinner. He merely sat down again with tidy finality and began to move the cigarettes about on the table-top.

With my needlework between my hands, I sat watching the two men, welded together by their near-fanatical interest in their subject, Mackie willing to defer to Twice's longer experience but not willing to be merely over-borne. I had always known that Twice was fond of Mackie but it was only now that I remembered how, during the time that Twice was critically ill, Mackie used to arrive on the veranda of the hospital and say: 'How is the Chief?' in a low scared voice and I could see again his drooped shoulders as he shambled away after receiving my non-committal reply.

'My slide-rule is through in the study,' Twice said, about to rise from his chair.

'Don't move, sir. I'll get it,' said Mackie and went through to the back of the house.

'You know,' Twice said to me, 'if I had a penny for every time Mackie has said those words, I'd be as rich as Croesus.' There was a curious vibration in his voice as he spoke and I looked into his face. He leaned forward and placed a hand on my forearm. 'Janet,' he said, 'Mackie is a good chap.'

'Yes,' I said, 'and I hadn't realised before just how good,' but I also meant that I had not known before of the close relationship that lay between Mackie and Twice. Like all lovers, I suppose, I had seen Twice only in relation to myself, had forgotten that life does not turn on a single axis like a small enclosed world but is as multifarious and complex in its nature as the solar system or the further galaxies.

We had just finished dinner when Sir Ian Dulac, the owner of Paradise, was upon us like a Force-9 gale in the words of Mackie, who sprang from his chair and made for the door as his employer entered. In a social way, Mackie spoke as few words as possible, Sir Ian spoke almost continuously in a loud barking voice and Mackie's instinct on his arrival anywhere, at any time, was to run, wide-eyed, as a hare runs when startled out of its form.

'Sit down, Mackie!' said Twice.

'*Me*, sir?'

'Sid*down*!' Twice repeated loudly as Sir Ian came into spate. 'So you're back, Missis Janet. Good to see ye, me dear. By Jove, you look well, twenty years younger, dammit, well, maybe not twenty but a goodish bit. Mother's delighted. She's been missin' you. Got old Maud Poynter stayin' round at the house, for company, ye know but it ain't workin' too well. Fightin' like Kilkenny cats, the two o' them, to tell the truth. Ye must come round an' see Mother as soon ye can, Missis Janet. Tell her about Scotland an' calm her down an' cheer her up.' His mind changed direction now and he glared from his sharp old eyes at Mackie whose head jerked to and fro on its long neck as his wild glance sought the far corners of the room. 'What you doin' round here?' Sir Ian barked. 'Should be down at the dance in the Bay like the rest. Good speech ye made this afternoon, though. Liked it. Give that bunch somethin' to think about.'

Mackie's skin was a dark gypsyish brown from the sun and his face seemed to grow black as the hot blood rose behind it while he tried to disentangle his long legs and rise from his chair.

'Sit *down*, Mackie,' said Twice and glared at Sir Ian, 'and you sit down too, sir. If you have come about what I think you have come about, I want Mackie here.'

Sir Ian's eyes sharpened as he stared into the blue eyes of Twice for a moment before he caught the back of a chair, pulled it out and sat down with a bump at the table. I had an urge to giggle.

'Some coffee, Sir Ian?' I asked.

'Rather have a tot o' whisky.'

'Certainly. I'll get it.'

When I handed him the glass, he said, 'Thanks, me dear. Well, no point beatin' about the bush. Missis Janet, Mother 'n' Edward 'n' I want Twice to manage this place for us. What d'ye think?'

'That is entirely up to Twice,' I said. 'I shall be in the drawing-room.'

'Sit *down!*' said Twice. 'I wish you would all stop going on like a bunch of fleas on a blanket.' As I sank back into my chair, he turned to me, 'What do you think?' he asked.

'It is what *you* think,' I told him, 'as long as you remember that I am no Marion Maclean. I could never give all those diplomatic parties and—'

'What has Marion Maclean got to do with it?' Twice

asked angrily. 'I am considering the management of Paradise, not turning myself into the sugar tycoon of the Caribbean like Rob Maclean.' He swung round to face Sir Ian. 'I am not tycoon material, sir. I hope you are clear about that. Given the staff I want, I could manage Paradise but I am not going to spend half my time sitting on my backside talking a blue streak at conferences and meetings of the Caribbean trade.'

'Nobody's talkin' about the Caribbean trade. I'm talkin' about Paradise,' said Sir Ian, 'so what sort o' staff d'ye want, me boy? Edward's in London. He can see about engagin' a Chief an' if—'

'Edward needn't bother to engage a Chief,' Twice interrupted. 'I have my own Chief right here.'

A sugar factory, in many ways, resembles a ship and one of its most important men is its Chief Engineer. Originally, Twice and I had come to St. Jago because Twice, as a consulting engineer, was to supervise the replanning and modernisation of Paradise factory and after his heart condition had been discovered, handicapping him for work as an active engineer, Sir Ian had taken him on to the estate staff as assistant to Rob Maclean, the manager. In the hands of Twice, however, the post had turned itself into that of Chief Engineer for, although he was no longer able to climb about the galleries or, in the words of Sir Ian, 'to hang from the girders by his toes,' he had an intimate knowledge of the huge complex he had planned and installed and even more important than his knowledge was his love for and pride in the thing he had done so much to create.

'Now, look here, me boy,' Sir Ian barked sternly, 'I know your health is remarkable. Was talking to Mark Lindsay the doctor chap the other day an' he says it's as remarkable a recovery as he's seen, but you are not fit—' he bumped his fist on the table four times, emphasising the four words '—to manage *and* chief the place on your own. No man is!'

'I know that,' Twice said calmly. 'I am not talking about

myself as Chief. I am talking about Mackie here.'

Sir Ian flopped back in his chair, while I looked at Mackie who spread his long fingers over the chest of his crumpled white shirt, his big eyes staring in wild surmise as he squealed out the words: '*Me*, sir?'

'Mackie?' Sir Ian breathed quietly and he blinked as he focused his eyes on the young man across the table as if he were seeing him in a strange new light.

'Why not?' Twice asked. 'Mackie was right here through the whole modernisation programme, under my bloody feet the whole time, not to put too fine a point on it. He knows more about the Paradise plant than any man you could bring in, no matter how experienced.'

'But, sir—' said Mackie and fell silent.

'What?' Twice asked and as Mackie simply stared bemused, he went on: 'Don't tell me you wouldn't *like* to be Chief of Paradise.'

'Oh no, sir,' said Mackie hastily. 'There isn't an engineer in the Caribbean who wouldn't like to be Chief of Paradise but—' There was another dark silence.

'But what?'

'I don't know. I sort of feel a fool, sir.'

'You are a fool, Mackie,' said Twice with affection. 'Look, off you go out of here, you awkward big clot and leave the rest of this to Sir Ian and me.'

'Yes, sir,' said Mackie with enthusiasm. 'Whatever you say, sir. Thank you for dinner, Missis—' His feet became entangled in the legs of his chair which fell over on its side with a clatter. 'Oh, sorry. Thanks for – er – everything. Goodnight.' He bumped into the edge of the door and debouched into the hall.

'Better start thinkin' o' gettin' married, Mackie,' Sir Ian barked after him, adding to the confusion. 'Can't have a bachelor Chief on Paradise. Mother don't approve o' them.' There was no answer other than a crash as Mackie fell down the veranda steps.

'I can't understand why that bloke is so clumsy as soon as you take him out of the factory,' Twice said thoughtfully. 'Round at the plant, he is as sure-footed as a Siamese cat.'

'Mackie,' said Sir Ian, staring at the wall.

'He is a good man, sir,' Twice said. 'You won't regret this. I can guarantee that.'

'I believe ye, me boy. It is just that ye don't notice time passin' an' the youngsters gettin' on. Ye get into the way o' thinkin' that people stand still. Of *course* Mackie is the man for Chief. Just never thought o' it. Kept thinkin' o' him as a junior, ye know.' He rose to his feet. 'Well, must get back an' report to Mother. She'll be delighted, me boy, about you an' Mackie an' everythin'. You'll come round to see her tomorrow, Missis Janet?'

'Yes, Sir Ian,' I said. 'Eleven in the forenoon?'

'Good. I'll send the car for ye, me dear. By Jove, Mother's goin' to be pleased about all this—'

While Sir Ian talked his way to his car, Twice going with him, I crossed the hall and sat down in my favourite corner of the drawing-room. When I had first seen this room, Twice and I had been migrants, on a visit to St. Jago from Britain, after which Twice might be sent to Africa, India or Peru, to any country that was developing technologically, but probably to one where sugar was grown, after his experience of the Paradise plant. This was how our future had appeared in 1950 but six years had worked their difference, making of that future something that could not have been foreseen. Instead of being a roving engineer, Twice had turned into the manager of Paradise, one of the figures of the Caribbean sugar trade.

'Are congratulations in order?' I asked as he came into the room.

'I think not.' He stopped in the middle of the floor. 'This appointment is not an achievement. It is more of an accident. By force of circumstances, I happened to be in the right place at the right time.'

'But you must be pleased, Twice. Half the sugar men would give their ears—'

'Naturally I am pleased,' he interrupted me, 'because

it means that I can run the thing the way I think it should be run. But we are getting ahead of ourselves. I haven't taken the appointment yet. I told Sir Ian I would give our decision in the morning.'

I noticed the phrase 'our decision' but did not speak.

'If you are going to worry yourself sick about my health all the time, the deal is off,' he told me bluntly.

I looked up at him for a moment before I spoke, choosing my words, trying to say precisely what I meant.

'I have abdicated from my post as worrier about your health,' I said. 'You manage very well without my worrying. I expect you to go on using common-sense, that's all. I don't think you could live as Rob Maclean lived, but it seems that you don't intend to do that."

'I don't. I don't want to be a petty power in the Caribbean. I merely want to run Paradise.'

'And you don't expect me to entertain oil men and—'

'The oil men and the rest can be dealt with in the office where they belong. It amused Rob – and Marion too, I suppose – to pit one oil man against another for the Paradise contract but it doesn't amuse me to watch a lot of ten per cent johnnies jockeying for position and lick-spittling around. I shall order the oils that suit the plant and that is all there is to it.'

'You make it sound very simple, Twice.'

'It is simple. I have always found it simple to be an engineer. It is my trade. They want to call me a manager now but I have been a manager before. I was Works Manager at Ballydendran once, remember?'

'I remember but it is a far cry from Slater's Works to Paradise.'

'It is still engineering. What is that thing Monica used to say – plus ça change—'

'—plus c'est la même chose,' I concluded. 'What you mean is that it is the same only different. Am I permitted to be a little proud of you when I write home to Tom and George?'

'I don't suppose I can stop you but, as I said, I don't

regard this as an achievement. It is simply something that has happened.'

'But if you weren't who and what you are, it would not have happened. What happens to us does grow out of us, Twice.'

He shrugged his shoulders, bored as he always was with the abstract and I returned to the practical. 'You said you will run Paradise as you think it should be run. This implies that it has not been run in quite your way in the past. How do you think it should be run?'

'All that money that Rob spent on charter planes to take him on speech-making trips to the other islands can go into a proper training scheme here at Paradise for a start,' he said. 'But at the moment, I don't want to talk about running Paradise, I want to talk about us. You have got the idea that I got better because you went away for a few weeks.' He paused and then added thoughtfully: 'In a way, maybe you are right at that. Remember in the few days before you went away how you lectured me till all was blue about being careful and not overdoing things? I did everything you said, went on with the old routine for about the first ten days. Then a queer little thing happened. I scratched my hand—' he indicated the broad back of his left hand '—on a rough edge of steel up at the workshop. It was literally a scratch but it must have opened during the night and there was a bloodstain on my top sheet in the morning.'

I watched him as he sat looking down at the floor. In the course of his work, Twice could get himself dirtier than anyone I have ever seen. He always seemed to be covered in engine oil but I had long since learned that engine oil, molasses or any other of the other by-products of sugar-processing did not qualify for the name of dirt. Dirt, in Twice's dictionary, signified body-soiled clothing, stained table or bed linen, unfresh towels in a bathroom.

'When I went to bed that night,' he was continuing, 'that bloodstain was still on that sheet and it went on being there for three days. Then I began to notice other little indications that the servants were taking a bit of a free ride. This is where you came in. It is difficult to describe how important it was that I should not be forced to miss you in this petty way as well as in all the other ways and I did miss you, you know. So I decided to do something about it, have all four of them in and give them a piece of my mind. That was the turning-point. After I had told Clorinda that they were all to come into the study, I thought for a few minutes that I had let you down at the end of two miserable weeks. Blood was beating in my head as if my temples were going to burst, I felt sick, my knees were wobbling, all the classic symptoms of the heart case who had gone too far. Then they came shambling into the study and I went into a flat calm. If Janet had been there, I thought, that sheet would have been changed. Things have got to be as she would like them and then I let fly and the house has run like clockwork ever since and I have felt better than I have felt for three years. Silly, isn't it?'

'Not silly,' I said, rising from my chair and turning away from him, 'not silly at all.'

'So you see,' he said from behind me, 'what happens to me doesn't grow entirely out of me. Some of it grows out of you. It is time we went to bed. You have got Madame to cope with in the morning, remember.'

But I felt that since my return thirty-six hours ago, I had been given a great deal that I did not deserve and that I must now confess my sins. 'Twice,' I said, 'when you left me at the Peak with Sashie yesterday forenoon and Miranda Beaumont was bitching away, I had such a hate for this island and everybody in it that for a moment I wanted to go straight back to Scotland. I just want you to know that I don't feel like that any more.'

'Pity,' he said, grinning at me, 'because, now, we might easily go back to Scotland one day. In the nature of things, my career as manager of Paradise cannot last long. Sir Ian and Edward still intend to sell this place when Madame goes and she can't last for ever although she is having a damn' good try. With my pension as ex-manager, we would be all right in a little place like Achcraggan, don't you think?'

'Oh, Twice—' I began but then the superstitious nature of what he called my Celtic Twilight took charge of me and I said: 'Twice, don't let's make plans. Let us just go on and see what happens. That is always best.'

The following morning, as I went about the house, I found myself glancing now and then at the wicker chair in the corner of the drawing room. At one point, I even picked up the chintz cushion from its seat and gave it a shake, in preparation for the visitant that might occupy it but even as I did so I was telling myself it was unlikely that the girl would come, that she might never come to the house again. She had taken on significance in my mind, I think, because she had touched some chord in Twice that made him speak of her in a way that was not characteristic of him. Twice was more given to firm opinions about people – 'Mackie is a good chap' – than to likening them to swallows that had come to nest in the eaves of his home. As a rule, I was the one to make such comparisons and the comparison having been made identified the girl in my mind with those harbingers of summer who used to make their homes under the roof-hang of the granary gable at Reachfar. Thinking of the girl, I could hear again the voice of Tom as he said to George: 'Be careful you, now, with that mortar up there. If you make the wall too different, the swallows may not like it when they come and if you frighten them off, the old people used to say, they will go away for seven years and take your luck away with them.' And my uncle, George, looked down from the top of the high ladder and said: 'Listen to the ould spaewife, Granny Tom, Janet but there is no need to be believing all you will be hearing.'

Still, he was careful with the mortar, I noticed, and did not damage with his trowel the weather-battered remains of the swallows' nests of the year before.

But on this morning, no girl came to occupy the wicker chair in the corner. What did come was Madame Dulac's car to take me round to the Great House which lay on the other side of the factory from Guinea Corner and the other staff houses round the park.

I had last seen the Great House a few moments after the earthquake when some of the great stone pillars that supported the first-floor verandas were lying like broken match-sticks on the lawn, but now, as the car deposited me at the garden entrance through the library, I saw that all the damage had been repaired. The columns of stone were back in place, the windows re-glazed and no trace of the earthquake remained. There was no trace of it anywhere now, I thought, except for the grave in the burial ground that held the bodies of Rob and Marion Maclean.

'Rubbish, Maud!' came the angry voice of Madame from within the library. 'It was *not* Beattie Denholm's grandson who played Red Gurk. It was Rob Maclean. All that that wretched young Denholm did that night was to try to shoot Mr. de Marnay. For a young woman, Maud, you have a very poor memory.'

'Here is Mrs. Alexander,' said Miss Poynter and Madame in her chair in the corner held out her two ring-laden fat little hands to myself in the doorway.

'Janet, how nice to have you back. Come, my dear, and sit down. Maud, go and tell them to bring us some coffee.' Miss Poynter went away and Madame continued: 'Dreadful woman. Ian and I thought we would have her here for a time because she must be lonely down there in that little house of hers all by herself although she won't admit it, of course. The Poynters were always very difficult unaccommodating people. And for a young woman, her mind is really quite decayed. She ought to get married. It would liven her up but only a fool would marry her. She is really very irritating, Janet, very irritating indeed.'

Madame was also very easy to irritate but I assured myself as I had done often before that this was no matter for wonder because during the last few years she had become stone blind. Before this disability overtook her, she had been very active in every way although she admitted to being 'in her eighties' while the rest of us were convinced, from historical evidence, that she was nearly a hundred years old. Before she became blind, she had interfered in the lives of everybody on the estate, had bullied every charity committee in the island, entertained lavishly, played execrable and very bad-tempered bridge and ruled her large house and garden staff with a Victorian sceptre backed by a will that was stronger than any iron rod.

Her reference now to Maud Poynter as a 'young woman' was misleading because, in comparison to Madame herself, everybody in St. Jago was young, although this was a fact that she preferred not to recognise unless it suited her. Maud Poynter was about sixty, an ex-actress who had achieved no distinction on the stage and I thought that Madame, now, must have forgotten what Miss Poynter looked like even at fifty when I had first seen her. Any man who married her would have to be blind as well as a fool for Miss Poynter, with her balding henna-ed hair, her rolls and bulges of pasty fat, her grotesque make-up and her clanking bracelets and necklaces resembled more than anything a toad dressed for a part in pantomime.

There was an underlying sadness in the fact that Sir Ian had brought her here as a companion for Madame. Miss Poynter was here because she and Madame were almost the only survivals in the island of a bygone day, the day of the 'plantation ladies', the 'white missis-es', those arrogant autocrats who were convinced that they were made out of a more regal clay than the rest of mankind. There was pathos in the fact of these two, together in this great house, quarrelling their frustrated days away.

'Now tell me about your holiday, Janet,' said Madame and at once, before I could reply, continued: 'I am most pleased that Mr. Twice feels able to take up the position of manager for us and I am sure that if he considers young Mr. Mackie qualified to be Chief Engineer, we have no need to worry. Now, there is the question of your house. At the moment, we have those people who have come to attend to the schoolchildrens' teeth at Olympus but as soon as their proper quarters are ready, we shall have the house redecorated and you must move up there.' Momentarily, I was glad that the old lady was blind, that she could not see the horror which, I was sure, was showing in my eyes. Olympus might be one of the finest houses in St. Jago but, to me, it was hateful, perched as it was on that vertiginous hill, its east and north walls rising out of sheer cliffs. Madame's butler came in with the coffee tray on which were two cups only. Miss Poynter had decided not to join us and I was thankful.

'Madame,' I said carefully. 'I would rather not move to Olympus, if you don't mind. Twice and I are very fond of Guinea Corner and—' I had a sudden inspiration '—my garden is very beautiful now. I should hate to leave it.'

Madame, in her more active days, had been very fond of her own garden and my liking for mine might be something that she would understand.

'There is no garden to speak of at Olympus, it is true,' she said thoughtfully. 'It is the site that makes the house. But our manager has always lived there, Janet, ever since we bought in the Olympus Estate. The house goes with the appointment.'

'But Twice and I are different from the Macleans, Madame. They had seven of a family, after all. Olympus is much too large for Twice and me and times have changed too. Servants are more difficult to come by these days. Your coffee, Madame.'

'Ah, yes, times change,' she agreed sadly as she groped for the coffee cup, while contriving silently to defy me to notice that she was groping. I edged the saucer towards her fingers and firmly she took it from my hand. 'So much change.' She sighed. 'Very well, my dear. If you prefer Guinea Corner, naturally you must stay there. I thought you would have preferred the larger house. When I was your age, even this house was never large enough for the entertainments I wished to give but times have changed, as you said.'

Her words sent me on a mental journey round the huge house, from its cellars, through the ground floor where we sat, on to the first storey which contained the drawing-room and the main bedrooms and on to the upper storey where there were more bedrooms. In my time in the island, when Madame was already old, I had seen buffet supper parties for over two hundred people in this house and dinner parties at which eighty guests were seated in the dining-room across the hall. My mind returned to the fat, blind little figure, upright in the straight-backed chair on the other side of the low table.

Sir Ian had said that I was to tell Madame about Scotland but there was nothing that I could tell her about my visit which she would understand. My brother, his wife and family pursued a way of life there that Madame Dulac could never comprehend, for she was fixed for ever in this world that had closed about her when she had come to Paradise as a young bride long ago. Nor did she want to be 'cheered up' by tales of other worlds. All she wanted was to remain the mistress of this world that she had ruled for so long, to remain unaware that it was disintegrating around her. I had learned long ago that the best way to amuse Madame was to encourage her to talk of the past.

'Just before you arrived,' she said now, 'Maud was trying to tell me that Beattie Denholm's son played the part of the villain in that entertainment we gave a few years ago. Really, Maud is very pig-headed and has no right to be so when her memory is so poor. It was Rob Maclean who played the part.'

In fact, David Denholm had originally been cast for the part of the villain, had then withdrawn and had been replaced by Rob Maclean but I said: 'Yes, Madame. It was Rob who played Red Gurk. It was a most exciting evening, if you remember.'

'Of course I remember,' said Madame and we went on to relive one evening of her long past.

When it was almost lunch-time and her chauffeur had brought the car to the door to take me home, she said: 'Now, Janet, what is the most convenient time for you to spend with me each day? What I should like is to send the car for you at two each afternoon and then Mr. Twice can come each day when he leaves his office and have some tea or a drink before he takes you home. But not on Saturdays or Sundays, of course. Ian will be with me then.'

'Very well, Madame,' I agreed, thinking of my plans for the back bedroom, trying not to grudge so much of my time to her, for she and her family had been very kind to Twice and me. Also, my friends George and Tom whom I had left at my brother's home came into my mind. They were not quite as old as Madame and they were not blind but I would not like to think of them sitting alone and lonely, while the changing world swept past them, if they ever became capable of letting anything sweep past them which, when I had left them a few days before, had seemed very unlikely.

'And one day,' Madame was saying, 'you must bring some of these girls who are staying at Olympus to call on me. One or two of them are dentists, I understand, a most sordid occupation for young women. I do not approve of it in the least and I cannot think what could make them take to such a profession.'

'I agree with you, Madame,' I said, which was true enough but the words were fortunate in that they were the only words that Madame genuinely liked to hear anyone speak but I now remembered that there was one item of news from Scotland that would interest her.

'When Roddy Maclean and I landed in London, Madame,' I said, 'he very kindly drove me up to my brother's home in Aberdeenshire.'

'Indeed? I am glad to hear that he was so considerate. A most unruly young man but I thought that he was settling down during his last visit here.'

'I think he is rather completely settled down now,

Madame. He and my sister-in-law's sister intend to get married.'

'My dear Janet, I am delighted! You must sit down again and tell me about the young lady. What is her name?'

I did not sit down. I felt that the little I knew about Roddy's prospective bride or, indeed, about anyone could be told in a few words. 'Sheila Murray, Madame. She is very pretty and she is a rather highly qualified nurse.'

'How very suitable. The nursing profession produces women of fine firm character, just the sort of person that that young man needs. Janet, this is splendid news. When you know when the wedding is to take place, you must tell me for I wish to send a gift to the bride. But, yes, you must get home for lunch, dear. Before you go, please find Maud and send her to me.'

'Yes, Madame,' I said and took my leave as she murmured: 'A nurse! Quite the finest profession for women.'

'Well,' said Twice over the lunch table, 'how are things at the Great House?'

'What our niece Liz would call droopy,' I told him. 'Madame and old Maud are irritating one another to death but I suppose that is better than each of them boring themselves to death on their own. And Madame wants me round there from two in the afternoon until drinks time from Mondays till Fridays.'

'You didn't say you would go?'

'I did. I felt a bit grudging but I agreed.'

'It is a bit of a demand. Just because they have made me manager doesn't mean that you have to devote your life to the Great House.'

'In my book, your being manager has nothing to do with it, Twice. Madame is old and blind and needs me and I can't explain properly. It is something that I learned at Jock's place. When I first arrived there, the children seemed to regard me as an old interloper, a sort of nuisance. They walked past me, ignored me, indicated that they had no need for me. It was horrible. And I think that deep down Madame feels that nobody needs *her* any more, that she has lived too long, even.'

'In a way, she has,' he said. 'She has outlived the only way of life she knows or likes.'

'I don't believe that anyone lives too long. If Madame is still alive, there is some reason for it. In fact, she must feel that she has something to do still or she would just die.' I was thinking of my grandmother who had seemed to decide, after my grandfather died, that her work was finished and she died within the same twenty-four hours. Anyhow, as long as Madame *is* alive, she has to be part of the life that goes on here and not just a body sitting in a corner of that house.'

'You are away over my head,' Twice said, 'but you must cope according to your own lights.'

'She mustn't be allowed to feel that life is going past her. I shall spend my afternoons with her as long as she wants me to,' I said. 'And she wants to meet some of the Teeth and Feet girls so we had better have some of them over here sometime soon so that I can meet them first. How shall I go about it? It seems a bit grand and Marion Maclean-ish for me to ring up Olympus and dish out a sort of royal command,' I said, irritated even as I spoke that even something as simple as this should be coloured in my mind by a shadow from the past.

'Percy didn't arrive this morning?' Twice asked. 'She usually appears at weekends. She will come in tomorrow likely. You can arrange it through her.'

'But if she doesn't come?'

'Ten to one she will but if not I can have speech with Vickers and Christie. They have been showing two of the girls around, a dentist and a nurse, I believe.'

'I wonder why it should be sordid for a girl to be a dentist and quite the reverse for her to be a nurse?' I said next and then answered myself: 'Something to do with Florence Nightingale and the suffragettes, I suppose.'

'Florence Nightingale wasn't a suffragette,' Twice protested reasonably enough.

'I didn't mean to say that she was. It was Madame. She approves of girls being nurses but not of their being dentists and I think it is because she approved of Florence Nightingale but not of the suffragettes.'

'Madame is a fat little bundle of prejudices as you well know,' he told me, 'and as illogical as they come.'

I could be as critical of Madame as anyone, was more aware of many of her less likeable characteristics than many because I had probably spent more time with her than anybody other than Marion Maclean, Sir Ian or her grandson Edward. But on this day I could brook no criticism of her, however legitimate, because she had contributed so much to our good fortune and happiness.

'We have all got prejudices and we can all be illogical,' I said, 'and Madame can be very reasonable too. When the Teeth and Feet Lot go, she wanted us to move up to Olympus—'

'Not on your life!' Twice interrupted.

'—but when I said we would rather stay here, she gave in without a murmur.'

'Just as well. I wouldn't live up there for anything. Besides, I have other plans for it.'

'What?'

'It will make an excellent barracks and school for my apprentices.'

'Tout lasse, tout casse, tout passe, as Sashie would say. It used to be one of the most exclusive white houses in the island.'

'To use it as a barracks and school is the only logical thing to do with it. Nobody would want it as a private house any more but the Yates are quite willing to move up there and turn it into a school. The Yates would live anywhere provided it was a school.'

Bertie Yates, who had lost his left arm in the 1939-45 war, had come to the island in 1946 as tutor to Sandy, the youngest son of Rob and Marion Maclean, but had soon extended his duties to form a small school at which the white children of the staff had their first lessons. He had married, a few years ago, Dorothy Davey, a young friend of ours and they now had two children but the Compound School had dwindled away, as the pupils grew older and went away to boarding-school. The Yates had remained, however, Bertie having been re-employed as steward of the estate Sports Club and general factotum, being one of those quietly useful people who could turn his one hand to almost anything.

'You are visualising a sort of boarding-school up there?' I asked.

'Yes, a fee-paying school for apprentice sugar men, engineers, chemists, field men – not a charity affair. It has to wash its face financially but it won't be too costly to the pupils or their parents. Yates will be the only salaried teacher, the theory man, mostly maths and chemistry. The apprentices will get the practical training in the old-fashioned way, on the factory floor, at the heels of Mackie, Vickers, Christie and the rest.'

'Your plans are very cut and dried. Does Sir Ian know about them?'

'Lord, yes. Edward too. They are delighted.'

'I am not clucking, Twice, but aren't you biting off rather a lot of work?'

'It will make no more work for me if it is properly organised – less in fact. At the moment, we have a dozen apprentices coming in and out from their homes and one can never be sure of having them all in one place at one time. If we have them all up at Olympus and Mackie takes a vapouriser apart, we can get them all down on to the vapour floor in a quarter of an hour.'

He spoke in a very calm way about his school but I knew that it was the realisation of a long-cherished dream. He had always disliked the system, prevalent not only at Paradise but at all the other sugar plantations in the island, whereby the senior and executive posts were all filled by men imported from Europe, so that no St. Jagoan could hope to rise in the hierarchy beyond the position of foreman.

Rob Maclean had not been interested in the training of native apprentices but in spite of this Twice, with the connivance of Sir Ian, during the last few years had been bringing on a few St. Jagoans towards more senior posts in the factory and as I looked at him now, his eyes bright as he looked to the future, I said: 'This is something you have wanted very much, isn't it?'

'Yes, it is. I am getting a lot that I want at the moment. I have got Joe Brown appointed as third shift man, under Vickers and Christie.'

Joe Brown was a St. Jagoan, the first apprentice that Twice had begun to coach.

'You *are* going it a bit, aren't you?' I commented.

He winked at me, one bright eye suddenly disappearing behind a black-lashed heavy eyelid. 'I am going it while the going is good, that's all. Not only is Joe appointed. He is to move into Bachelors' Bungalow with Vickers and Christie.'

Here, history in a small way was being made. Joe Brown would be the first coloured man to live in a house on the Staff Compound.

'But that dump can't contain four of them,' I protested.

'Mackie is moving out. One can't break with tradition altogether. You have to mark the difference between the Chief and the rest of the grease-wallahs. Mackie will move into School Bungalow when the Yates go up to Olympus.'

'Will he like that?'

'Mackie doesn't care one way or another where or how he lives. Giving him a place of his own is more of a sop to Madame and Sir Ian. There is a touch of the mad genius in Mackie. He is never completely conscious except when he is at work in the factory. The rest of his life is a sort of dream.'

'He seemed to get on very well all those years with Vickers and Christie. It seems a pity to break them up.'

'He didn't get on with them in the ordinary sense. It

was more that he didn't notice them. Mackie isn't really much aware of other people.'

'He is aware of you.'

'That is sort of different.' Twice rose from the table, suddenly embarrassed, as he always was when made to think of the world, so mysterious and mentally defeating to him, of human relationships. 'I think he regards me as a sort of adopted father or something. Well, it is time I was back up at the office.'

He went away, leaving me to think that there were no phrases like 'sort of' and 'or something' in his speech when he discussed his practical plans for apprentice schools and staff housing, that these phrases made themselves heard only when he was emotionally involved.

That night, Twice and I were awakened at about midnight by a combination of the flashing beams of car headlights, the continuous roar of motor horns and a large number of loud voices raised in raucous song. Sitting up in bed, we watched through the window the car lights wind round the corkscrew drive to the top of Olympus hill, where the house had something of the outline of a huge light-bedizened Christmas tree against the dark sky.

'That lot have really got the wind under their tails tonight,' Twice said, lying down again as the noise died away.

'Does this happen often?'

'Never to this extent before, the selfish young brutes.'

I giggled. 'I don't mind your getting middle-aged,' I said, 'but don't get smug and crusty, will you? Remember that night it was your birthday away back and somebody put that dead alligator in the bath?'

'Don't,' he said. 'The very memory makes me tired. That was the night that that oil man from Texas and I had the race to the top of the palm trees.' He sat up again and looked down at me in the moonlight, his eyes stern and accusing. 'That was the night that you danced the Highland Fling at Bachelors' Bungalow and danced yourself off the table on to the floor and went on dancing without missing a beat. By all the laws of dynamics, you should have broken both your legs but you didn't.'

'Stop it,' I said, rolling over so that my back was towards him and pulling the sheet up round my ears, sorry now that I had disturbed our over-energetic ghosts. 'Go back to sleep.' But sleep for a long time was not possible. After a few moments, there came a loud whoosh across the moonlit park which brought us bolt upright to see about a dozen rockets light up the sky over Olympus and after some more fireworks the air was rent by someone playing a very bad rendering of Tipperary on what sounded like a trombone. Olympus was certainly making a night of it. 'Speak of the spring and foison of the year' I thought, as I lay down again. The heady atmosphere of St. Jago was affecting these young people just as it had affected Twice and me when we first arrived.

I do not know what time it was when I fell asleep but I awoke shortly before six, at first light, as I always did and went out to the garden to cut some flowers for the house before the sun became bright and hot. Early morning was the best time of the day at Paradise. The sun popped over the horizon as suddenly as it had disappeared on the evening before but, as it began its climb to the zenith, there were long bands of shade across the grass which was dewy and cool underfoot. As I let myself quietly out of the back door with my flower basket and secateurs, Caleb came out of his quarters at the end of the arbour and began to erect a tent of palm fronds over his bed of cauliflowers, to shade them from the later sun of the day.

'Morning, ma'am. The time is hot. There is a blow out to sea maybe.'

By 'a blow' Caleb meant hurricane and I now noticed the humid stickiness of the air, the heavy pressure of hurricane weather. The eye of the blow might be a hundred miles away but its sullen oppressiveness spread over a wide radius.

'I hope it stays out at sea then,' I said.

And now the other hurricane that had struck Olympus

about midnight had blown itself out and there was a deep Sunday-morning stillness over the park as I carried my flowers into the pantry and began to put them into vases.

Sundays were the most social days at Paradise, the days when the Yates might drive across the park for a pre-lunch drink or Sir Ian call for what he called 'a bit of a chat' and in the afternoons the younger members of the staff would join their factory colleagues round at the Club to play tennis or the favourite cricket if there were enough of them gathered together to form two teams. There was no cricket season at Paradise. It was played all the year round by everybody, from Caleb and the other yard boys up to the old pensioner who swept up the loose cane trash in the factory yard.

Having filled some six vases with flowers, I set out to carry the first and largest to the drawing-room but in the doorway of the room I stopped dead. Beside the wicker stool in the corner, there lay a pair of small white sandals and on the stool itself there were two slim bare legs and small feet. The legs were crossed at the knees, where the stool joined the edge of the big chair and I thought at once of the pointed wings of a swallow showing under the eaves of the granary gable at Reachfar. I was about to tiptoe back to the pantry when a small face wearing the largest, heaviest-looking blackest-rimmed spectacles I had ever seen poked round the edge of the wicker cave.

'Good morning, Mrs. Alexander,' the girl said, getting to her feet. 'I am Percy Soames. Maybe Twice told you about me?'

'Yes, he did,' I said. 'Good morning. Do sit down, Percy.' I put my flowers down on the table where the arrangement of hibiscus had been. 'Would you like some coffee? I am going to have some. I have been in the garden.'

'Thank you.' She sat down on the stool and put on her sandals.

Pouring coffee, I said: 'You are an early bird this morning' and then noticed that the cliché contained the word 'bird'.

'I have been here since just after midnight, actually,' she said. 'I hope you don't mind. It is fun when people don't lock their doors.'

'You haven't been to bed?'

'I slept right here.' She indicated the chair and stool which together more than contained her short length.

She was very small, with fragile bird-like bones and although she had slept in the white shirt and shorts, she still looked fresh and airy, as if she had just flown in from the high sky. I watched as she gathered her shoulder-length hair, so fair that it was almost white, into a bundle, pulled it back from her face and with a deft movement between her fingers and an elastic band, fixed it into a pony-tail that dangled from high on the back of her head.

'I got tired of the party,' she said, 'and I knew Dram wouldn't bark if I came. He knows me.'

'The party seemed to be quite a wingding,' I said, remembering.

'Pam Durrant and Eddie Muir got themselves engaged yesterday afternoon,' she explained. 'That started it.'

Drinking her coffee, she retired into silence. This was not of a hostile kind, but rather a withdrawal into a private world which, I felt, might be governed by laws that did not apply to the world I inhabited. To sit across the room from her was, I thought inevitably, like sitting near a tree where a bird was perched, watching it pursue its secret way of life for a moment, before it spread its wings and took to its own element, leaving me bound to the earth. And as I would have watched the bird in silence, in silence I watched this girl for I had an instinctive feeling that to question her, to try to know her or place her would cause her to take wing.

'I like this chair and this house and Twice,' she said after her prolonged silence. 'I hope you won't mind if I come here sometimes.'

I felt as if one of the swallows were paying a formal call at the door of Reachfar, asking for permission to build a nest on the granary gable.

'Of course not,' I said. 'Come any time but if you tire of another party, there is a bed ready in the first room on the left at the top of the stairs. And as you know, we do not lock doors so you can always get in.'

She turned her small head and looked at me through the enormous glasses. She had a shy wild trick of never looking at one directly when she spoke, seeming to address some point beyond one's shoulder. Her eyes behind the lenses were large and blue and obviously myopic.

'Thank you,' she said. 'You are kind.'

In spite of her air of shyness, she had a poise and self-possession which reminded me of my niece Liz, a poise that I had not had at her age. Like Liz, this young person was the result of an upbringing less repressive than mine had been, an upbringing that did not contain the adage that the child should be seen and not heard. My upbringing had made me more predictable to my elders, I was sure, than Liz or this young woman were to me. My elders must have known that, to a large extent, I would react according to the strict code of behaviour that had been imposed on me but this young woman was not a puppet controlled by any code and she would react, I felt, to any situation in a manner that was entirely personal.

'Bruce said you were kind,' she said now and added : 'at least he didn't say that. He said you were a good egg. So often when somebody says something like that, it doesn't work, don't you think? I mean when somebody says you will like so-and-so, you hate the sight of them as soon as you see them.'

'That is true,' I said, amused, 'but tell me, who is Bruce?'

She looked at me with a puzzled frown that caused the heavy-framed glasses to slide down to the tip of her small nose. Before replying, she pushed them back into place with the tip of her forefinger. 'Bruce? You must know him. He is around Twice all the time – Bruce Mackie.'

'Oh, Mackie!' I said, feeling that I had made a strange and exotic discovery until I became conscious of the girl's blue-eyed stare of blank amazement. 'It is one of those things,' I explained confusedly. 'I have known Mackie for years but he has always been called Mackie. I didn't know his first name was Bruce. Silly, isn't it?'

'No,' she said solemnly, after a thoughtful pause, 'not really. You can know people for years and not know lots of things about them and there are other people that you feel you have known for years the very moment that you meet them. But names are queer,' she added, changing direction. 'Sometimes I think it would be better if we all had numbers tattooed on our foreheads.' She held her wrist up to her ear. 'Listen, has my watch stopped? I have got to see about breakfast for that lot up there even if it is only alka-seltzer and iced water. Is it only about half-past seven?'

'It can't be much more. I went out to the garden at six. That lot on the hill won't be awake for hours yet. I don't think numbers on our foreheads would work very well, though. I would feel that Number Seven and all the multiples of seven and all the numbers with seven in them had been born lucky and had an unfair advantage. Why don't you like names?'

'It isn't that I don't like them exactly. It is that if you don't know somebody's name you are lost and if you do know somebody's name it makes you think things. Our headmistress at school was called Janet and *she* wouldn't have given a stranger coffee at seven in the morning. I meant to be off back to Olympus before you got up, actually,' she confessed now.

'Then I am glad I caught you. I wanted to see you.'

'Why?' she asked a little sharply.

'Because of Madame Dulac.'

'Madame Dulac? The old lady at the Great House as they call it?'

'Yes. She has asked me to bring a few of you girls at Olympus to call on her. Apart from that, I would like to meet the members of the Mission and Twice and I thought we would have a little party here soon. He said you would

77

know the best time and day to have it, to suit the Olympus people, I mean.'

'They would go to a party anywhere at almost any time,' she told me, 'but Sunday for drinks before lunch or in the evening would be the most sensible. Do you want them all? There are seventeen of us, if you count me.'

'I should certainly count you. Yes, the invitation would be to them all but the ones who don't want to come don't have to.'

'Oh, they will come all right.'

'Then shall we say about eleven-thirty next Sunday? Shall I write a note or will you tell them?'

'I'll tell them and stick a notice on the board in the hall.'

'Thank you. And you must tell me which ones are dentists, girl dentists, I mean. I don't think I should take girl dentists to the Great House just at first. Madame doesn't approve of dentistry as a profession for women but she will come round to it in time. She is rather old-fashioned,' I apologised.

'And I will tell you something,' said Percy with grave emphasis, 'she is quite right, not approving of women dentists, I mean. I suppose some people have got to be dentists but imagine having your horizon bounded by two rows of teeth and some of them rotten at that.'

The girl was reminding me more and more of my niece Liz, with her emphatic independence of mind and utterance. Liz was only eight years old and this girl was about twenty, I estimated but Liz had taken after my brother's and my side of the family, who are all tall while Percy was so small in every way as to be almost a miniature. She was very little taller than Liz, while I was sure that the sandals she was wearing would never have contained Liz's feet.

'Do I qualify to call on Madame Dulac, not being a dentist?' she asked.

'But certainly, if you would like to.'

'I would. I like old people who have lived for a long time. She is old, isn't she?'

'None of us know how old but I think she is in her nineties, although it isn't polite to mention it.'

Percy laughed softly, indulgently. 'My mother was like that about her age,' she said then with her sudden gravity.

I remarked the verb 'was' and waited quietly but she changed direction again. 'Just fancy a place being called Paradise.' The thought of Liz flitted across my mind again at the phrase 'just fancy'. 'Names again,' Percy said. 'I never thought I would live at a place called Paradise. In fact, that is partly why I came here, the idea of living at a place called Olympus, Paradise.'

'I see your point. When I first came to the island and was invited to dinner at Mount Ararat, I felt my head going round. How do you come to be at Olympus? Twice told me that you are not a member of the Mission.'

'You know how it is – Doctor Livingstone, I presume and all that. I came out to the Caribbean last May. I went to Trinidad first, then I poked round some of the smaller islands, then in July I landed here in St. Jago. Shortly after the earthquake, I was walking along Harbour Street down in the Bay when who do I meet but Nancy Marsh and Mary Crockford, two girls I was at school with at home. They are both members of the Mission. They told me they were living in this old house called Olympus because the earthquake had knocked down half of the hospital and how awful it was because nobody had time to manage the servants and there was never any food and it was all filthy. I offered to run the house for them in return for a bed and my board and here I am. It was partly because it was called Olympus, Paradise, like I said and partly because I was bored with being on my own.'

'Where were you during the earthquake?'

'In a guest house called Mount Segoya out near Hurricane Point. There was no earthquake there at all though. I could hardly believe it when I heard about all the people who had been killed at this end of the island.'

'That is how earthquake goes. It seems to run along a certain stratum or something.'

'It was quite bad here, wasn't it?'

'Yes, pretty bad. If you had been at this end of the island you would have wished that you had never come to the Caribbean at all. Why did you come in the first place?'

She frowned, causing the spectacles to slip down her nose and I thought at first that she was annoyed by my curiosity but as she replaced the heavy frame with a small straight forefinger, she smiled. 'I am not very good at whys,' she said. 'There is never one simple answer. But I like the sea and ships and I had had pneumonia and the doctor said I should have a holiday somewhere in the sun. Then I draw and paint a bit and I had seen an exhibition of paintings by West Indians. It was exciting. But it is just a silly mix-up of reasons, you see.'

'Actually, it was just a silly question on my part,' I said. 'I can never understand anybody coming to these islands, you see, unless they have to. All these tourists down in the Bay wearing funny clothes and frying themselves lobster-red in the sun strike me as being demented.'

'You don't like it here?' she asked.

'Yes, *I* like it but that is different. This is my home and Twice is here—'

'And he is a good reason for being any place,' she interrupted me. 'He is the nicest man.' She pursed her lips suddenly, staring at me through the large lenses. 'I shouldn't have said that. I spend a lot of time by myself and you get into the habit of saying things to yourself that you shouldn't say out loud but sometimes I say them out loud.'

'But I am very glad that you think Twice is a nice man,' I assured her. 'He is my own favourite man, as my niece Liz puts it.'

'How old is Liz?'

'Eight.'

'You saw her when you were away?'

80

'Yes.'

'Has she any sisters or brothers?'

'Two brothers when I went there and a third one got himself born while I was actually there.'

'It must have been fun.' She sounded wistful. 'You enjoyed your holiday?'

'Yes, very much.'

'I like babies,' she said and rose to her feet. 'I must go up there and see what that lot are doing.' She suddenly looked older, businesslike, conscious of her duty, informal as her arrangement at Olympus seemed to be. 'Thank you for the coffee and – and—'

'For not being the same sort of Janet as your headmistress?' I suggested and she laughed.

'Something like that,' she said and as we went to the veranda door: 'I am walking but it isn't too hot yet. I didn't bring my car down last night. That *would* have make Dram bark. Goodbye and I'll tell them about next Sunday.'

I watched her go down the driveway and out on to the road across the park that led to the base of Olympus hill. She would walk a few steps, then skip a few, the pony-tail of hair bobbing at the back of her head, then she would pause, looking down at the ground or up into the branches of a tree before beginning to walk or skip again. She looked secret and unpredictable, like a creature of another kind, whose motives were not to be estimated, as one might try to estimate the motives of another human. Face to face with me over the coffee cups, she had been the essence of candour, a likeable, highly communicative and social young creature but now that she was alone – 'I spend a lot of time by myself' – and unaware that I was watching her, she seemed to have moved into another world, governed by laws other than those of the social world that she had just quitted. Twice's simile of the swallow, I thought as she disappeared into the shrubs that bordered the Olympus drive, had been very apt.

*　　　*　　　*

In the end, the numbers for the Sunday forenoon party swelled to nearly fifty at the instigation of Twice.

'I suppose we owe the Compound a drink on the strength of Mackie's and my new jobs,' he said, 'and if we are having a shindig we might as well go the hog and get it over with.'

'And you will disappear into the study with Mackie and some of the staff and leave me holding the hog,' I told him. 'There is just one thing. Are all the staff people pleased about these new appointments? I am no Marion Maclean to stand about leering in triumph. If I give a party, it is a *party* so that people can have fun, including me.'

'Mackie and I are a popular win,' he assured me, 'especially Mackie. After all, Vickers and Christie could never have expected promotion over Mackie's head. They are reasonable blokes although dutiful rather than gifted engineers. And the manager has to be an engineer so that the chemists and field people prefer me as the devil they know to some other devil from outside.'

'All right, let's go the hog,' I said. 'I'll lay on a buffet lunch and give the staff wives a change from their own catering while I am about it.'

'That is going to be a lot of work.'

'Not too much. Sashie will lend a hand.'

When I telephoned Sashie to ask if he would have a turkey and a ham cooked for me in the efficient kitchens of the Peak Hotel, he said: 'Darling, don't worry about a thing. Forty-eight, you say? Call it fifty including Don and me for you must have *me*. It is much simpler to do the whole thing from here. Just see that your refrigerator is empty on Saturday evening and don't lift a finger otherwise.'

On the Saturday evening, he arrived with two of his staff who stuffed the refrigerator with roast turkey, baked ham and salads and then unloaded crockery, glasses and cutlery from his car into the pantry.

'I feel very grand, like Lady Cunard or somebody,' I

told him. 'Especially when I remember what a sweat a thing like this used to be in the old days. I suppose you will charge me the earth what with waiters and everything?'

'It is all between friends, my sweet,' he told me. 'In return, you can do a tiny thing or two for me.'

He gave me his sidelong glance and went through from the pantry to the veranda where he sat down, arranging his crimson trousers with his finicky fingers.

'What sort of thing or two?' I asked, standing over him and speaking very slowly and rather loudly.

'Darling, you distrust me?'

'Of course I do. Come along, out with it.'

'Caleb plays the guitar very well,' he said, causing me to stare at him dumbfounded until he looked up at me and added: 'I could use him down at the Peak.'

'No, you don't!' I said angrily as Twice got out of his car and came up the steps. 'Don't you dare, Sashie de Marnay! You can take all that turkey and ham and you know what you can do with them but you are not taking Caleb down to that gin-palace to make a lickspittling gigolo out of him.'

'Janet—' Twice began.

'You keep out of this,' I told him. 'Now, you listen to me, Sashie de Marnay—' I broke off, too enraged to find words for what I wanted to say.

'By Jove,' said Sashie in the voice of Sir Ian, 'the red rag is fairly streamin' from the mast-head, what?'

'What is going on?' Twice asked loudly and sternly.

'*He* wants to take Caleb—' I began but Sashie broke in on me and explained his proposal lucidly to Twice who turned to me and said: 'Janet, this is a matter for Caleb.'

'But, Twice—' I felt tears rising to my eyes, tears not only of sorrow but of frustration for it was nearly impossible for me to express the depth and complexity of what I felt. When we had first come to St. Jago, the tourist boom was just beginning but it was now the main industry of the island. It brought in vast amounts of revenue, mainly American dollars, but it was drawing the young men and women away from the fertile plains and valleys into the concrete and chromium jungle of what we called the Platinum Coast, the white-sanded beaches of the island's north coast which was a vast pleasure ground. It seemed to me that the life there was, for the negroes, nothing more than a new and more corrupting slavery than that from which they had been emancipated little more than a hundred years ago. The former slavery had been an evil thing but this new form was, to me, just as evil, if more subtle, in its falsifying of values, its subservience to quick returns for shoddy services.

I had not realised until now how much I loved Caleb, how far his small ambitions had been my ambitions too and I saw this development as a threat too dreadful and at the same time too subtle to be put into concrete words.

'Janet,' Twice said quietly, 'if Caleb has the talent and the opportunity to earn more than we can give him, we have no right to stand in his way.'

'It is not just a question of money and Caleb has a minor talent only,' I said dully, coldly. 'He would last at the Peak for a season, maybe two, before the tourists tired of him and needed a new diversion and what then? Would he ever come back to his way of life here, his *real* way of life? You know he wouldn't. He would turn into a hanger-on round the clubs and bars, scrounging for tips like all the rest.'

'But—'

'You be quiet, Twice Alexander, and hear me out. Given a few more years, Caleb will have enough money to buy a few acres of bush. That is what he really wants, what all St. Jagoans want if they are not corrupted, what they call a lickle piece o' lan'. And I can't think of a better thing for people to want than a little bit of the earth's surface that they can work to make a living. And given his few acres, Caleb could make a good living for himself, a wife and a family. He may have a slight talent for music but he is a natural born cultivator, as he calls it.'

'A crofter, you mean, like yourself,' Twice said, 'but nevertheless, you can't stop Sashie asking him if he would like to sing at the Peak. That would be beyond your rights.'

'It isn't a question of my rights,' I said and appealed to Sashie: 'Sashie, I am serious about this. Caleb came here to me six years ago as a skinny under-nourished little boy but he is a man now and I think he is a good man. I know he has done things that are typical of his race and tradition, things that separate him from our race and tradition but that doesn't make him less good as a person. He has had two illegitimate children, maybe more and he wears coloured shirts that would frighten a matador and has enough stinking hair oil in his room to float Paradise. In those ways, he is outwardly like all those touts down in the Bay but inside he is not like them. He is not corrupt as those hangers-on are corrupt. Given a few more years he will be able to buy his piece of land but he will never do it if you take him down there and make a monkey on a stick out of him.'

'But, darling—' Sashie began.

'This is a waste of time,' Twice interrupted. 'I can't sit here and have Caleb disposed of as if he were some sort of moron. Sashie, if you have a proposal to make to him, go and make it. He is in the back garden. Janet, you have always known that the time would come when Caleb would go. If you didn't know it, you should have.'

'It is all very well for you—' I began and broke off helplessly. It was useless to say hurtful things but Twice had not nursed Caleb through measles, had not worked with him in the garden day by day, had not grown fond of him as a child he had reared, as I had. I went out to the corner of the house and called his name: 'Caleb!'

He came round the house and on to the veranda, coal-black and shining and gave me the broad gentle grin that showed the glittering rows of teeth.

'You called me, ma'am?'

'Mr. Sashie wants to speak to you, Caleb.'

With polite dignity, he turned to face Sashie.

'Would you like to make some more money, Caleb?' Sashie asked.

'I always in the market for more money, sah. How?'

'Would you like to be singer and guitar-player at the Peak Hotel?'

I knew that Caleb was as startled as I had been when he replied. When Caleb had first come to me, he had spoken the dialect of the island but now, as a rule, he spoke fairly standard English although with, some people said, a slight Highland intonation which he had caught from myself. At this moment, however, his speech became very St. Jagoan.

'You mean leave me cultivation an' da Missis heah? Oh no, sah. Thank ya, sah, but not leave me cultivation an' da Missis an' da Chief, sah.'

I wanted to burst into tears of pride and joy yet tinged with shame that I had under-estimated Caleb in thinking that he would fall to the lure of the Platinum Coast. But now Sashie spoke again.

'You would not have to leave Guinea Corner, Caleb. We would send a car up for you three nights a week, say and you would be back here about midnight.'

'I see, sah.' Caleb looked solemnly at Sashie for a moment before turning to me. 'Please, ma'am, what you say?'

I suddenly felt as if I were airborne, intoxicated with delight and had to make an effort to speak calmly. 'It is up to you, Caleb, but after all you are never in bed before midnight anyhow. You might as well play your guitar down there and get paid for it as play it up here for nothing.'

'Okay, ma'am. You will arrange 'bout me with Mars Sashie?'

'You bet I will, Caleb,' I said and he went away back to his vegetable patch and his hosepipe, unmoved, as if nothing unusual had happened.

'Now for it,' said Twice to Sashie. 'I hope you brought your fattest cheque book with you?'

'We will not quibble over trifles, Janet,' Sashie said.

'Oh, won't we?' I thought, wondering if I should ask for five pounds a week and come down to four or start at four and come down to three pounds ten.

'Five guineas an evening,' said Sashie, 'to rise to ten if he makes a hit. From about mid-October until about March – the platinum season only.'

'Holy smoke!' said Twice.

'It is a deal, Sashie,' I said, trying to sound as if I made such contracts every day. 'But you will try to see that he doesn't get any nonsense ideas?'

'He won't get any what you call nonsense ideas, darling, not that one. I thought I had seen most things under the St. Jagoan sun but I did not expect to meet under it a coal-black Reachfar Highlandman. I congratulate you, my sweet. I shall let you know later which evenings we shall want him down at the Pit of Corruption.'

'Sorry, Sashie, I take it all back.'

'Not at all, dear. We *are* rather corrupting but only to the corruptible.'

'Just fancy,' I said to Twice, 'fifteen guineas a week! Caleb!'

'Sashie,' Twice said, 'do you think we could knock a pound or two out of old Minna singing De Blood ob de Lamb?'

Sashie smiled. 'If the day ever comes when I hold a revival meeting at the Peak,' he said, 'I promise to call upon Minna. Meantime, I have another favour to ask of you. I did not know until this summer that Caleb was such an artist nor, until I had heard him, did I know that this island had such a wealth of folk-song.'

'Caleb learned them from his old Uncle Abel,' I said. 'He used to be a lumber headman at Mahogany Hall.

87

He is about a hundred years old, I should think.'

'This is my point. When Uncle Abel and a few others like him die off, these songs will be lost for good.' He glanced at Twice before turning to me with a mischievous smile. 'Do you think, darling, that I could pay for some of the corruption I have created at the Peak by recording some of Uncle Abel's songs?'

'Sashie, what a wonderful idea! Make recordings of them, you mean?'

'That too, perhaps, later on. But first I should like to get them down on paper, in notation, you know.'

'You can write music?' I was always interested in discovering facts about Sashie who was very sparing of personal information. He brushed my query aside as he always did. 'I am not a latter-day Beethoven but I can put a melody into notation, yes. Only, Heaven knows one could not put God Save the King into notation down at that parrot-house where I live so I wondered if I might bring my little piano up here. It is quite a pretty piano, French, you know and it would look charming in the far corner of the drawing-room there, by the window.'

'Quite soon, we'll be starting to truck sugar sacks up from the warehouse at the wharf,' Twice said. 'I'll send big Sammy to the Peak and the piano can come up among bales of sacks. Will that do?'

'But splendidly. Thank you, Twice dear. And I shall not be a nuisance, Janet. Should you require total silence at any time, I shall not tinkle a single note. And it is only temporary. As soon as Silver Beach is habitable, I shall move the piano down there. Don't you think this is a good way of beguiling my retirement?'

'You will never retire!' I scoffed. 'You are like my grandmother. You will always have to be *at* something.'

'You are probably right, my sweet. And now I must go,' he said. 'I shall arrive in good time tomorrow to manage this little entertainment as Madame would call it.'

* * *

88

The party was very much like the many others I had given and attended during my years at Paradise, except that formerly my own contemporaries had predominated while, on this occasion, the average age of the guests was much less. Twice and I, it was brought home to me, were truly the seniors at Paradise now, for even the staff couples, like the Yates, were only in their thirties. Sir Ian, of course, was the eldest of all present, very much a father figure, in his element among all the young people, especially the girls, whom he treated with a twinkling gallantry which, I noticed, brought forth all their femininity. Even a big raw-boned girl dentist who, I was sure, would become a power in her profession, took her hands out of the pockets of her slacks and took up a less manly stance and even began to flutter a little after a few moments of Sir Ian.

I spent most of my time with Sashie, partly because we were jointly responsible for the management of the food and drink, partly because most of our young guests seemed to stand in awe of us two, an attitude quite different from their attitude to Twice. It did not surprise me that they gave Sashie a fairly wide berth because this was the attitude that he invited but I was a little hurt that they were so formal in their approach to myself.

'Hasn't that Madonna-looking girl on the arm of Twice's chair got the most beautiful and sexy legs?' I said to Sashie at one point.

'I have seen better and sexier, darling,' he told me. 'Why are you wearing a dress instead of your usual shorts today?'

'An oblique and doubtful compliment. I consider that I am too old to wear shorts in public any more. Sashie, what makes them gather round Twice like chickens round a hen?'

'I think it is the enthusiasm,' he said thoughtfully. 'Twice has never lost that crazy sort of enthusiasm that young people have and all these Mission people are enthusiasts. That is why they are here. They are volunteers who believe that this Mission of theirs can make the world a better place. You don't believe that any more, do you?'

'Do you?' I countered.

'Darling, I never did believe that anything I could do would make the slightest difference but I imagine you did, once upon a time.'

'I don't think I ever had the sense of dedication that these youngsters seem to have,' I said, 'I think I was bent more upon making the world a better place for one person, namely me.'

'And very healthy too. Do you suppose that little red-haired girl is being taken in by that smouldering line that Don is handing her? Ought I to separate them?'

'If she is the type to be taken in by a line, she will be taken in sooner or later so you might as well let it rip.'

Twice's contribution to the party, of a practical kind, had been to bring his record-player through from his study to the veranda, so that our guests might dance if they wished. During the long convalescence after his illness, Mackie had built an ingenious trolley which ran on castors, carrying the player and a fair number of records on a rack below. This rack usually contained Twice's collection of recordings of Beethoven but these, today, had been replaced by a heterogeneous medley of recorded island calypsos and ballads. Suddenly, somebody said: 'George Formby!' and Twice sprang up.

'Don't put that on the player,' he said. 'It shouldn't be there at all. It dates from about 1935.'

The young people round the player, who all hailed from George Formby's part of England looked momentarily disappointed, whereupon Twice said: 'If you want to hear it, I'll get you my little old portable.'

'I'll fetch it, sir,' said Mackie and brought from the study the shabby little old gramophone that had gone with Twice over half of the world during the six years of the war. It was set on a table, wound up and began to grind out the sound of a ukulele and the voice of Formby singing:

'I'm leaning on a lamp-post at the corner of the street
Until a certain little lady comes by.
Oh me, oh my—'

It sounded very nostalgic and old-fashioned but the young people were as fascinated as the excavators of the tomb of Tutankhamen, which caused Caleb to fetch from the study a dusty cardboard box which yielded up among other things Harry Lauder singing 'Tobermory', Gracie Fields singing 'The Biggest Aspidistra in the World' and an American torch singer singing 'I Cover the Waterfront'. Many of the listeners had heard the Lancashire singers in person but the voices of Fields and Formby on these scratched old records, in this exotic setting so far from Lancashire seemed to fascinate them and the little gramophone and the cardboard box became the stars of the party. And these relics from the past continued to amuse the young people. Later on, they played the old records every time a few of them came to visit us.

The party went on from eleven-thirty in the forenoon until shortly after four when Sashie caused tea and bread and butter to be served, after which the guests dispersed.

'Nothing like bread and butter to remind them of time and their manners,' he said. 'Sandwiches and cake have nothing like the same effect. Did you enjoy your party, Twice?'

'Very much.'

It was in the time that followed that the party showed its significance, however. Before it took place, the only young people to come around the house had been Percy and Mackie but, after the party, there was seldom an evening when a few of the inhabitants of Olympus did not visit Guinea Corner. This, I came to understand, was what had been happening while I was away and this was what Twice had meant when he said: 'They all got a habit of popping in in the evenings.'

They required no entertainment. They sat around, mostly on the floor, talking and arguing. Sometimes they danced on the veranda and sometimes they would choose classical records and listen. They did not develop for me the familiar confidence that they displayed towards Twice but they ceased to stand off, seeming to accept me, in the words of Mackie, as 'a good egg'. It seemed that in my absence my quality as an egg had been in some doubt and that on my return they had decided to move with caution.

'It was fun last night,' Percy said one morning early in December, 'but if you get sick of us all being over here all the time, Janet, just say so.'

Percy seemed to have no doubt of my quality as an egg, for which I was grateful and she spoke her mind with less and less reserve. 'I don't think I shall get sick of you all,' I told her, 'but I don't quite understand why you all come here when you could be dancing at the Club or the Bay or wherever.'

'Sometimes you are real dumb,' she informed me. 'This is a home, don't you see? We are all institution people.'

'Institution people?'

'Yes. We have been in institutions all our lives – schools, universities, training colleges, hospitals, common rooms, dormitories, institution food and beds. Olympus is one more institution, that's all.'

She made it all sound very barren, very different from my own young life which had been spent entirely in what she called 'homes'.

'I see,' I said. 'Then you and they are all the more welcome although you are not really an institution person like the others.'

'I am, practically. After Olympus, I shall go back to the boarding-house in the Bay, another institution, if I stay in the island, that is,' she added before changing direction in her sudden swerving way. 'Look here, Mary Crockford and I had an idea last night.'

Mary Crockford was the girl with the long sexy legs

and the serene face of a Madonna. She was also one of those I had taken to visit Madame for she had a deep musical voice which, I knew, would make her distinctive in Madame's mind, depending as she did so much on her acute hearing.

'You sit with Madame every afternoon from Monday to Friday, don't you?' Percy was asking.

'Yes.'

'Well, we wondered now that we have been round there whether we could go sometimes and give you an afternoon off. Nancy and Selina would join in too. They have nothing to do on their days off anyway until the others come off duty in the evenings.'

'This is very kind and thoughtful of you all, Percy,' I said, 'and I am sure it can be arranged.'

'Kind and thoughtful nothing,' said Percy. 'It will be fun. I can go any afternoon and Mary is usually off on Tuesdays and Nancy on Wednesdays and Selina on Thursdays so just let us know. Listen, don't you think Pam Durrant and Eddie Muir are awful bores with all that huggery-kissery?'

'I have noticed them doing rather a deal of it,' I admitted, 'but I thought my being critical was just old-fashioned.'

'Then I am old-fashioned too. So is Mary. I don't think people should be private in public. Anyhow, I am not sure about all this falling in love business.'

I had been watering the plants on the veranda while we talked but now I put my can down in a corner, sat down and looked at her.

'Aren't you?' I asked.

'Do you believe that it happens?'

'Yes,' I said, 'but I think there is a lot of rubbish talked about it too. I don't believe in the novelette stuff where somebody looks into somebody's eyes and drowns in love as if he had fallen off a pier and then they go on to live happily ever after. Then Sashie said something once that made me think a bit.'

'Sashie says a lot of things that make one think. What was it?'

'We were talking about Edward Dulac, Sir Ian's son. Sashie said that Edward was about to fall in love because he was ripe for it. Sashie said that people get ripe for love like apples on a tree. They fall off their twigs, as Sashie put it and when they fall they suddenly see the nearest woman as having the body of Aphrodite, the intelligence of Einstein and the spirituality of an archangel.'

'What nonsense!' Percy sounded a little cross. 'Janet, I was being serious,' she protested.

'So am I being serious,' I told her. 'There is a lot in what Sashie said. Romantically-minded people talk of falling in love as if the victim were suddenly struck by a meteorite or smitten by some other agency that is not of this world or part of this life but it is not a simple accident like that. It is the culmination of a process, I think, like most other things in life. Take me, the only case I really know about. I reached the age of thirty-five without ever falling in love—'

'What about Freddie and Alan and all these people that Twice was so funny about at the party?'

'Oh, those. I was always *imagining* I was in love. I even got engaged a time or two but always came to my senses and broke it off but at the age of thirty-five I met Twice and here we are.'

'Did you know right at the beginning when you first met him?'

'I think I did but since I have grown older I have begun to wonder a little about it and I think the truth is, Percy, that there is a lot in what Sashie says. I was thirty-five, in danger of being left on the shelf as people said in those days, my family wanted me to marry, our employer Mr. Slater and his wife wanted Twice and me to marry, my friend Muriel kept on condescending to me as a successful married woman condescends to an unwanted spinster and one way and another, things forced me to pursue Twice until I ran him down.'

'I don't believe a word of it,' Percy said.

'Darling, I am not being funny. I honestly think that my family and Muriel and other circumstances had a lot to do with it. I have even wondered if the man I met had been lanky and dark-eyed like Mackie instead of being broad and blue-eyed like Twice, if he had been a dyspeptic banker instead of a Rugby-playing engineer, I might not still have fallen in love with him just the same. I was a ripe apple, ready to fall, like Sashie said, but it is not as dreary as it may sound. No matter how it happened or what the causes were, I am still very glad that it happened. What set me off on this story of my love life?'

'I asked,' said Percy. 'Mary and Selina and I were talking about Pam and Eddie last night. Selina said Pam only wanted to marry Eddie because she is the greedy sort and wants a bit of everything she can lay her hands on and Mary said she must think she loves him or she wouldn't dream of marrying him. Then Selina said that this business about love was a lot of rubbish, that it was only a sex thing that lasted for a short time but it made you lose your head and with the laws like they are, there you were tied to some man who would bore you for the rest of your life.'

'And what did you say?'

'Nothing much. I am not sure what I think, like Mary and Selina are.' She frowned, the spectacles slipped and were re-positioned. 'I met a fellow at a party once—' The spectacles slipped again and were allowed to remain with their bridge on the tip of her nose as she broke off and turned away.

'Yes?' I said.

'That is all. I never saw him again.' She turned to face me, pushed the spectacles into place. 'I am going over to Bachelors' Bungalow. That place has got to be cleaned up. It is a wonder those three don't get scabies or something.'

'I didn't know you had taken over Bachelors' as

well as Olympus. By the way, does Mackie know?'

'Bruce? Yes. I called in there at lunchtime yesterday. Do you know what they were eating? Tinned stew and tinned potato. Tinned potato with the vegetables there are in this island! I told them it just wouldn't do.'

I looked at her very hard. She was the first person I had ever known who had dared to tell the denizens of Bachelors' anything about their way of life. My staring eyes seemed to make her feel that she must explain herself.

'I can't bear homes not being properly looked after and people living in squalor,' she said. 'And I like house-keeping and arranging about meals and things.'

'Have you ever thought of having a little home of your own?' I asked.

I did not know her financial position but she had made this trip to the Caribbean and she owned her little car, which indicated that she had some sort of income.

'Perhaps I may sometime,' she said, 'but that is not the same. In a real home, the kind I like, you have to have people to look after, to feed and so on.'

'There is plenty of so on at Bachelors',' I said. 'Watch out for all those pulleys and blocks and tackles.'

'And don't touch Bruce's drawing-table. I know,' and she was gone, skipping across the park.

Watching her go, I thought of the time during my child-hood when the young swallow had, somehow, penetrated under the eaves and into the Reachfar granary itself and then could not find its way out. Tom, George and I went up there one wet day to sweep and clean the granary anent the coming harvest and found this creature in demented senseless flight from wall to wall, from floor to roof, bruising itself against our man-made barriers. We opened the door wide, opened both skylights in the roof but, frantic with panic, the bird could not find these channels to the open sky. In the end, we crowded it into a corner and George caught it between his big gentle hands.

'Here, Janet,' he said, 'you take him out to the top of the steps and let him go. Maybe he will mind that it was you that set him free and take you for a holiday to Spain in his mind when he goes off at the back-end o' the year.'

Careful, I took the delicate creature between my hands and went out with him to the little landing at the top of the granary stair. Seemingly exhausted and beyond hope, he made no movement except for the frantic pulsing of his heart and even when I took my left hand away, he lay on the palm of my right as if unable to move.

'Hold him high, Janet,' Tom said. 'Let him feel the air and see the sky.'

I raised my arm, holding him out beyond the rail of the granary landing and now the small head lifted and suddenly he was away on a long swoop of scimitar wings that took him down towards the grass of the Little Parkie and then up into the rainy sky above the dark fir trees of the moor.

Percy, like the swallow, it seemed, needed to feel the air and see the sky and also like the swallow, she felt a need for a nesting-place, a home. Unlike the swallow, however, she did not know by instinct where to go to build her nest. She seemed to be searching for a suitable place.

By hearsay and by remarks made by herself, I knew that she spent much of her time around the docks in St. Jago Bay. Ships and their movements seemed to fascinate her, to take her on imaginary voyages. She had made friends with all the wharf managers and Customs officials and had acquired the liberty to go almost anywhere she pleased among the warehouses and piers of the port and she knew the movements of all the ships, both passenger and cargo. But despite her charm and the ease with which she made acquaintanceships, there was about her something of the solitary, of the creature that belonged to another element, lived by different laws. Although she came about Guinea Corner as confidently and familiarly as if it were her home, I sensed in her something transient, something of the visitant who would one day respond to some strange urge peculiar to her secret nature but when I tried to express to Twice something of what I felt, he merely laughed at me, accusing me of a departure into the Celtic Twilight as an escape from the St. Jagoan sun.

Christmas and the New Year, what Madame called 'the festive season', formerly a marathon of parties at Paradise, passed quietly. At Guinea Corner, we had a Christmas day lunch, attended by Percy, Mary Crockford, Sashie and Mackie. Mackie's presence was another little step towards changing his image on the estate, separating him from the jollifications of the junior engineers and the people at Olympus, while Mary was invited at Percy's suggestion to balance numbers. Mary was Percy's particular friend at Olympus and in outward aspect they could not have been more different, Mary tall, dark and stately in contrast to Percy's small swift frailty.

As soon as New Year's day was past, the great annual change came over Paradise, as the estate made the final preparations to go into Crop. By long tradition, Paradise factory and distillery began to process – went into Crop, as it was called – on the first Tuesday of the year but in 1957, New Year's day itself fell upon a Tuesday so that the big day did not come until the eighth of the month. On the second, however, the preliminary activity began.

There had been plenty of music round Guinea Corner during the last weeks with Twice singing at his drawing-board in the study, Caleb with his guitar, Sashie with his piano and the young people with the record-player in the evenings but now the music of Crop began to sound from beyond the garden walls. The livings of some four thousand people depended upon Paradise and now the army of cane-cutters with their women and children too young to be left at home began to come down from the surrounding hills, to camp round their cooking fires in the corners of the cane pieces. The sugar cane which had grown in these corners had been cut by the flashing cutlasses of the men and was lying in great bundles, tied with chains, ready to be picked up by the tractors with their trains of trailers. These first bundles would be consumed before the start of Crop proper, when the crushing mills were run up for their final test and each bundle carried the tally-mark of the family which had cut it, a long blade of cane tied round one of the chains in an ingenious distinctive knot. These tally-marks would be used on every bundle throughout the six months cropping period, for the cutters were paid by tonnage cut, but these first bundles sent to the mills for the run-up always seemed to me to have a peculiar significance, as if they were a faith-offering from the workers to the complex plant on which their simple lives depended.

The men and women sang and laughed while they worked, the children sang and laughed while they played and as Crop Tuesday came nearer, the factory began to add its accompaniment to the music. Smoke began to issue like a long black plume from the tall stack and as steam was raised and the turbines were run up, a humming vibration filled the air and this became an orchestrated mixture of notes as more and yet more of the complex was brought into test action until at last the faith-offerings were swung on to the conveyor belt, their chains falling away with a crash like giant cymbals and the real song of Crop reverberated across the park as the jaws of the mills took a grip on the great mouthfuls of tough cane.

But this was only the final rehearsal which lasted for about an hour while those first bundles went through the mills and the engineers stood by with their giant wrenches, ready to adjust the heavy rollers on the advice of the chemists and agronomists, that the maximum of juice might be extracted from the tough stalks. Very soon, the deep greedy groaning of the mills died away, not to be heard again until after the siren blew at six o'clock on Tuesday morning but the cutting in the fields went on and the tractors and trailers rattled from fields to factory, stock-piling the cane yard anent the big assault.

The start of Crop was always exciting but also anxious and especially this year for the earthquake of the year before had done considerable damage, so that parts of the factory had had to be re-built. Even worse than the visible damage that could be repaired, however, was the insidious damage that earthquake could do by shaking foundations, by causing shifts in levels, damage that might not show until the plant was in full production.

Throughout the trials, I watched Twice very carefully and as unobtrusively as I could, ready to note the first signs of over-strain, but even after the mill trials he was serenely calm and confident and made me aware that I had not been as clever as I had thought when he said on the Monday evening: 'You can relax now. I haven't blown a fuse or anything.'

'The mill trials were all right?'

'Steady as a rock. If we have any trouble, it will be with some silly little thing like a valve or a feed pipe. That place up there is a bit like life. It isn't the big things that make the trouble but the little things that can go wrong and have an effect out of all proportion.'

Paradise was not the only factory in the island going into Crop. There were many others, all with their traditional starting dates between January and March and there was competition between the factories and their crews, the aim of each one being to start grinding and continue processing for the six-month period without a hitch and they were all watching one another, ready to commiserate with patent insincerity if anything went wrong. 'Retreat is in trouble again' the crew of Summer Hill would say with satisfaction and 'Summer Hill had to shut down after four days' would say the crew of New Linlithgow with scornful patronage. But if some of the estates watched some of the others, they all watched Paradise, the most up-to-date plant in the island which, this Crop, was to run with a new manager and a new engineer, the youngest Chief in the island. It would be wrong to say that the others wished Paradise ill, but they would have been more than human had they not wished us a week's shut-down for the good of our souls.

'It is all madly exciting,' Percy said, dancing into the house on that Monday evening.

'A bit too exciting,' I said. 'I hope all that new equipment settles down all right.'

'What happens tomorrow?'

'They don't fire rockets or anything. The siren will blow at six in the morning, that rumble you heard today – that's the mills – will get deeper and deeper and louder and louder and will go on, we hope, till about the middle or third week of June and Crop will be over.'

'You are trying to make it all sound very ordinary, Janet, but it isn't. It is just as exciting as a big ship putting out to sea.'

She had a trick of standing on the ball of one foot, with the point of the other perched on tiptoe and standing thus now, she looked more than anything like a gull about to take flight from the rail of a ship.

'You like to watch big ships putting out to sea, don't you?' I asked.

'Yes and Twice's factory going into Crop. That is how to say it, isn't it? Going into Crop?'

'Yes. That is how to say it.'

She jumped into her little car and drove away while I listened to the silence, broken only by a faint hum and hiss of steam now. The sounds of the last few days now seemed like the stirrings of some god out of his six months sleep but he had now settled down again to wait for tomorrow's dawn. There was a tense hush over the valley as if the sky and the surrounding hills were waiting for the scream of the siren that would announce that the god was fully awake and going about his business of providing another year's sustenance for those who lived by him.

When I awoke in the darkness before five the next morning, the waiting silence seemed even more intense and I moved softly on my way down to the pantry. But

Caleb had forestalled me. The tray with the tea and bread and butter was ready to carry upstairs.

'You are going up to the factory, Caleb?'

Every male on the estate would be crowded into the cane and transport yards when the siren blew.

'Yes, ma'am. You need anything before I go?'

'No, thank you. Off you go.'

I stood for a moment by the pantry window. It would not be light until shortly before six but already the sky was growing pale in the east. For me, this first morning of Crop was a repetition on a grand scale of the thrilling morning at Reachfar during my childhood when the sun rose behind a golden curtain of mist and the horses were yoked to the reaper and driven into the first field of ripe oats.

As I picked up the tray, I had an acute awareness of the cycle of the year from spring, through summer to the first day of harvest and although winter was to come, winter would lead on to another spring.

In the hall, Percy stood like a pale sprite in her white shirt and shorts.

'Hello,' I said, 'where have you come from?' for she might, I thought, have come from another planet or down through time from another era.

'From Bachelors'. I have been seeing that they got breakfast. But I wanted to be right here at Guinea Corner for the start of Crop. Is that all right?'

'Of course it is. Get yourself a cup from the pantry and come upstairs and have some tea.'

Twice was up now and already dressed, like Percy, in the white shirt and shorts that he always wore and was pulling on his knee-length stockings.

'That stocking won't do,' I said. 'There is a hole at the side of the heel.'

'It isn't much.'

I took another pair from the drawer. 'Take it off, Twice, please. I wish Minna would learn not to put away things that need mending but I suppose she never will.'

He took off the stocking and handed it to me, began to put on the pair I had given him. 'You are a superstitious old crone,' he said.

'Don't you go calling me an old crone.'

'As if a hole in my stocking would make the mills seize up!'

'Twice, to see that you are fed and clean and decently dressed is all I can contribute.'

'You under-rate yourself,' he said, pulling me down on to his knees.

'Look, Percy is here. She is coming up. Put your shoes on. Oh, stop it, Twice. She will think we are demented.'

He released me and stood up as Percy came into the room. He seemed suddenly to be very large, very dominating, vibrant, filling the room with energy. 'Good morning, Percy,' he said. 'I hope you are not thinking of coming up to the factory? We can't do with odd bodies, however fetching, up there this morning.'

'Credit me with a little sense,' said Percy. 'I only wanted to be here at Guinea Corner when the siren blows.'

He looked at his watch. 'Another half-hour yet,' he said and in that moment two beams of light swept across the darkness beyond the mosquito mesh of the windows. 'There goes Mackie, Chief Engineer. You know, Percy, it is the Chief who takes off a sugar crop, not the manager-wallah like me.'

'That's not what Bruce Mackie thinks,' Percy told him. 'Norman Vickers fetched Mary and me over to Bachelors' last night to try to cheer him up. He had had a fight with Bob Christie and was in a black rage. He wouldn't even have a glass of beer and kept saying that if anything went wrong today he would shoot himself.'

Twice laid aside his teacup. 'I had better get off up there. Mackie has the temperament of a bloody prima donna. He will be all right once we start rolling but he might throttle Christie or the millman before the whistle blows. See you at breakfast around nine,' he said, kissing me and then he picked Percy up, kissed her and set her down again. 'That's for luck,' he said and ran downstairs.

'I just love that man,' said Percy, executing a pirouette in the middle of the floor. 'Oh, Janet, look at the sun coming up! Isn't the dawn in this island the most marvellous thing?'

The blazing disc that was the sun came up behind the distant wooded hills and in silhouette against it was the black smoke-stack of the factory, like the baton of a conductor calling his orchestra to readiness. Then, into the silence of the morning, came the scream of the siren, reaching out to the hills and reverberating back to die away as the groaning rumble of the mills came across the park and the cane-cutters began to sing as their cutlasses flashed in the new early light.

'Well, Percy,' I said, 'we are in Crop.'

She took her spectacles off and two big tears rolled down her cheeks. 'That was about the most splendid thing ever,' she said, turned swiftly away and ran downstairs.

The more I saw of Percy, the more akin to her I felt, liking, as we did, the same people, moved, as we were, by the same events and I wished to bring her closer to me, to know more of her and feel her more securely mine but, following this little moment at the start of Crop, she disappeared for three days and I had to accept that she inhabited a different world from my own, that world governed by different laws.

To me, that world was as remote and mysterious as the spring sky above Reachfar had been in my childhood, when the wind-borne clouds would now cover the sun, now reveal it, while the swallows swooped and flashed as they pursued their different and secret way of life.

PART TWO

'And summer's lease hath all too short a date'
from a sonnet by SHAKESPEARE

AT the end of twenty-four hours, we began to feel that this 1957 crop was going to be trouble-free.

'And so it should be,' Twice said. 'There was none of Rob's paint-it-red-and-make-it-do about that overhaul last year.' This phrase, 'paint-it-red-and-make-it-do' dated from the time of Twice's apprenticeship when he had worked under an old foreman in south Scotland who was never known to be pleased with any piece of work. The most that he would say after inspecting work that had been done was: 'If that's yer best, pent it ridd an' mak' it dae' and even this was pronounced grudgingly.

'I didn't know that Rob went in for paint-it-red-and-make-it-do,' I said now.

'Rob was all right on the big spectacular things,' Twice told me, 'but he did not fuss if a hidden bolt was an eighth too short or too long. Mackie will turn the entire stores block inside out to find the right bolt. I suppose that is the difference between the basic tycoon and the basic engineer – the spectacular or the right bolt.'

He rose from the breakfast-table, went to the window

and looked across the park at the plume of smoke drifting from the stack. He then looked downwards, his head cocked to one side as he listened. To my ears, the factory made one single humming noise, punctuated by a few groans and clanks, but for Twice this noise could be heard in its component sounds, as the woodwind and strings of an orchestra can be heard separately by a conductor. And I think that, for Twice, this noise was music of a kind, each component of it true in tone and in balance.

'She sounds all right,' he said after a moment. 'I won't go up till later. I am going through to the study to write that letter.'

'What letter?'

'To old Alex about the boy,' he said, looking surprised.

His son had not been mentioned between us since the evening of my return from Scotland when the discussion had ended with his saying: 'I will have to think about it a bit more.' During the some four months that had passed, Twice had been thinking about it and was surprised now that I did not know he had been thinking and had reached this decision to institute enquiries about his son. Obviously, while he had been thinking, my position in regard to the matter had been an important consideration with him and he now felt that, instead of thinking quietly in the privacy of his own mind, he had been discussing the matter with me down these weeks that had passed.

'I am very glad you have decided to do that, Twice,' I said.

His expression changed as he became aware that I could not have known about his decision until now. 'Stupid of me,' he said. 'I have become accustomed to your knowing most of what I am thinking but you couldn't know about this.'

'Does old Alex know about you and Dinah?'

'No. He is going to get quite a shock and he will be very disapproving but he will also be discreet.'

Discreet was an understatement in regard to old Alex,

who was Twice's only living relation and the driest and dustiest of Edinburgh legal men. He was so cautious that he would hardly commit himself to a remark on the nature of the weather. Thinking of the arrival of Twice's letter on his leather-topped table, while faced by this strange new development in our lives, I was betrayed into nervous laughter. 'I am sorry, Twice,' I said at once, 'but I was thinking of old Alex opening your letter. It has its funny side.'

'I didn't think that anything connected with Dinah or me could ever be mildly funny but you are right,' he agreed. 'Of course, old Alex may not want to touch the thing with a barge pole. That firm does nothing as a rule except prove rich old women's wills.'

'But he will know of a firm who will handle our unrespectable but human little affairs, surely,' I said.

Twice put an arm round me. 'Thank you for calling it our affair.' He frowned. 'I have a feeling it is not going to be easy. Dinah didn't use my name for one thing. I don't know what she called herself and of course, then, I didn't care. And the last time I saw her, her father had died. Her mother died long ago. There were no other relations that I ever heard of.' Down the weeks, he had been marshalling his facts. 'I gathered that she was going to sell up and move away from Belfast. At that time I only wished she would move away to hell for preference,' he said savagely, 'but I wish now that I had been more matter-of-fact. Well, I'll go through to the study and see if I can put what is relevant down on paper.'

When he had gone, I went to my writing-table in the drawing-room. This was where I did my 'public' writing as opposed to my attempts to write a novel in the secrecy of the bedroom upstairs. I was the family banker, paying all our bills and I was also the family correspondent, writing all the letters to our friends. In my earlier time at Paradise, I used to maintain a large correspondence with people we had known before we came to the island but during the time of Twice's illness, I had allowed this to drop away. It is difficult to write letters when there is nothing but anxiety to report and nowadays I wrote regularly only to my family, while the rest of my correspondence had degenerated into cards and short notes exchanged at Christmas. My life now centred between two poles, the immediate pole of Paradise and Guinea Corner and the distant but constant pole of my family at home in Scotland. The other people I had known were now distant landmarks on the landscape of the years, even my friend Monica with whom I had been more intimate, probably, than with any other person except Twice and the members of my family. It seems that the human capacity for intimacy is limited and that the intimacy of marriage leaves little room for other intimacies and when Monica married Torquil Daviot at about the time that Twice and I first left Scotland for St. Jago, distance had opened between Monica and me. During my holiday in Scotland, I had spoken to her once or twice on the telephone but, although she lived only about a hundred miles from my brother's home, I had made no effort to visit her or she to visit me. We explained to one another that we were busy but, as I have always believed that one is never too busy to do what one really wants to do, this meant that I preferred to cook for my brother's children and George and Tom while my sister-in-law was in hospital giving birth to my new nephew to visiting Monica, and Monica preferred her activities at her home at Pountdale to visiting me. Thinking of this, I reminded myself, not for the first time, that nothing in life is for ever, that the essence of the process is change. At first, as I looked at the card that held no more than a conventional Christmas message, I felt sad but soon decided that this was merely sentimental, that there was nothing to be sad about, that what had been between Monica and me was now, as the saying goes, an old song. The important thing was that it was a song in memory and not a jangling discord.

Not all of the letters in the Christmas flood of mail carried conventional greetings, however. There was one that made the past seem very near and at the same time very far away. Twice and I had sold our Scottish home, Crookmill, to two friends, Lucy Wilton and Daisy Ramsay, the pair to whom we always referred collectively as Loose-an'-Daze, the pair famed for their fooshionlessness. They were muddle-headed but kind women and they had turned Crookmill into a small home for elderly people who were left alone, but who could pay a small sum for care and attention. 'We have had a sad year,' their letter told me. 'In June, we lost Mrs. Slater. She came to us after Mr. Slater died last March but it was no use from the very beginning. She had lost all interest and just went steadily downhill. Then in November, old Mattha died. You know how thrawn he was. We had a spell of hard frost, he would not stay in the house and he fell in the garden and broke his thigh. Then he developed pneumonia and there was nothing we could do. We miss him more than any of the people we have had with us, just because he was so thrawn and difficult likely. Although he went six weeks ago, we were just saying to one another today that we still expect to hear him shouting at the others and then stamping out of the house in a temper.'

Thinking of old Mattha made the early days of my life with Twice come very close momentarily and then made them recede down the tunnel of the full years that had elapsed since that time. In one sense, Mattha would live in my memory for ever, a 'thrawn' yet curiously lovable old man who seldom uttered a civil word while in another sense his death was like the falling of a leaf of some distant summer and nothing more. And this letter that told of his going was the first of a number of letters of a similar kind that marked that year.

The process was a logical one, although it carried with it the poignant sense of man's mortality. These people who died were people who had been old when I was young and the deaths made plain that the spring of my own short year was over. Yet, after the first initial shock, the news of the deaths of Mr. Rollin, of Granny Gilmour,

of Danny the Beeman, of the Reverend Roderick Macken-
zie took on the character of the slow beat of a very distant
muffled drum, a sad music that was of the very long ago
and far away.

But there were the survivors too for Tom, George and
my old stepmother Jean were still at Achcraggan, my
friend Martha wrote to say that her aunt was now a widow
again and had taken up a new brand of religion and
Madame Dulac was still round at the Great House, quarrelling with Miss Poynter.

I had written a letter to Loose-an'-Daze and cheques in
payment of one or two accounts when Caleb brought me
that morning's incoming mail. There was one letter addressed to myself and several business-looking ones for
Twice and I took the latter through to the study. Twice
was standing at his drawing-table, his slide-rule in his
hands, while he whistled the air of 'Drink to me only
with thine eyes' from which I understood that he was
in the preliminary stages of planning some new
lay-out.

Before his illness, Twice had whistled and sung all the
time he worked and he had unconsciously chosen certain
tunes which indicated to me and eventually to Caleb in
the garden outside the open windows the stages of his
work and phases of his thought. He had immense power
of concentration so that, now, he was unaware of my
presence in the room as he stared out at the sky. Suddenly,
in mid-note, 'Drink to me only with thine eyes' broke off
and there came a few quick bars of 'There was a wee
cooper who lived in Fife' while he manipulated the slide-
rule, then that tune too was dropped as he picked up a
pencil and ruled a line on the paper, singing: 'By yon
bonnie banks and by yon bonnie braes, where the sun
shines bright on Loch Lomond'.

'Things are goin' nicely, ma'am,' Caleb had said to me
one day long ago in the garden, 'we are doin' Loch
Lomon'' and Caleb, now weeding the rosebed beyond the

window, began to sing a soft negro accompaniment to the tune from inside the room.

'Sorry,' Twice said, turning round and seeing me, 'I didn't know you were there.'

'Letters,' I said, handing him the bundle.

Sitting down to read my own letter, I now noticed on the table by my chair the envelope addressed in Twice's hand; 'Alexander Ferguson, Esq., Messrs. Ferguson, Darling & Bell, W.S.,—' The small white rectangle lying on the dark wood of the table seemed to have tremendous presence, as if it were aware of being a symbol of great and mysterious import and my voice felt uncontrolled as I said: 'I have a letter from George and Tom. They are getting reckless. This is the second in a month.'

George and Tom, in their own words, were not 'great hands at the letter-writing' and this letter was their customary blue air-letter form, about a quarter of which was taken up with my brother's address and the date. George began: 'Dear Janet, We left Castle Jemima and came down to Jock's place for the New Year but we did not fight with Jean this time. We are here to dance at Sheila and Roddy's wedding in a fortnight's time and wish that you and Twice could come to dance along with us. Shona bought our present for them and it is blankets but we got young John the Smith to make them a poker for the fire with a ram's head on the handle as an extra. Tom will give you the rest of the news.' The letter now continued in Tom's hand: 'We have gone right past ourselves and have a new suit each to go to the wedding and Liz is fair past herself too at being the bridesmaid—'

'Janet,' came the voice of Twice from behind me, 'Old Alex is dead.'

I turned round and at once noticed that the skin of his face looked too tightly drawn over his jawbones and temples. 'Sit down,' I said, dropping my own letter on his desk and taking the white typewritten sheet from his hand.

But Twice did not sit down. He picked up the letter

he had written from the table by the door and ripped it across and then across again, then stood looking down at the scraps of paper in his hands. I read the brief message from Cousin Alex's firm, looked up and said: 'But, Twice—'

'This is not the moment,' he said and dropped the scraps of paper into the wastebasket. He sat down at his desk. 'Maybe that—' he looked at the letter I was holding '—is a reminder that one is not always allowed to choose one's own moments, that one can't just reach out when one feels like it and grab at something – or some*one* – that one has ignored for so long.'

I felt stunned, as if I had been running very fast and had crashed into a stone wall. Twice caught me by the arm and pulled me down on to his knees. 'Darling, don't look so stricken.'

'Twice, are you all right?'

The strained look had left his face and he smiled. 'Physically, perfectly all right, mentally rather back on my heels. I feel that I have over-reached myself and have been given a salutary lesson.'

'What are you going to do now?' I asked, getting up and laying the sheet of paper on the desk.

'I don't know yet. Wait a bit, I think. This is not something I can ask any old legal wallah to tackle for me.' He frowned staring down at the letter. '*That* gives me the feeling that I ought to do nothing for the moment. Is that silly?'

'No, I don't think it is silly. Twice, you said we might go back home one day. If we did, maybe you could go to Ireland—?'

'Maybe. Maybe that is it. At the moment, I just don't know. Poor old Alex, a stroke, they said.'

'How old was he?'

'Somewhere between sixty-five and seventy. Not that old.'

It is in this way that we escape from the momentous incidents of life that threaten to overwhelm us. We seize upon the trivia, the immediate cause of the death, the age of the one who has died. We do not contemplate death itself and Twice and I did not contemplate the change in our plans that this particular death had caused. We turned away from the moment that Twice had felt so strongly to be not the right one for what he had planned to do and having turned away, we buried the shock of the moment under lesser and more manageable thoughts and words. What looked like the upheld warning finger of fate was not to be defied or even contemplated with equanimity.

We settled into the routine of Crop. Very few moments of life are momentous; most of it is a going on from one moment to the next, a dealing with the little events that come to hand. By most plantation wives, Crop was regarded as a stretch of monotonous boredom which led to much petty quarrelling among the beleaguered women in the estate compounds, for the men folk were tied to the factories that processed day and night and there was little social life.

I had been fortunate in my upbringing on a remote hilltop in Scotland where I had always had to create my own amusements, which was a good preparation for these six-month cropping periods when passing time was marked only by the scream of the siren at six in the morning, at two in the afternoon and at ten at night, when the shifts of factory workers changed over. I had never been at a loss to fill my days and this Crop they seemed more full than ever, so that I could not find as much time as I should have liked to spend on my secret writing upstairs. Sashie's piano had been installed in a corner of the drawing-room before Crop began and most evenings when Twice and I came home from the Great House we would find him there, with his large sheets of staved paper and often Percy too would be in her wicker chair in the other corner with her sketch-book on her knees. Percy invariably went back to Olympus to see the evening meal served to her charges but frequently Sashie would have the meal with Twice and me and then Percy and some of the Olympus people would come over to spend the rest of the evening.

Twice's post as manager sat lightly upon him, for which Mackie was largely responsible, with his devoted watch over the factory plant.

'I have never known a crop with fewer alarms and excursions,' I said to Twice.

'Thanks to Hawk-eye Mackie. He can see, hear, feel, smell a fault before it brings the whole thing to a sticky halt.' The word 'sticky' was used literally. Sugar is a sticky substance in all its stages of processing and if any part of the complex came to halt, the engineers were faced with pipes full of juice that rapidly clogged into something like half-cooked candy.

Twice divided his working time between his drawing-table in the study and his office at the plant and spent his evenings with the young people or in discussion with Mackie and I spent as much time as I could in the back bedroom where I was growing more and more engaged in what I was trying to do there. A change had taken place in our way of life. We spent less time alone together than we had done formerly.

It does not take long for a pattern of living to develop, for habits to form and so gradually, naturally and quietly that I did not notice what was happening, Madame, Sir Ian and Miss Poynter at the Great House, Twice and myself at Guinea Corner and the young people at Olympus became welded into a heterogeneous family of three generations. It was as if I awoke one morning at the end of January and discovered that this had happened. Looking back, it was impossible to say how or when the process had begun but I think an important factor was the offer of Percy and her friends to replace me at the Great House on some afternoons.

The first visit, when Percy and Mary went unescorted by myself, was a ringing success and when I saw Madame the following day, she was filled with enthusiasm for the Health Mission and its members. She had always been interested in the health services of the island and in her early days in St. Jago, indeed, she had been a member of the committee that founded the first hospital. Gradually, the hospitals had come under government administration but Madame had continued to devote much of her time and money to them.

'Miss Crockford is a most intelligent and interesting young lady,' Madame informed me with approval. 'She is the statistician of the group, you understand, and collates all the information for the others. It must be a great deal of work for they intend to make a health record of every school child in the island and they have a separate section for the little ones under five.'

'How very interesting, Madame,' I said.

Naturally, I already knew from talking to the young people the nature of their mission but Madame liked firstly to command and secondly to instruct and it was my habit to indulge her.

'And little Miss Soames is charming. She is very tiny, isn't she, Janet?'

'Yes, Madame. She stands less than five feet and is very slimly built.'

'I thought so,' she said with satisfaction. 'Her hands are so very small. But, as I said yesterday, she is probably the most useful person of the whole mission for I gather she is most capable at catering and running their establishment for them. Janet, I should like very much to meet the others. Do you think that would be possible?'

'I should think so, Madame.'

'Not all at once, of course. I shall not give a formal party for them. I cannot cope with large numbers any more,' she said, with one of her few outbursts of impatience with her blindness. 'But I should enjoy meeting them one or two at a time if they would like to come. When would be the best time to invite them?'

'Friday evenings, probably, Madame,' I said. 'They

finish work for the week at five on Fridays and as a rule they all come home and spend the evening at the Club or with us at Guinea Corner. Friday is the one evening when they all seem to come home. Other evenings, some of them work late or stay in town and on Saturdays they swim or play tennis all day and dance all night.'

'As well they might when they work so hard,' said Madame. 'Very well, you will convey to them that I shall be delighted to see one or two of them any Friday evening.'

'Yes, Madame.'

The young people were goodnaturedly co-operative. At first, they regarded the visits to the Great House as a duty which they owed in return for their accommodation on the estate and on the first Friday evening Twice and I stayed on with Madame to sponsor the two young doctors who had volunteered, but after the visit they were enthusiastic and their enthusiasm spread to the others. Sir Ian with his genuine liking for young people was the most comfortable of hosts, Madame with her real interest in their work made conversation easy but I think an even more important factor was the age and feeling of tradition that hung over the house itself. To these 'institution people', as Percy had called them, four thousand miles from their own homes and families, this rooted place with its blind châtelaine still a commanding figure in her straight-backed chair had an attraction to which they responded with something like bemusement. They looked about them at the tasteless amalgam of old furniture and Victorian bric-à-brac and pictures that Madame had introduced as a bride, at the old servants, at the lush perfectly-kept garden beyond the windows, at Madame herself with their eyes wide, like the eyes of children in a historical museum. After that evening, I could look out from Guinea Corner at six o'clock on a Friday and be sure of seeing one or two battered old cars come down from Olympus and cross the park to the Great House on the other side of the factory.

'Whose car is that?' I asked Twice one Friday evening as a vehicle rolled out of the Olympus driveway.

Cars, for me, have no personality. They are all alike. More than once, having arranged to meet Twice at our car after having been to the shops, I have been found beside the wrong car but Twice can assign cars to their owners by sound as well as sight. He glanced across the park. 'That is young Lydgate's.'

'Good. Madame likes Tony Lydgate.'

'I wonder if she still would if she knew all?'

'All being what?'

'Lydgate calls the Great House the Biggest Aspidistra in the World'. When we had finished laughing, he added: 'Of course, you can't be sure that Lydgate is in the car. I have never seen such a bunch of sharers-out and muckers-in.'

'I know, and all the girls wear each other's clothes, except Percy, that is. She is too small.'

'But in spite of Edward's worst fears, they don't seem to be muckers-in in bed,' Twice said. 'They are a very orderly lot. We are going to miss them around the place when they go.'

'Go?' I felt my heart sinking. They had become a part of the place so familiar that I had almost forgotten that their stay at Paradise was a temporary makeshift.

'Their Chief 'phoned Sir Ian today to tell him that the hostels would be ready at the end of next week.'

'Goodness, we *are* going to miss them, Madame and Sir Ian as much as anybody.'

'Janet,' he said hesitantly, 'I want to make a suggestion.'

'All right. Suggest.'

'It is about Percy. She can't go to the hostel with the rest of the girls. She will have to go to a boarding-house. I thought perhaps we could ask her to stay with us for a bit. What do you think? But not if she would be a nuisance of course.'

'You silly ass, as if she could be a nuisance. I should like to have her, if she will come, that is.'

'You don't think she would?' he asked gravely.

'I am not sure, Twice. I shall certainly ask her. But she is a rover, that child, a real modern-day tramp. I don't think she likes having a fixed abode. When I first came home, you likened her to a swallow, remember? It was very apt.'

'She comes here a lot,' he said, frowning. 'I thought she would like to stay.'

'Popping in and out as she does is different from being a house-guest. She might not like regular meal-times or even having to say that she would be out for a meal. This is only an impression I have, of course, but look at her attitude to Olympus and Bachelors'. She could have a salary for what she does at Olympus, I gather from Mary Crockford, but she doesn't want a salaried post. Percy likes suddenly, some morning, to decide to spend the day around the docks and she arranges the evening meal and off she goes. As Mary puts it, she is very conscientious about what she has undertaken to do but she does it in her own way and in her own time. Of course, she could do just as she pleased here. Anyway, I shall ask her if she would like to come, Twice.'

Almost subconsciously, I was trying to warn him of what I felt to be the nature of Percy. I was aware in a doubting uncanny fashion that he might be growing too attached to Percy for his own future happiness and this made me add: 'She did say to me once, though, that she might leave the island after the Teeth and Feet Lot left Olympus.'

'I can't get used to the idea of that little thing roving round the world all on her own,' he said. 'She has never said any more to you about her parents?'

'Not a word. I am fairly sure that her mother is dead though and that she has no connection with her father. Again it is an impression only. She simply has the air of being completely on her own and of liking it that way, let me point out. *You* haven't gathered any more about her?'

'Not a thing but then I am never alone with her as you are.'

'She might talk to you, given the opportunity.'

He shook his head positively. 'No, she wouldn't. She will ask me what I think about this and that and she will talk about you and me but never about herself.'

'That is one of the most interesting things about her,' I said. 'Unlike most people, she doesn't seem to think that she is in the least interesting.'

Percy, exactly as if she knew by instinct of our little plan to capture her, suddenly became very elusive and although I told myself that there were logical reasons for her never appearing at Guinea Corner alone, I could not rid myself of the idea that she suspected us of an attempt to cage her. Indeed, everything about her was elusive, especially the relationship between Twice and herself. He was regarding her more and more as a daughter, speaking of her in the slightly possessive tone that he used in speaking of Mackie but the bond on her side was more difficult to define. At times, I would think that it was merely his appearance that attracted her as an artist, for she never tired of sketching him or parts of him – the side of his head, his big hands, his well-proportioned legs and feet which were always bare when he was in the house. Twice could never have been called a handsome man but he was very individual, unlike any other man I had ever seen and I knew that this was not only my own view. His facial features were contradictory, as Sashie had once pointed out. 'That soft mobile mouth,' he had said, 'above that hatchet of a chin is a contradiction in terms.' Thus, sometimes, I would think that it was Percy's pencil that was fascinated by Twice but at other times, when she bent a soft thoughtful glance on him while his attention was concentrated upon something else, I would wonder if she saw in him and felt for him something that she might have seen in and felt for her lost father.

Whatever his attraction for her, however, it seemed to be in abeyance during this last week of her stay at Olympus. She came to the house only once, one evening with a group of the others, to invite us to their farewell party.

'It will be just a drink and a salted peanut,' they told us, 'and we'll even have to borrow glasses because we want it to be on the very last night and everything except our beds will be all packed up.'

Percy, I heard from Mary and the others, was spending all her time either at the docks or round at the lake in the garden of the Great House. There were sound Percy-ish reasons for the time spent at both places for it was February, when the St. Jagoan weather was at its best. The docks were at their busiest, with cruise ships carrying fugitives from the European and American winters calling every day and the lake was its busiest with migrants of another kind. These were large white wading birds with long red legs which Madame called 'Red-legged Stilts' and which Caleb called 'Gawlens'. They were very beautiful whether wading or preening or in their slow languid flight and Percy's pencil was busy with them.

In the days of the Macleans, Olympus had been graciously and elegantly furnished and on the night of the party I found pathos in the large bare hall, empty except for a mountain of luggage, topped by a heap of tennis racquets and golf clubs. On one wall, there was a notice board with one notice which said: 'If you don't collect your laundry before you leave forget it. Soames.' The party was being held in the large drawing-room where so many distinguished people had been entertained but now the only furniture that I could see was a number of wicker chairs, some painted blue, some green. I had a momentary time-slip back to the anteroom of my officers' mess during the war and would not have been surprised to see the red-gold hair of my friend Monica above the back of one of the wicker chairs.

'Percy has a cold,' Mary Crockford told me, handing me a glass. 'She is in bed. Isn't it a shame?'

'It is. Could I see her?'

Mary led me up the wide bare stairs and up again on a slightly narrower flight to the top floor, opened a door quietly and said: 'Percy?'

From inside the room there came a little grunt, Mary switched on the light and we went in. 'Percy?' Mary said again on a sharper, more anxious note.

Percy looked at us from wide too-bright eyes, groped for her spectacles on the green-painted metal locker by her bed but gave up the effort and let her hand fall back limply to her side. On her pale cheeks there were grotesque crescents of scarlet flush, running out towards her temples and from where I stood in the middle of the floor, I could hear her short laboured breathing.

'She is worse,' Mary said. 'Janet, she is really sick.'

'I had had pneumonia,' said Percy's voice in my memory.

'Is Doctor Gurbat Singh downstairs?' I asked. This was the estate doctor, an old friend of mine on whom I could rely.

'Don't spoil the party,' Percy whispered at us.

'We won't,' I assured her, taking hold of her wrist. 'Mary, get Gurbat Singh and ask Mackie to come up too.'

'Bruce Mackie?'

'Yes.' Mary did not wait for the explanation which was due but went away downstairs. I could explain to her later that I would not nowadays ask Twice to carry even Percy's light weight to the car but Mackie would carry her.

Gurbat Singh merely stood beside the bed, looked down at Percy and left the room again with me behind him. Mackie, with his dark eyes searching round the bare walls stood beside Mary.

'Hospital,' said Gurbat Singh. 'She can't stay here.'

'Guinea Corner?' I said. 'I can nurse her.'

'Whatever you say,' he agreed.

'Mackie, will you carry little Percy down?' I asked.

'Has the Chief got his big car here? Are the keys in it?'

'Yes.'

He turned to Mary. 'Go down and get Vickers on the quiet and tell him to run the Chief's car round to the back door.' He now turned to Gurbat Singh and me. 'You wrap up the baggage,' he said. 'I'll take it down.'

Percy, wrapped in her blanket, was a very small bundle that seemed to be a very long way from the ground as Mackie crossed the back yard with her and got into the back of the car, bundle and all. I sat beside Vickers in the front, Mary stayed to pack Percy's things and bring them to us and Gurbat Singh went round by his clinic to fetch what he required. Percy, in the big four-poster bed in the main bedroom at Guinea Corner looked even smaller but at least she no longer looked like a child abandoned in an institution as she had looked in that hospital furnished room at Olympus. Gurbat Singh did not take long to complete his examination and tell me what to do and when we came out on to the landing, Mackie was standing there, awkward, all arms and legs that looked utterly beyond his control, so that it was an effort to recall the cool gentle neatness with which he had handled the 'baggage'.

'Here, Missis Janet,' he said urgently, 'I'll have to go and get the Chief. I'll get a proper rocket if I don't. If there is any trouble he has to know.'

'All right but don't—' I broke off. I had been going to say 'Don't alarm him' but I had learned that, down the years, Mackie had given as much care as myself to not alarming Twice.

I left Mary with Percy and Gurbat Singh and I was on the veranda when Mackie came back with Twice.

'She will be all right,' the doctor said at once.

'What is the matter with her?' Twice asked and the

bones of his skull seemed to be about to burst through the skin.

'Pneumonia, I am afraid,' Gurbat Singh said in the weary tone of one who knew from long experience that only the bare truth would serve. 'She will be all right,' he repeated with energy. 'We caught her in time.'

'Where the hell has she been?' Twice enquired of me with angry accusation. 'What has she been doing?'

I recognised this outburst as a release of tension and anxiety and so did Mackie but he was quicker in his response than I was. 'All of us get a chill an' a fever sooner or later, sir,' he said. 'You know that.'

The use of the negro phrase 'a chill an' a fever' lightened the atmosphere, caused the dark spectre to dissolve and Twice sat down, relaxed.

Percy was very ill indeed for three days but at dawn on the fourth morning she showed that indefinable change that comes with the turn for the better. Physically, she was probably weaker than she had been at dawn on the previous day but I was certain nevertheless that the life force now had the upper hand. When Twice put his head round the door of the room, I pointed to the sleeping girl and whispered: 'Better.' I then began to cry and went across the landing to our own room. He followed me.

'Sorry,' I said, mopping my face. 'It reminded me of the morning that Caleb got better and the cable came telling us that Dad was dead.'

'Don't, Janet. It can't be like that this time,' he said. 'Here is Clorinda with the tea.'

'Good morning, sah. We askin' 'bout Miss Percy, ma'am.'

'She is better, Clorinda,' Twice told her. 'Much better' and when she had gone downstairs, he repeated: 'Much better. Janet, when I wanted her to come to stay with us I didn't mean it to be like this.'

'Things have a way of happening as one didn't mean them to,' I said, 'but no matter how it happened, I am glad that she is here. I have never seen anything so awful as that bedroom at Olympus. She shared it with Mary. Two hospital cots, two metal lockers, two metal cupboards, two canvas chairs. It was worse than my tin hut in Buckinghamshire during the war.'

But now I remembered that I had been happy in the tin hut which had had a discomfort unknown to the room at Olympus, for it had had a damp cement floor, was permanently cold and if I made a fire of fallen wood in the little black stove, chill beads of dirty water used to gather and slide down the curved metal walls.

'But when one is young it is different,' I said, almost talking to myself. 'I felt that if I had to live at Olympus, I would turn into a number, a sort of non-identity, a mass-produced thing like the metal cupboards but in the tin hut I didn't feel like that. When one is young one is so sure of who and what one is, somehow.'

'So sure,' Twice pointed out, 'that one rises above being a number even. In the Air Force, you were a number first and then a name, remember?'

'That's true. It would be logical to think that one becomes surer of oneself and one's identity as one gets older but it isn't like that. It seems to work in reverse. Twice, I am tired. I always burble when I am tired but I shall be able to sleep today and come to my senses. Mary will manage on her own. You slept all right?'

'Given Gurbat Singh's pills, one can't help oneself,' he said. After he had gone to the factory, Mary, who had been granted a week's leave, took up duty in Percy's room and I had a bath and went to bed but although I was tired, I could not sleep. I lay with every muscle tense and at last I had to admit to myself that I was waiting and listening for the pattern of that morning when Caleb's illness showed its first abatement to repeat itself. Hard as I tried to reason with myself, curse as I might my superstitious Highland nature, the waiting and the listening were there and not to be ignored. I got up, put on a dressing-gown and went downstairs to ask Cookie for some coffee and as I reached the hall, Mackie came up the veranda steps. I saw the envelope in his hand, an airmail letter, not a cable.

'Percy is better, the Chief tells me,' he said.

'Yes, much better.' I held out my hand for the envelope but Mackie merely looked wildly round him, at me, the furniture, his own feet on the step as if he could not imagine what he was doing here, face to face with me in a dressing-gown at this unlikely hour of the morning.

'I am on my way out to Halfway Cane-piece,' he said, as if reminding himself of why he had come here before he brightened and added: 'Oh, the Chief said to give you this, said you would be glad to have it. Good-bye.'

He thrust the envelope at me, I saw on it the large handwriting of my niece Liz and for the second time that morning, I began to cry but from relief this time. News sent by Liz could not be other than good.

'Dear Aunt Janet, This is to tell you about the wedding. I was the chief bridesmaid and the only one as well and I had a white dress with a blue sash. I really wanted to wear the kilt like the boys but Dad said you would look pretty silly in the kilt with flowers in your hair and carrying a gold basket full of blue hyacinths. I had the basket so that it would go over my arm when I had to hold Aunt Sheila's bouquet when they put the ring on her. Roddy looked very good-looking but was very quiet. I thought he was feeling sick but he said not. Uncle Alasdair was an usher and Dunk and Gee were an usher between them and Sandy Tom slept in his pram in the church porch the whole time. George and Tom wheeled him from Granny's to the church and had on their new suits and flowers in their buttonholes. Sandy Tom had a flower too but fixed to his pillow with a nappy pin. George did it. After the minister had done it we all went to a hotel and had a slap-up lunch. It was soup and fish AND roast turkey like Christmas and pudding and the

Cake and we all had wine but the bubbles itched my nose. – I have had my dinner between that bit and this bit. – That is all about the wedding. It is very cold and a sleet storm today. That is why I am writing. There is nothing else to do and Dunk and Gee are very fightable. Gosh, I forgot the main thing about the wedding. One of my front teeth came out into an apple the day before and Dunk said fancy a toothless hag with flowers in her hair but Dad said a toothless bridesmaid was very original and deestinkay. I am not sure about that last word and Dad is not here and the rest of us do not know. I think it is French. Tom and George are still here because the weather is too bad to work at the garden at the cottage anyway. We like it when they are here. We all send our love to Uncle Twice and you as well of course from Elizabeth' – then a different hand – 'Duncan' – yet another hand – 'George' – and now 'X Alexander Thomas, his mark' in the handwriting of George senior.

Life did not have patterns or run true to expectations. I carried my letter upstairs, re-read it, then fell asleep and did not awaken until after dark in the evening.

Percy was very weak and made slow progress and when I remarked on this to Gurbat Singh, he astonished me by saying: 'She has had a nasty go but she is very robust, you know. She will come along all right.'

'Robust? She has bones like a bird and they are all on display!'

'But she is sound, Missis Janet.'

'She has had pneumonia before, too,' I protested.

'And she lived to have it again,' he told me with his cool East Indian calm. 'But she must have got a very severe chill and she shouldn't get another. Keep on with the tablets. I shall look in again tomorrow.'

'I like that Doctor Gurbat Singh,' Percy informed me from the four-poster. 'He looks like an intelligent peacock and should wear greenish-blue robes. Listen, what day is it?'

'Thursday.'

'So yesterday was Wednesday.' She took on her thoughtful look and then protested: 'But the party was on a Friday.'

'That's right. Last Friday. You don't remember the days?'

'Not much. Bits. I didn't think it had been so long.' She looked round the room. 'This is upstairs at Guinea Corner?'

'Yes.'

'Somebody carried me downstairs at Olympus. I remember going down but not coming up.'

'Mackie,' I said. 'Bruce Mackie carried you.'

'Kind of him. What a bore.'

'What about sleeping a little more?'

'All right.'

She was docile in a considerate way. because she did not want to be a nuisance. 'Couldn't I get into the bath?' she would ask while I was sponging her. 'I am such a nuisance.'

'You would be more of a nuisance if you got another chill.'

'That's right,' she would agree.

I had thought that the transfer of the Mission from Olympus to their quarters in St. Jago Bay would withdraw them from the life of Paradise, but this was not so. At first, they came up in groups to enquire about Percy, when she became convalescent, they came to visit her in the evenings or on their days off and some of the girls spent their free afternoons with Madame while I was nursing Percy. In time, they were pursuing their work in all the schools of the island, sleeping at their hostels but spending the rest of their time at Paradise which they had adopted as their home. The reason was partly financial. Their salaries were not great. They could not afford the hotel dance floors, the tennis courts, the swimming pools or even the Coca-Cola of the Platinum Coast, while at Paradise they had all the amenities of the

Estate Workers' Club of which Sir Ian had made them free.

Percy's legs were the last part of her to return to action and obey her will and in spite of her dogged patience, she became very bored, enclosed by the four walls of her bedroom. She tried not to show this but one would go upstairs and find her on the window-seat, looking hungrily out at the sky like a caged bird.

Eventually, one evening when she had been incarcerated for about three weeks, Mary and two of the other girls arrived to see her and Mackie arrived at the same time to see Twice.

'How is she?' Mary asked.

'Very bored with her four walls but she still can't manage the stairs even with my help,' I said.

'Shall I get her?' Mackie asked on impulse and at once became all hands and feet. 'I mean, I carried the baggage up. I could bring it down, that is, if it is all right, I mean and wouldn't—'

'Thank you, Mackie,' I said. 'I shall parcel her up and you can bring her down into that chair.' I pointed to the wicker chair in the drawing-room. 'Mackie is going to carry you downstairs,' I told Percy. 'Roll over on to this blanket.'

'But—' she protested, looking towards Mackie in the doorway.

'It's m-me or the factory crane,' he said.

On a further three evenings, Mackie arrived and said: 'Shall I get the baggage?' but on the fourth evening, Percy had come slowly downstairs on her own wobbly legs and poked her face out of her wicker cave in the drawing room when he arrived to say: 'Sucks to you!'

'Dammit,' said Mackie, 'I am fired,' but he had grown as easy in his manner with her as he was with Twice and as he was with no other female, even myself, in spite of my awareness that he liked me.

When Percy had grown strong enough to spend most of the day downstairs and to go about the garden and a little way into the park beyond the wall. I remembered what Gurbat Singh had said.

'Percy,' I said to her, 'I don't think you understand this climate. You can get a chill and develop sudden pneumonia in a way you never could at home. Can you remember feeling suddenly cold before you got ill?'

'You bet I can,' she said. 'I was sitting in a tree round at the lake, watching the gawlens and I fell in. You would never believe how cold that lake is.'

'It is spring-fed, for pity's sake. What did you do?'

'Came out and dried off in the sun.'

'No wonder you got pneumonia. If anything like that ever happens again, run like blazes for the nearest hot bath. Promise me.'

'I promise. I would have to, wouldn't I, after the pest I have been? You should have slapped me into hospital. Next time Mary comes up, I shall ask her to find a room for me in the Bay.'

I paused carefully before I said: 'Percy, when the Mission left Olympus, Twice and I were going to ask you to stay here for a bit. Would you like to?'

'Here? At Guinea Corner?' She raised her eyebrows, causing the spectacles to slip. 'I would like that,' she said, pushing the spectacles up again before adding with strong decision: 'if you would let me pay. I couldn't just stay without paying. That would not be right.'

'You think not?'

'You must let me pay,' she said firmly.

'Very well,' I conceded. 'You may pay what you would at a boarding-house.'

'Boarding-house,' she said scornfully. 'It is the loveliest house in the world.' She became solemn. 'Why do you ask me to stay?'

'Because we like having younger people around and we like you.'

'You don't really know anything about me.'

'Does that matter?'

She gave her little laugh. 'Perhaps not. There isn't much to know. I don't know much about myself.'

'Does anybody? How old are you, Percy?'

'Twenty-one. I was twenty-one the day of the Olympus party.'

'What a birthday!' I said.

'It is the sort of thing that happens. I had the big act all ready, about how, in the middle of the party, I would say: You all know something? This is my birthday and I am twenty-one and they would all drink my health and none of them would have had to give me a present for none of them can really afford it and what happens? I get pneumonia. Plans never work out. It is the things you don't expect that happen. When I came out here to the West Indies, for instance, I never imagined anything like meeting Twice and you and being asked to stay here.'

'What *did* you imagine when you came out here?' I asked.

'I don't know. Sometimes I think I don't know anything.'

She was listless and depressed much of the time, which was only partly the aftermath of her illness, I felt, for she invariably became brighter when Twice was in the house, had less of the air of the caged bird. It seemed to me that she had changed since her illness, had become even more of a solitary. When the Mission had been at Olympus and she had lived there, she had appeared to be one of the group, with Mary Crockford as her particular friend, but now her apartness from the group and even from Mary became apparent. It became more and more obvious that their visits merely bored her and that she preferred the company of Twice, Sir Ian or myself, people of an older generation. When she had been well and mobile, I now came to understand, she had moved around with the group, taken part in their activities only up to a point, but she had had a habit of withdrawing quietly, going off to the Great House lake or down to the docks. Of course, her poor sight had excluded her from games like tennis but there was more to her isolation than this physical disability. She was simply not gregarious by nature and this I could understand, for I have always liked to spend part of my days by myself but the difference between Percy and me was that I was happy in solitude and she did not seem to be so.

I felt that she was suffering less from post-illness depression than from some deep unhappiness which the illness, taking advantage of her weakness, had brought to the surface but I could see no way of helping her. I felt that if I said something direct like: 'Percy, why are you unhappy?', weak as she was, the bird would take wing and fly out of reach. I did not speak of this to Twice, because it might have worried him, but I hoped that she might disclose to him something of what her thoughts were, he seeming to be closer to her than anyone. Meanwhile, she was growing physically stronger from day to day and the phase might pass.

With Percy convalescent, the music broke out around the house again, Sashie and Caleb busy with the piano and the guitar, Percy and Twice with the player in the evenings and I resumed my upstairs writing in the mornings between Twice's going to the factory and Percy's coming downstairs. I also resumed my visits to Madame in the afternoons.

One morning, I was in the back bedroom, wrapping up the manuscript of my second novel in brown paper, ready to put away in the linen cupboard when, suddenly, Twice materialised beside me as if he had erupted through the floor. Between my startled hands, the stiff brown paper sprang apart, exposing the written sheets. Long ago, Twice had indicated very clearly that he disapproved of this activity of mine. He had a curious attitude to it which reminded me of my grandmother's reaction to something that was too strange for her comprehension. 'No good can come of it,' she would say in a voice deep with foreboding. Twice did not use these words although I was sure that they expressed what he felt. He used other arguments which he considered more rational. And now here he was, looking very large and what Liz would call 'fightable' and here was I caught in the act, betrayed into carelessness by those long years when he had not been able to come upstairs and take me unawares. Naturally, I felt guilty that I had been taking advantage of his weakness, doing something he did not like, cheating him and perhaps less naturally but, for me, very naturally, because I felt guilty, I became angry.

'What are you doing in here?' he snapped at me.

'Shut up! You'll wake Percy. What are *you* doing in here? Is anything wrong?'

'I forgot that draft I wrote in bed last night. Then I heard you in here.'

This made me angrier although I do not pretend to know why. He heard me, went my train of thought, when I wasn't making a sound and I didn't hear *him* coming upstairs, the cat-footed fox-eared beast that he is!

'So you have got that writing bug again?' he said.

'Not again. I have always had it.'

'You are mad! People like us don't write books.' He was scornful. I became angrier still.

'What are we people like?' I asked.

He poked his face forward. 'Don't start that. You know bloody well what I mean – ordinary people—'

'You were the first person to point out to me that there was no such thing as an *ordinary* person.'

This was true, it made him angrier now and he changed his ground. 'We are plain unimportant little people. We have no high-flown connections with the arts or even with sex drama like Roddy Maclean.'

'I think plain unimportant little people are very interesting and I don't see why I shouldn't write about them as I see them,' I said.

'You will only make a fool of yourself and me too!' he said loudly. 'I don't see why—'

'Now, look here, Twice Alexander, that's enough of that—' I was saying more loudly still when we heard the steps on the landing, followed by the gentle closing of the bathroom door. The rage seeped out of us.

'Hell,' I said, 'what are we fighting about? Twice, I am not doing any harm. Nobody knows about this.'

'Sashie does.'

'Oh, him. He doesn't matter. Twice, why are you so annoyed about it?'

He looked shamefaced. 'I don't know. It is something to do with your going where I can't follow. Something that pushes us apart.'

'Darling, you take it too seriously. It will never amount to anything.'

He turned away towards the door with a defeated air. 'Do you know where I put that draft I wrote?'

'Yes. I'll get it.'

When he had gone back to his office, I did not return to the back bedroom. Never before had I taken a stand like this about my secret pastime and I was a little astonished at myself, but I did not want to think of the stand I had made or of my implicitly declared intention to go on with my writing. This 'difference' between Twice and myself was too strange for immediate contemplation and had to be absorbed gradually.

I went out to Caleb in the garden where our work absorbed my attention until Clorinda came to tell me that Percy was downstairs. When I came into the room, she was sitting in her wicker chair and she looked up at me with a mischievous smile. 'Now, look here, Twice Alexander, that's enough of that,' she greeted me. 'I heard you upstairs. I couldn't help it.' She studied my face which probably looked disconcerted. 'That is all I heard, honestly,' she added.

'It was nothing important,' I lied. 'I had done something Twice didn't hold with. I often do. Sometimes I wish that I didn't but I do.'

'You do?' She looked pleased, as if this were welcome news. 'But you love him a lot, don't you?'

'Yes, I think so but you can love people quite a lot and still do things that annoy them,' I assured myself more than Percy.

'Have you a lot of things to do this morning?' she asked.

'Nothing at all. Why?'

'If I am going to stay here and I seem to *be* staying, you ought to know something about me. I don't want to be a bore, but—' She broke off.

'I don't bore easily,' I said.

'No, you don't,' she agreed. 'You seem to be interested in everybody and everything. I would like to tell you about my mother, my mother and me. I have never talked to anybody about her before. I don't know if I *can* talk about her.'

Her big eyes looked at me and then round the room as if there were a presence there somewhere which she could not identify.

'You can try, if you are sure you want to,' I said, 'but first I am going to fetch your milk drink and my coffee.'

I went through to the pantry, leaving her alone, that she might have time to reconsider, to edit what she wanted to say, to change her mind and say nothing at all if she thought the better of it. Hitherto, she had been so independent and self-contained that I did not want the weakness following her illness to betray her into giving confidences that she would afterwards regret. Nothing is so destructive of human relationships as the mis-placed or mis-timed confidence which is regretted afterwards with grudge and bitterness.

I spent an unnecessary amount of time mixing the patent food that Gurbat Singh had recommended into the glass of milk but when I returned to the drawing-room there was a look of collected decision on her pale little face.

'I like the way you and Twice argue,' she said, and I

decided that she had indeed changed her mind. 'It is all so direct and straightforward.'

The argument of that morning had not been 'straightforward' in my view for our difference had not been resolved but merely marked into a new definition and determination in my mind. Circumstances, including Twice, had stopped my attempts at writing for many years but I was determined suddenly to defy these circumstances as I had never defied them before.

'I don't know if direct and straightforward are the words for it,' I said, 'but if they are, our arguments used to be a great deal more so. I have broken more crockery than you could shake a stick at, heaving it at Twice. We are a little more civilised now, though.'

Percy laughed and then became grave. 'That is better than just pinching and scratching as Mother and I used to do. And then quite suddenly, she died and it was all awful. Then I got pneumonia and came out here.' She was silent for a little before, with a sudden change of direction like the swoop of a swallow in flight, she said: 'It is queer. My talking to you like this starts with Twice but I could never talk to *him* about it. I think I sort of fell for Twice because of my father. That Mrs. Beaumont down at the Bay talked about me being his girl-friend but that is a lot of rubbish. You know that. And that woman Beaumont would be a nymphomaniac, only she hasn't got the face or the build for it.'

This made me laugh for I had never heard a better summing-up of Miranda Beaumont.

'Twice gave me a feeling of somebody who had once loved me, so it must have been my father because there has been nobody else. He ran away and left my mother and me when I was four but I still think he loved me. I sort of remember it and yet I don't. I don't blame him for running away either, because I can sort of understand why he did it.' She paused, drank some of her milk and said: 'I had better start at the beginning. We lived in Manchester. My father was an art teacher and he made extra money in textile design. Before they were married, my mother was a hairdresser. She worked in one of those fashionable expensive salons. They got married and I came along and we lived in this little bungalow. I don't remember much about it except that there was a rockery in the garden with cushions of blue flowers in it, but Mother always called it that awful little bungalow. Then my father ran away. I don't remember much about that either but when I got older Mother told me that he had gone off with this woman who was an old friend of his and Mother divorced him and he married this friend. Mother was never nasty about him. You know, I think she was quite glad he had gone. You never hear about it being like that but I think that was how it was with Mother. Does it sound silly?'

'No, it doesn't.' Naturally, I thought of Twice and Dinah, the only parallel of which I knew. 'You are probably quite right about how your mother felt.'

'Good luck to him, she used to say, but that was later. At the time, everything, for me, got very exciting. Mother sold the bungalow and we went to live with Gran, Mother's mother, in Liverpool, down near the docks. In Gran's kitchen, there was a chair exactly like this one—' she patted the arms of her wicker chair with both hands '—not the leg-rest part but this part. It had been Grandad's chair and Gran would not part with it.' She paused, took off her glasses, examined them short-sightedly and replaced them. 'The important thing is that my father left Mother the bungalow and most of their savings. That is where it all began. It gave her the chance to do what she really wanted. But it was 1940 and the war had started and Mother couldn't begin just yet so she went off and joined the women's part of the army. What was it called?'

'The A.T.S.,' I supplied.

'That's it. She had a khaki uniform and she used to come home on leave and got promoted and was an officer. She and Gran and I were happy. Gran and I were happy all the time.' Percy spoke in short sentences, building up her picture as if with short strokes of a pencil on paper. 'It was a flat, four rooms altogether, above a butcher's shop and all the men round about worked at the docks, the ones who weren't at the war, that is. There were air raids and Gran and I used to go down to the butcher's cellar. I thought it was all very exciting.' She smiled at me fleetingly. 'And then the war was over and Mother came home but then Gran died. Everything got different. I was ten at the time.'

When she said this, I felt a keen kinship with her for, in my own life when I was ten, 'everything got different' after my mother died. 'My mother died when I was ten,' I said, 'I think I know the sort of difference you mean.'

'Mother gave up Gran's flat and sold the big chair and all the things. It sounds as if I am blaming her, but I am not. After all the bombing, those old streets down by the docks were condemned and we would have had to move out anyhow. Mother got a place in another part of the city, not a smart suburb or anything. It was a shop with two rooms at the back in a street of shops, not smart shops but chain stores and bakers' and green-grocers' shops where working people came to buy their food. She opened a hairdressing shop, called it Polly's Parlour. She didn't like the name Polly – her own name – but calling her shop that showed the special kind of cleverness she had, I think. The customers she was after had never been in a hairdresser's shop in their lives – at least a lot of them hadn't – and if she had called it the Salon Pauline or something fancy, they would never have come in. They came into Polly's Parlour, though. This is why I said it was important that my father left her with the bungalow and some capital. It gave her a start.'

'And, of course, you were still at school,' I said.

'Yes, but it was a different school now. I was sent to boarding-school, quite an expensive one called Belvedere near Morecambe Bay.'

Here was the link between Percy's speech and the mean

dockland streets, the link that resolved a seeming inconsistency that had been puzzling me.

'Mother couldn't cope with me as well as the business, you see,' she said and quickly added: 'There it is again, as if I were blaming her, as if I were saying—' her voice became a whine '—she liked the shop better than me, boohoohoo!' She pushed the spectacles back into place. 'It wasn't like that at all. She was very good and kind to me. She wasn't all cosy and loving like Gran, but then she was quite a different person from Gran and far cleverer. People *are* different and they can't help it. And Mother *was* clever. Quite soon, she had three shops, all in the same sort of working people's districts and she buzzed round them in a little old car, managing them. She learned to drive when she was in the army. She had a way of picking up anything that would be useful to her.'

After another thoughtful pause, Percy seemed to go off at one of her tangents. 'You know how Sir Ian calls the Health Mission the Teeth and Feet Lot?'

'Yes, but I didn't know that you knew it.'

'Twice told me and I told the rest. When he first told me, expecting me to laugh, of course, I didn't laugh at first. It made me think of Mother, as if I had heard a sort of echo and I thought: Mother was the Hair and Feet Lot. I remember the night she had the idea. It was during the Christmas holidays and she was sitting with her feet in a bowl of water. She suffered with her feet. She stood on them too much, I suppose. Anyhow, she suddenly said: That's it. Feet! And she hired three chiropodists, put one in each shop. That was the cleverest idea she ever had. Sort of ridiculous, isn't it? By the time she died she had thirty-seven shops all over the industrial parts of the north and the Midlands, all looking after women's hair and their feet. She was the Woolworths of the hair stylist and chiropody business.'

Percy fell silent and after a moment I said: 'She was still quite young when she died?'

'Forty-three.' She smiled. 'She admitted to being thirty-five and looked about that.'

'When did she die, Percy?'

'It will be a year ago in April. By the way, that is my proper name – April Soames. It was my father who nick-named me Percy and that is one of the things about Mother and me. Mother insisted on calling me April because it wasn't what she called common like Polly or Annie. Annie was Gran's name. But after my father went away and people asked me what my name was – you know how people do with children – I always said I was Percy Soames. I think now that it was my way of remem-bering my father. But it always made Mother angry, not because of my father but because she did not think it was as pretty as April. These were the silly little things that we pinched and scratched about. I don't think I really cared whether I was called Percy or April but I wouldn't give in over it and neither would she. I think this is why I am so fascinated by names – people's names, place names, trade names, names of ships, any names.'

'Probably,' I agreed, 'what our psychologist friend on the Mission would call an imprint. We all have them.'

I was thinking of the woman who had achieved so much and had died when she was three years younger than I was at this moment, while I myself seemed to have achieved nothing.

'We pinched and scratched all the time,' Percy was saying, 'especially when I got a bit older and left school. It wasn't that we didn't like one another because we did, but we thought different things were important. She liked me and yet she sort of despised me, in the way that she had liked and yet despised my father. She could not understand why I did not want to be a hairdresser when so much money could be made at it.' Percy squirmed in her chair and momentarily I thought it was the first tremor of another chill but it was a shudder of revulsion. 'All that smelly hair and smelly shampoo and smelly waving-machines!'

'And the feet,' I thought, my sympathy with Percy.

'And yet she tried so hard to be understanding. I said I would like to do a domestic course. She paid the fees. I then wanted to go to art school. She paid the fees. But when I wanted us to buy a proper house to live in, she would have nothing to do with it.'

'Did you still live at one of the shops after she had created this – this little empire?' I asked.

'Oh, no. We lived in hotels, several different ones but all exactly alike if you see what I mean. She said we were not going to spend our lives sweeping and dusting like in that awful little bungalow. Later on, she always said, we would travel, see the world, but it was always later on, when she had got the next Polly's Parlour opened and staffed and running. But there never was any later on. She died.'

'That is very sad, Percy.'

She frowned, the spectacles slipped and were allowed to rest on the tip of her nose while the large eyes looked over the top of the frame, but probably without seeing, at the parkland beyond the garden wall.

'The saddest thing is,' she said quietly, 'that she died disappointed and it is my fault.'

'Disappointed?' I repeated.

'I had never been what she wanted me to be, had never done what she wanted me to do.'

Percy, I told myself now, clear-sighted as she seemed to be about her mother's nature, had really loved this woman for I knew in my own experience the regret and guilt that comes at the death of the truly loved. I was thinking of the death of my father and of my own feeling at that time that I had never even tried to achieve what he had wanted me to achieve, that I had taken all he had to give and had given nothing in return. I had been too busy, always, in the pursuit of my own ends.

'I think this is a feeling that comes to most of us at the death of someone we love, Percy,' I said. 'You are not the only one to have felt like this but it seems to be a rule of life that we have to do what our nature prompts us to do, even if it disappoints and even hurts other people that we may be very fond of. The ugly truth is that we all seem to love ourselves more than we can love anybody else. You can see it in that letter that Liz wrote about the wedding. The letter was not about the wedding. It was about Liz, egotistical Liz. We are all pretty much like Liz but as we get older we try to cover it up more than she does. Yet when some big thing happens, like death, we see ourselves as we really are and we feel guilty about it. Still, I don't think we can help being as we are.'

Percy nodded her head, concurring. 'In an ordinary reasonable way, I know that Mother would have died anyway,' she said next, 'no matter what I had done or not done. She had cancer but it was the way it happened that made it so terrible. Do you mind if I tell about it? I have never told anybody before.'

'Yes, tell me, Percy.'

'If I *can* tell it, that is.' She was silent for a moment as if she were marshalling her facts. I had the impression that she had been over this ground in her mind many times before, in an attempt to rationalise the emotional shock of death which cannot, in the end, be rationalised. All that can be achieved is acceptance. 'I did a year at the domestic science place and then enrolled at art school,' she began. 'Before I went to the dough school, Mother used to say that there was no point in us having a proper house because I knew nothing about housekeeping and she certainly wasn't going to do it. After I had gone to dough school and had learned quite a bit about cooking and everything – you can always learn about things you like to do – she still would not take a house. Then I said I wanted to go to art school and by the spring of last year I had been there for a year and a half. Mother paid the fees, like I said, but she thought the whole thing was silly and often said that she could make more money in a month than my father had made in six. That was true too, I believe. Anyhow, I had just won a poster competition and this made her sit up and take notice, as it were. It was like the time she said: That's it. Feet! She said that when I had finished at Art School, I could take over the design of all the display material she needed for the shops.'

Percy looked at me with wide sad eyes. 'I still am not sure,' she said, 'why I didn't go along with this. It was something that I would have enjoyed doing and would have done quite well, I think. If another firm had offered me a job like that, I think I would have taken it. But I hated these shops. I think now that I saw them as the side of Mother that had made my father run away and all the scratching between her and me were because of them. It was as if she were addicted to them as if they were drink or drugs and I felt I had to stay clear of them at any cost. Anyway, all that doesn't matter now. We began to quarrel because I wouldn't promise to do what she wanted, our usual sort of quarrel, not loud or shouting but just scratching at one another. She was tinting her hair. She spent all her evenings attending to her appearance or doing accounts. By this time, she didn't like to have me actually around any of the shops – I gave her age away. I would have been all right designing display material in our rooms. I sound as if I were criticising again but I am not. Her own looks were one of the best advertisements she had. She was dark and pretty, not like me. I take after my father. So there she was tinting her hair and I was getting ready to go out to a party with the winners of the other sections of the competition and we were clawing like anything. I said some terrible things about her not caring for anything except shops and money and then went slamming out to this party. I don't usually drink anything much and I didn't drink much that night either but I think I got sort of high, mostly because everything seemed to be so horrible. We went to a supper and dance place and there were some officers off a ship who joined us. One of them was called Peter. I liked him and things got better. I began to enjoy the party. Then they had to go back to their ship and the Peter one wanted to take me home but I wouldn't go. I can't tell you how much I hated living in hotels, especially that night. I was ashamed of living there, ashamed that this Peter should find out that I did not have a proper home. I see now that this was silly but that is how it was that night. He might think that I was a liar or even a tart and there was no time to explain how things really were. I arranged to meet him the next night and he went away.' She paused again. 'I didn't meet him the next night or any other night. The next night, Mother was in hospital and we were waiting for her to come out of the anaesthetic after the operation. She died twelve days afterwards.' Percy now made one of her sudden changes of direction which, this time, astounded me. 'I swear that during that whole awful twelve days, I did not think once about that Peter or even remember him,' but I felt that this last was addressed to herself more than to me, a repetition of something that she had told herself many times before.

'You didn't?' I said quietly.

'No. It was only after it was all over that he came back, back into my mind, I mean. I remembered dancing with him, being happy, while Mother was all alone, in sudden terrible pain, *needing* me and I was not there.'

'Where is Peter now?' I asked.

'I don't know. I never saw him again.' I had heard her speak these words before. 'There are lots of Peters in the world and that is all I know about him, that his first name is Peter. Not that it matters. It is just that I can't forget him, he was so mixed up with that awful night, part of the guiltiness and the shame.'

It was notable to me that none of the others with whom she had gone to the party seemed to be part of the guiltiness or the shame but only this stranger that she had met for an hour or two but I made no remark about this. She took off her glasses, rubbed a hand over her eyes and said, trying to smile: 'Anyway, you know a bit about me now and why I am on my own, bumming around the world. The solicitors sold all the shops for me and they look after the money. Mother left me everything except for the little bit that she left to my father.'

'She left something to your father?'

'Yes. I think it was a sort of repayment for the bungalow and the money he left in the bank when he went away. That is the fair-minded sort of thing she would do.'

'Where is your father now?'

'In the south of France. He is married like I said and they have three children – teenagers. They have a guesthouse and he still paints, sells quite a lot of pictures. They wanted me to go there to them but I said not yet anyway. They seem to be happy and I was not going to risk upsetting things for them because you never know what you may do without meaning to. I may go for a visit sometime. I tried to explain in a letter. I am not much good at writing just what I mean but he seemed to understand. I suppose you think I am a muddle-headed sort of idiot, don't you?'

'No more muddle-headed than anybody else. And you have lots of time to sort your muddles out, Percy.'

'I must make up my mind what I am going to do,' she said.

'Take your time. The first thing you have to do is to get properly well,' I told her.

It seemed to me that, in the past, she had given all her time and energy to fighting what she did not want to do and that to reverse the process, become positive and make up her mind as to what sort of future she wanted would take a little time.

In the days that followed, I did not go up to the writing table in the bedroom but spent all my spare time working in the garden with Caleb or in a corner of the veranda with my current piece of tapestry work and while I sewed, I thought that life resembled the work between my hands. It was a complicated design of birds, flowers, leaves and branches upon a pale grey background and I found that when I had stitched in a black-outlined leaf in colour, the colours of the bird adjacent to it altered and that when I stitched in the grey background between the two, the characters and colours of both bird and leaf underwent a subtle alteration, as if the light upon them had changed. And in texture, too, the work had a character resembling that of life, in that it was made up of many complexly interwoven strands of which the basic ones were rendered invisible by the surface design while, yet, on the surface, less than a third of the coloured thread was to be seen, the remainder being concealed in and behind the basic canvas.

Percy's decision to tell me of her early life had been triggered by her overhearing part of that argument between Twice and myself and by what I had said to her afterwards. The crux had been my remark: 'You can love people quite a lot and still do things that annoy them.' This chance remark had altered the light in Percy's mind upon her past relationship with her mother, had taken some of the guilt out of the 'pinching and scratching' over their differences and had decided Percy to tell me of those differences. But in telling her story, Percy had altered the light in my own mind and as I worked at my tapestry, I was thinking of her mother who emerged from what I had been told as someone to be admired, yet not without question. It seemed that her discontents and frustrations with the sweeping and dusting of the awful little bungalow had led to the break-up of her marriage but the fact remained that she had been a success in her chosen field and had caused no major unhappiness to those around her. Her former husband was now happily married again, and her child, Percy, was a very fortunate young woman' by worldly standards as a result of her efforts. The fact remained, however, that Polly Soames had died in loneliness, with no relationships other than a broken one with her husband and a tortured one with her daughter. At the end, after all her effort, had she known any satisfaction? Or had she died at the peak of her effort, still planning the next shop she would add to her little empire, dying too soon to know either the satisfaction of achievement or, perhaps, the dissatisfaction of learning that a fortune made by hairdressing is not enough?

Polly Soames, it seemed to me, had had the dedicated will and ruthless determination, which I had never had, to go her own way, to declare her own identity without regard for the people around her but, hearing of her at this time, when I had taken my small stand against Twice, had the effect of stopping me in my tracks. How far was it permissible to go in declaring one's identity? In any case, I told myself as I went on with my needle-work, I was not the sort of person that Polly Soames had been. Whether the motive drive behind her little empire had been the desire for money, the desire for petty power or an urge towards self-aggrandisement by making a commercial mark on a commercial society, I had none of these desires or urges. And this, I told myself, was just as well, for my writing would never bring money, power or aggrandisement. It brought only its own satis-faction and to me alone. Was it mere selfish self-indulgence then to continue with it in the face of Twice's disap-proval?

This disapproval, which even Twice himself could not explain in logical terms, was a real and very deeply-rooted thing which I had come across before. It had been nur-tured for centuries by the Calvinistic sternness of the Scottish church which regarded pleasure as evil, so that an activity which brought pleasure to the doer as well as to the beholder of the finished work was doubly evil. In addition to being nurtured by the church, the dis-approval was sanctioned by a utilitarian society and was thus invested with the power of both camps. Utilitarian society asked of what use was a picture, a book, a stained-glass window? How much could you get for it on the open market? And the answer was that nobody in his right senses would pay for something that was of no utilitarian value. And down the centuries, the few eccentrics who insisted on painting pictures and writing poems had come to be regarded as no better than vagabonds and parasites, no better than the tramps of my childhood who, in my grandfather's words 'would neither work nor want'.

I knew that it was the firmly embedded residue of all this ancient prejudice that was at work in Twice and this I would have swept aside but for the few words – 'something that pushes us apart'. This was not unreasoning prejudice. This was a simple truth for the only times that Twice was not the uppermost thought in my mind were those times when I was busy in the back bedroom. In the midst of every other activity, he was there. The few days and nights when Percy was critically ill, she had not been dominant in my thoughts while I nursed her. The hovering ever-present anxiety had been: 'I hope this crisis in the house is not going to upset Twice, worry him, harm him in any way.'

The question, therefore, that kept me in the garden or on the veranda was not whether I would defy Twice by pursuing a harmless pastime that he happened to dislike but whether by obeying this urge that had been with me for so long, I would cause a gap to open between us by indulging in something 'that pushes us apart'. Having recognised the problem I did not try to come to a decision for I have never planned or decided or lived consciously by the will. I did what I have always done, went on from day to day, taking the trivia of life as it came along and it was a feature of life at Paradise that there was always plenty of triviality.

February gave way to March and my forty-seventh birthday came along with Twice making the annual joke: 'You poor old woman!' for his own birthday was not until April and I was six weeks his senior. In addition to the remark, he presented me with a pretty antique brooch and otherwise the event would have have passed unnoticed, for I did not consider forty-seven an age for celebration, had not Sashie arrived.

For Percy, who did not know about the birthday, the day had its own significance for she was at last completely recovered and announced her intention at breakfast of driving down to the docks. 'Is it all right,' she asked in her considerate way, 'if I drive down to the Bay today?'

'Of course, if you are sure you feel well enough,' I said.

'I shouldn't be surprised,' Twice said, 'if the entire dockland has disappeared, you not having paid it any attention for such a long time.'

'That is just what I feel,' she told him. 'How did you know? It is time I checked up on it.'

There was a gay comfortable companionship between them which seemed to make Twice younger and myself older when I was with them so that my real identity died down to a flicker and when they had gone their separate ways, I took to the corner of the veranda with my sewing again.

It was not yet nine in the morning when I saw Sashie's car stop at the gate and Sashie begin to walk up the drive. Instead of approaching the veranda door, he took the path to the back of the house to look for Caleb. I knew that he often called quietly like this in the forenoons while I was upstairs, usually on matters of hotel catering, for Caleb could always tell him where a crop of fruit or vegetables was ripe in the valleys among the hills. I waited till he was just outside the screen from where I sat and said: 'Why are you sneaking around here at this hour?' which made him give a little start before he retraced his steps and came up on to the veranda.

'You ought to be upstairs minding your own business,' he greeted me. 'I only came to see Caleb for a moment.'

'Are you in a hurry or will you stay for a little?'

'I am never in a hurry away from you, darling.' He was wearing wine-red trousers, a pale blue shirt and the strap of his wrist watch matched the trousers. He arranged himself in a chair beside me and flicked a speck of dust from one of his small suede shoes before handing me the package he had brought.

'I wish you happiness and many more years of usefulness, my sweet,' he said.

When I opened the package, it contained an inner package of quarto typewriting paper and a very good fountain pen. The paper was of the very make that I used upstairs in the back bedroom.

This was typical of Sashie. As if by a sixth sense, he had come to know of my secret activity a few weeks after we had first met, although at that time even Twice did not know of it. Sashie was not inquisitive, did not actively enquire into the intimacies of other people but he was extremely observant and curiously sensitive, so that he seemed to acquire knowledge of the people around him as if they were transmitting stations whose signals only he could receive.

'Thank you very much, Sashie,' I said, laying the package aside. 'I shall go on being as useful as I can.'

'But not too useful . . . I met your patient on the gorge road on her way to the Bay. Now that she is discharged, I thought you would have been being useless upstairs.'

'No. I seem to be stuck for the moment.' This was the first time I had openly admitted to him what I was trying to do.

'Then a little chat with me will be *just* the thing, darling.' Deliberately, he veered away from the subject that was uppermost in my mind but which I did not want to discuss and this again was typical of him. 'How long is Percy staying?' he asked.

'As long as she likes. She is a paying guest, you know. She insisted on it. She brightens the place up, as Sir Ian would put it.'

'She is a strange little creature, curiously unpredictable,' he said. 'She gives the impression that she is seeking for something.'

'Aren't we all? Isn't that what life is about largely?'

'I suppose so. But I wonder why she chose to settle here?'

His use of the word 'settle' brought the bird image to my mind again, as if Guinea Corner were the branch of a tree. 'I think the reason is sadly simple. She referred to herself once as an institution person. I gather she has never had what she calls a proper home.'

'I suppose that would account for her aura of transience,' Sashie agreed. 'The world is full of transients these days, passing on from they don't know where to they don't know where.'

'I think the Peak Hotel makes you take a depressed view.'

'You are probably right, my sweet. We are at the end of our long winter of discontent down there.'

'During which you have made a great deal of money,' I reminded him for it was during the winter season that the wealthy tourists who could pay the outrageous prices came to the island. With the hotter weather, the cheaper package tours would begin, bringing people less rich.

'Oh, of course, darling,' Sashie agreed, 'but I really prefer the packaged lot. They enjoy themselves more because they are bent upon enjoyment. Wealth is a peculiar thing when people believe in it as if it were a god, when they come to expect it to do everything for them. They arrive at the Peak, the wealthy ones, pay their money and expect it to bestow on them enjoyment and happiness. These things are generated from the inside outwards and no amount of money can bestow them from the outside inwards. It is very depressing. The sooner Silver Beach is habitable, the better. Perhaps when I can live there, I shall be more cheerful company. Life even among the coconuts must be less sterile than life among our guests at the Peak.'

'You are tired of the Peak simply because it is complete,' I told him. 'You liked it well enough all those years you were building it up into what it is but you are not interested in the finished article. You are just like my hen, Chickabird that I had when I was a child.'

'A *hen*, darling, called *Chick*abird?'

'Every spring, I used to put thirteen eggs under Chickabird and she would hatch out twelve or thirteen chickens. Then she would spend all her time scratching up worms and insects and things for them to eat and she would preen them with her beak and tuck them under her wings and peck my ankles to make me bring food for them and generally cherish them. Then a day would come when they were half-grown and she would round on them, peck them, chase them away as if to say: Gerrout, I'm sick of you. You are on your own now. That is how you are with the Peak.' I paused, took thought for a moment before adding, to my own surprise: 'And you are quite right. As Ecclesiastes no doubt said: There is a time to stay and a time to go. You are finished with the Peak, Sashie, and there is no point in hankering about it.'

'I am glad that I have your formal permission to retire,' he told me smiling.

'You are not retiring,' I said. 'You are only moving on, like Chickabird. She hatched out another flock of chickens every year until she died of old age or when she felt too old to be bothered with another flock of chickens. Have you any idea of what you are about to move on to?'

'The house at Silver Beach, naturally, as soon as the builders have made it weather-tight – the decoration of the inside, I mean. After that, I am not sure. I have a notion that, if I put my tiny mind to it, I might paint a passable picture or two and then there are the religious songs of the island.'

'Sashie,' I asked, 'is there anything that you can't do?'

'A great number of things, darling.' He paused and a curious light came into his eyes. I looked hard at those eyes of his, the blackest I have ever seen. St. Jago was an island of dark eyes, the soft luminous dark brown eyes of the negroes but Sashie's eyes were of a different darkness, more changeable, hard rather than soft, brilliant rather than luminous. 'I think I can make my meaning clear or as clear as I wish to make it in conversation with someone face to face, as now, but I do not speak well on the telephone and I cannot convey my meaning, as some people can, by the written word.' He rose to his feet. 'That is partly why I travel so frequently to London and the States and it is why, indeed, I should like to go now and have a word with Caleb on the subject of pineapples. May I?'

'Of course. And thank you again for my present, Sashie.'

'My pleasure and I shall probably bring you another one soon. I am going up to the States for the next two weeks on a short promotion trip.'

'Promotion my left foot!' I told him. 'The truth is that you simply can't stay out of aeroplanes.'

Again, this was something that had not occurred to me until this moment but it was true. Sashie left the island several times a year on trips that seemed to involve a great deal of flying and very little time spent on the ground although they were all made ostensibly on behalf of the hotel.

'You are in a very perceptive frame of mind today, darling. Very well. I do admit to a liking for being airborne.'

'Goodness knows why. If anybody should hate aeroplanes, you should.'

'We all have an element we cannot forsake, I think. Mine is the air, just as yours is the earth, you grubber about among common clay. Stop digging me, my sweet, and go and work your garden, as Voltaire had it.'

His car was hardly out of sight when Percy's little car came up the drive and she came on to the veranda.

'Is anything the matter, Percy? Are you all right?'

'I am perfectly all right. I just came back, that's all.'

I sank into my chair, remembered what Twice had said that morning. 'Have the docks disappeared then?'

She smiled, then turned away to look across the park. 'Actually they *have* sort of disappeared, for *me*, that is,' she said. 'I got down there and there was lots doing. The

Orinoco and the *Carpathia* are in and the *Reina del Pacifico* is due this afternoon. But I suddenly thought this is all silly and I don't know what I am doing here so I came back.' She turned to look at me, still smiling, as if at some folly of long ago. 'I think I have grown out of the docks and ships. After all, I am twenty-one now.'

'Oh, well, you have lost a pastime,' I said, 'but no doubt you will find another one.'

'I think I shall run over to Bachelors',' she said. 'I'll bet it is in a fine old mess by now.'

'There is no doubt of that,' I agreed and off she went.

While Percy had been ill, a Mad Hatter's Tea Party of sorts had taken place around the park. The Yates had moved up to Olympus, Mackie had moved into the Yates' bungalow and Joe Brown had moved in with Vickers and Christie at Bachelors' Bungalow. In St. Jago, everything was rapid. Daylight gave way to dark in a matter of minutes, flowers bloomed only for a day and changes were quickly absorbed, so that already Caleb and the others like him were referring to Olympus as 'School' and to the Yates' bungalow, formerly known as 'School Bungalow' as 'Engineer's House'.

Madame and Sir Ian were delighted with the changes, Madame deeming them all 'very convenient and suitable' while Sir Ian welcomed anything that could be called 'somethin' doin'' around the place for Crop is damnable dull'. He was spending his time driving from one house to the other, interfering in a benevolent way with the furniture and its arrangement, drinking bottles of beer and directing anyone who was available for direction. Mackie, according to Twice, ignored the whole matter of the move, stayed at the factory and allowed Sir Ian to furnish his new home from the cellars of the Great House. Mackie did not care what goods and chattels he was given provided they comprised his drawing-board, his bed and a refrigerator for the chilling of beer.

During lunch, Percy informed us that the chaos at

Bachelors' was greater, if anything, since Joe Brown had taken Mackie's place there.

'The muddle has spread out into the garden now,' she said, 'with Joe's nets.'

Joe was a member of the Paradise cricket team, a valued batsman and it could have been foreseen that practice nets would be erected in the garden.

'Better not interfere with those, Percy,' Twice advised. 'Joe is part of the backbone of the cricket team.'

'But does he have to have all these newspaper cuttings on his walls? There is even a picture of an old man with whiskers and a cricket bat on the ceiling above his bed.'

'Moderation is a little known quantity among Paradise engineers,' I said. 'If you simply see that they get their meals, you will be doing a great service. Never mind the press cuttings.'

'It would be another service,' Twice said, 'if you extended your attentions to Mackie's place. I told him this morning that he would have to give a house-warming and he nearly ran up the smoke-stack. But he will have to do it. The factory hands expect it.'

'What sort of party?' Percy asked.

'A few drinks and sandwiches at mid-day on a Sunday would be best,' he told her. 'We run at half-cock on Sundays while we clean and do odds and ends of maintenance and even the hands on shift could get over to Mackie's for an hour or two. Do you think you can talk him into it, Percy?'

'I can try. He isn't all that difficult, you know.'

'Incidentally,' Twice asked me next, 'was there any overseas mail today?'

'Only one,' I said, 'from Edward. It is on my table in the drawing-room. Read it if you like but I wouldn't recommend it. It is unconscionably dull.'

'Miranda Beaumont will tell you that Edward is a boy-friend of Janet's,' Twice said to Percy, 'but I leave you to judge for yourself.'

'You should be ashamed of yourself, Twice Alexander,'

I said. 'You know that Edward and I never had a thing in common except the Macleans and now they are dead all that is dead too.' I had spoken hastily and now I added: 'Heavens, how awful that sounds!'

Percy sensed my discomfiture and said quickly: 'What is he like, Edward, really? Sir Ian and Madame aren't dull.'

'He is a proper old maid of a fellow,' Twice told her. 'And the older he gets the more old-maidish he gets.'

But this, for me, was too much. I had no feeling for Edward more than a mild liking, born as much of the fact that he was Sir Ian's son as of himself, but I thought I knew him better than Twice did and I was vaguely sorry for him as a man with little capacity for human relationships.

'I wish you would stop being old-maidish *about* Edward,' I said crossly.

'What do you mean — old-maidish?' Twice asked, reasonably enough.

'You are always picking at him, being funny about him, like Tom and George and all of them about the Miss Boyds at home!' I burst forth. '*They* couldn't help being old maids and if they set their caps at some man, George and Tom and all of them laughed as if to split themselves. That is how you are about Edward. No matter what he does, you laugh at him.'

'Are you up with the hounds, Percy?' Twice asked. 'I am miles behind.'

They sat staring at me, two pairs of bland blue eyes in two half-smiling faces.

'Oh, forget it,' I said impatiently. 'I can't explain what I mean but just let Edward alone, that's all.'

Twice reached a hand across the corner of the table, laid it on the back of Percy's small hand and said solemnly 'Percy, as a subject, Edward is off.'

'Off,' Percy agreed and they both laughed at me and I laughed too. There was a great deal of this sort of laughter, family laughter and family signs and language around our table, originating mainly between Twice and Percy, much of it at my expense but I did not resent it. One does not resent the loving laughter of friends.

When Twice had gone back to his office, Percy went out to the veranda with her sketchbook and I went upstairs to change before going to the Great House. Fetching a clean towel from the linen cupboard, I saw the brown parcel of manuscript on the shelf and thought: 'There should be a second package there,' whereupon I went to the back bedroom, completed the tying of the parcel that Twice had interrupted nearly two weeks ago and carried it to the cupboard. Standing there in the dimness, with my hand on the parcel, my mind reverted to my accusing Twice of being 'old-maidish' about Edward.

It was no wonder that he had not understood my use of the word, for it was a word from my childhood, used in the way I had used it then, when I thought of the Miss Boyds, the six maiden sisters who came to live in our local village of Achcraggan. People laughed at their single state but laughed even more at their attempts to woo the local bachelors and I, in my childhood mind, described this attitude of the populace as 'old-maidish'. Grappling with an attitude that I could not understand, an attitude that seemed unreasonable, I had misapplied in my mind the words 'old maid' that were on everybody's lips and I had misapplied it again today.

While I washed and changed, I thought of the Miss Boyds and of that long-ago time when I was eight years old, when the world and all the people in it seemed to stand secure and steady, waiting for me to explore and come to know them. Each day, I discovered something new and placed it carefully in the storehouse of my memory. Perhaps it would be another folk-name such as 'Scrambled Eggs' for the field flower that George and and Tom called 'Stinking Willie', perhaps it would be a new long word such as 'circumnavigation' or perhaps it would be the remarkable fact that, in Australia, people were attached to the earth by their feet and hung upside-down and did not stand upright in a proper civilised fashion as we in Scotland did. At this time, the world in my mind was not subject to change. It was simply there, in all its vastness, for me to discover and come to know. Brushing my hair, I remembered that it was at the time of the Miss Boyds, that the shifting changing nature of life had first declared itself to me. Something happened that made the Miss Boyds change from figures of fun to figures of tragedy and with the change in them, all the other people I knew underwent a change too. It was difficult to identify the nature of this change because life went on as usual, with my chickens to feed, the eggs to collect, my going to school and having games with Tom and George but, suddenly, at quiet moments, you could remember people laughing at the Miss Boyds, then remember that they did not laugh any more and you were aware of the change for a few seconds, like the shadow of a wind-borne cloud drifting across the hills. For most of the time, though, you forgot about the change because other things were going on, just as, now, I told my reflection in the glass that this was no time to reminisce about the Miss Boyds when Madame's car was waiting at the door for me. Still, walking downstairs, I could see the frilly blouses and hear the silly giggles of the Miss Boyds as I had first known them and I stopped halfway down, gripping the banister rail in concentration. Why not write my memories of that long-past time, why not set down the Miss Boyds I had known in words that were impervious to change? Maybe, one day, my niece Liz would be interested to read about these people who had lived near Reachfar so long ago.

Percy, standing below in the hall, brought me back to the present. 'Madame's car is here,' she said. 'Listen, why don't I go instead? Would you rather get on with your sewing?' I wanted to turn and run up to the back bedroom but I did not speak and Percy continued: 'After all, you were round yesterday. Madame won't mind and I have nothing to do.'

'All right, Percy,' I said. 'You go. Madame will be delighted.'

The car drove away and I went upstairs, filled the new pen that Sashie had given me and stared at the wall while I contemplated the contrary nature of life and of the people who live it. Twice did not like my writing but he by his own words had started this train of thought, had fired this desire. Twice would have preferred me to spend my afternoon kindly and sensibly at the Great House but he himself, by attaching Percy to our household, had provided the means whereby I could abscond from that duty. 'Twice,' I apostrophised him in my mind, 'in spite of all you say, if I ever dedicate a book to anyone, I shall dedicate it to you' and with an unholy fervour and glee, I pulled a sheet of paper on to the blotter and began to write.

Mackie's house-warming party, arranged by Percy, was an unqualified success. 'A very enjoyable affair,' Sir Ian pronounced. 'Makes a break. Crop's damnable dull.' Sir Ian was not in the least interested in the factory unless something went wrong, which he classed in one way as 'somethin' doin' around the place' and in another way as 'bad business this. Got to get goin' again an' stop these perishers up at Retreat laughin' at us.' From his point of view, therefore, the 1957 crop was more than usually dull for there were no crises at the factory, not even the stupidest labourer, as he pointed out, falling into the molasses tank or being swung aloft on top of a bundle of cane by the factory crane.

As soon as Mackie's party was behind us, Sir Ian began to look forward to the Easter 'shut-down'. I have said that the factory ran continuously through the first six months of the year but this was not strictly true. There was a planned stoppage from Thursday morning until Tuesday morning over the Easter weekend, during which no cane was milled but steam was maintained by a skeleton staff to avoid the unwanted stickiness at the restart of operations.

Traditionally, in the island, a meeting took place at the racecourse and a regatta took place at the Yacht Club on Easter Mondays and although when he was younger, Sir Ian had been a horse-fancier and polo player, since he grew older he had transferred his allegiance to the regatta, because he was on the committee of the Yacht Club which gave him the right to wear what he called his 'sea-goin' hat'.

'Well, what about the regatta, Missis Janet?' he asked me one Sunday forenoon.

I was about to refuse when Twice said quickly: 'Yes, Sir Ian. We were thinking of going down this year.'

'Good. I'm gatherin' one or two for lunch. I'll expect you two an' little Miss Percy, of course.'

'Percy likes boats,' I said.

'Don't know one end o' a boat from the other meself,' Sir Ian said, 'an' I wouldn't set foot in one o' these nut-shells if ye paid me but when I'm in me sea-goin' hat nobody is any the wiser. I hear young Candlesham has a new boat this year?'

'Yes, sir,' Twice said, 'specially designed and built in the States.'

'Believe in British bottoms meself. Never sail except under the British flag they used to say here in the old days. Of course, that's all changed now. Is Mackie crewin' for Candlesham this year?'

'Lord, yes. Don won't race now without Mackie in his crew.'

'You know, Sir Ian,' I said, 'I think I should stay with Madame on Regatta Day.'

I was remembering former regattas when she had domi-nated the scene and I did not like to think of her, relegated to her chair in the library with Miss Poynter snoring out her afternoon nap in another chair.

'No need for that, me dear,' said Sir Ian. 'Mother'n' Maud'll be at the racin'.'

'They are not going to the Race Meeting!' I protested.

'On the radio, ye know. They're at the racin' every Saturday now since the season opened. Tony the Millman puts their bets on for them an' they bet against each other as well. Mother's makin' a packet but I don't think Maud's doin' so good.'

'I think Madame is just terrific,' Percy said, after Sir Ian had gone away, 'just like my Gran. Gran used to have a shilling on a horse every week and half-a-crown each way on the Derby.'

On the morning of the regatta, Percy came down in navy slacks, white shirt and navy canvas shoes, her pony tail tied back with a fluttering bow of navy blue ribbon. While she waited for Twice and myself to be ready to leave, she was playing on the lawn with Dram who, standing on his hind legs with his fore-paws on her shoulders, was slightly taller than she was.

'Pretty, isn't she?' Twice said to me on the veranda steps.

'Very pretty,' I agreed and added: 'That hair ribbon is what Monica would call a Suivez-moi-jeune-homme and some young man is going to obey it one of these days.'

'She is young yet,' Twice said and went round to fetch the car, unwilling to think as yet of being parted from his daughter as he was coming to regard Percy more and more.

He and Percy watched the sailing from the Peak Cliff in the grounds of the hotel, but the sailing was a secondary consideration for the regatta, for the sugar people especially, was first of all a break in the routine of Crop, an opportunity to talk to people other than those on the staff of one's own plantation. I however, disliking the sycophantic attitude of the wives to myself, spent more of the day with Sashie, going out to the cliff-top only to watch the race in which Don Candlesham was sailing his new yacht, Amaryllis II with Mackie as one of his three-man crew.

'It is all very dull and foregone as a race,' Sashie said, 'but Don has become a regatta institution, bless him.'

'It all started with that marvellous win over the Whiteman brothers that year Cousin Emmie was out here,' I said. 'I am no sportswoman but that win was one of the highlights in my time in this island.'

'It did have a certain drama.'

'And Don doesn't look a day older. He is as handsome as ever, Sashie.'

'I think one has to be intelligent before one can grow old.'

'What a bitch you are!'

'No, my sweet. Truthful, as I see it. And don't mistake me. I am devoted to Don and love him for his sweet simplicity. If he has a brain, however, he does not use it, except in the way he is doing now, to take that contraption of wood and canvas over a certain distance of water more rapidly than anyone else. Maybe he is wise. The use of the brain is very ageing. Well, they are off,' he ended as a shot rang out from the Yacht Club tower.

'Brains or not,' I said, 'Don and his contraption are very beautiful.'

'That I grant you,' Sashie conceded as Amaryllis found the breeze and went skimming away, a bird with a black body and scarlet wings that took flight without any apparent aid from Don and his crew.

'That boat is like a bird,' I said. 'Surely it takes intelligence to render animate a contraption of wood and canvas?'

Sashie looked at me, his eyes like black slits. 'Darling, you are such a comfort. Perhaps Don is not a moron after all.'

I thought I had never seen anyone so brimming with sheer enjoyment as Percy was that day. She liked the yachts, of course, as everyone present must have liked them, skimming about as they did like multi-coloured butterflies on the blue water but Percy herself resembled a butterfly, swooping and loitering over a flowerbed, as she moved from one group of people to the next.

'You are having a good time, Percy?' I asked her in a quiet corner.

'A wonderful time!' she said and turned as Twice left a group of men and began to walk towards us. She waved to him and turned back to me. 'This is the very first time in my life that I have been out as a family,' she said. Perhaps I looked non-plussed, for she explained: 'In the holidays, families round us used to go to Blackpool or somewhere. We never did.' Her face had become grave as she remembered but Twice had reached us and she smiled again.

'Having a good time, Percy?' he asked.

I saw her face pucker as she turned away from him and towards myself. 'Percy considers it as good as Blackpool,' I said, smiling at her. 'Well, Amaryllis has done it again.'

'And goodness, isn't Mr. Candlesham handsome?' said Percy, recovered from her emotional little moment.

'So is a cobra in its own way,' I said.

'If that is a warning,' she told me, 'save it. I don't like too-handsome people. And will you look at Pam Durrant and Eddie Muir? Why do they have to hang on to each other all the time? Nobody wants either of them. Listen, is it all right if I stay for the dance at the Yacht Club? They say it is all right to go to it in slacks. I have no car but I can surely get a lift back.'

'Mackie will bring you back,' Twice said.

Later on, when Twice and I were about to leave for home, I happened to be present when Mackie was told by Twice – rather summarily, I thought, as if he were being given an order at the factory – to see that Percy was brought home after the dance.

'I am not staying all evening, sir,' said Mackie. 'I want to be back by eleven to see to the run-up.'

For a moment, Twice looked as startled as if Mackie

had told him to check his steam gauges himself, then recovered and said: 'No point in running up before six in the morning. The cane yard is well down. You had better stay at the dance.'

'Whatever you say, sir,' said Mackie and went away.

When we were in the car and driving out of the gates of the Peak, I said: 'You didn't ask me but if you did, I would say that you want to remember that Percy isn't part of Paradise sugar and rum complex.'

'What are you talking about?' he asked although he knew very well.

'You can't *order* Mackie to play sheepdog to her.'

'Are we to leave her there to come home with any Tom, Dick, or Harry? Half of them will be as drunk as they can hold before the night is out.'

'Darling, she isn't a Victorian miss straight out of the schoolroom.'

'You are quite right, of course,' he said in his generous way after a moment's thought and the subject lapsed but the little incident interested me by throwing a sudden light on his attitude to Percy. She is as precious to him and he is as possessive of her, I told myself wryly, as Paradise Factory so that only Mackie is to be entrusted with her.

The next morning was a less dramatic repetition of the first day of Crop. I got up at five to make tea and Twice drove up to the factory as the siren, which had been silent over the weekend, rent the air at six and when he came back for breakfast at nine, the full orchestra of Crop was sounding across the valley once more.

'No trouble with the re-start?' I asked.

'Not with the plant but Mackie is in one hell of a temper.'

'What about?'

'God alone knows.' He jabbed his spoon into a half grapefruit. 'I don't see why any bloke has to get into a state like that about anything,' he said. 'He is going round that place up there like the Wolf of Badenoch.'

'*Boom-ta*-ta-*ra*-ra-*ra*-ra!' I began to hum the tune of 'Scotland the Brave' and Twice clenched his teeth, his eyes beginning to glitter as I said: 'I don't know why blokes get into these states either but I don't think you are in any position to criticise blokes getting into states.'

When I had first known Twice, his temper and temperament would have made any display by Mackie seem milk-mild by comparison, I was sure and Twice had always 'run up' to his explosion by whistling 'Scotland the Brave'.

'He will get over it,' I said. 'Something must have annoyed him.'

'Something must have annoyed who?' Percy asked, coming into the room.

'Are you up already?' I asked. 'When did you get in?'

'A little after midnight. The dance got boring. Too many people got drunk.' She patted Twice on the shoulder and took her place at the table. 'I did the right thing by you,' she said. 'I came home with a sugar man.'

Twice merely smiled but I said: 'You did? Who was he?' which made Twice look at me as if I were half-witted.

'Hugh Mac-something. He is a shift engineer at Retreat and his father is Chief there.'

'Oh, Hugh Macbeth,' I said, trying not to look at Twice and not to laugh. 'Hugh is a nice fellow.'

Percy, unmoved by the silence that now descended, ate her grapefruit, then picked up her cup of coffee and went out to sit on the lawn with Dram and Charlie the cat.

'Well,' I said to Twice, 'you were the prime mover in Mackie's state and *you* will have to get him out of it.'

'Damn and blast it! A *shift* man from *Retreat*!' said Twice with a mixture of venom and scorn.

This was not, it must be understood, a simple case of Percy having been squired home by someone other than Mackie. Even in a simple matter like this, life as we live it is complex and explosive and very often it is the innocent, like Percy, who act as the detonator.

Paradise was regarded as the leading sugar plantation in the island and if Paradise came first, the last place was surely occupied by Retreat, yet Retreat had two things in common with Paradise that the other estates had not. Like Paradise, it was not part of the big sugar empires but was privately owned, not by a family like the Dulacs but by a group of six men, three Scots, two Englishmen and a Welshman, who also managed it and occupied its key staff positions. And, like Paradise, it had one of the best cricket teams in the island. Here the resemblance to Paradise ended but around Retreat there hung that aura of independence and ancient lineage, of the time when all estates were privately owned, of the time before the big battalions of the sugar combines. Retreat was like a poor relation, if of good blood – a ne'er-do-well relation that paraded shamelessly its rags, tatters and makeshifts. Its factory was a shambles of second-hand throw-outs bought cheaply from or donated by other factories; its transport consisted of a few broken-down tractors from which old ox-drawn carts had to take over after the first week of Crop. Retreat, in the words of Twice, was a triumph of the 'paint it red and make it do' but, as if to make nonsense of any fair and logical order of things, Retreat could field one of the best teams in the annual Sugar Cricket Tournament. Only the year before, Retreat had beaten Paradise for the fifth time in succession in the final and as if this were not enough, Percy had now passed over the Chief of Paradise and had chosen as her squire a mere shift engineer from Retreat.

I found the whole situation, from Mackie's rage to Twice's puzzled bemusement as to how to cope, ludicrously funny and would not for the world have indicated to Percy the comic enormity that she had committed, so after she had seen Twice into his car, as was her after-breakfast habit and had come into the house, I said: 'I am sorry that the dance turned out badly. A lot of the sailing set drink too much.'

'It didn't matter, she assured me. 'It was such a lovely

day all day and thank you for taking me. If it hadn't been for me, I don't suppose you and Twice would have gone?'

I decided to be honest. 'No, I don't think we would have, but we enjoyed it too.'

'Except for the plantation wives,' she said. 'You don't like them hanging around. You are a private person, different from my mother. She liked being a public person, I think.' She altered course. 'Hugh Macbeth is dotty about cricket.'

'The whole island is dotty about cricket,' I told her 'and Hugh is a very good – Caleb—' I called through the window '—is Hugh Macbeth of Retreat a batsman or a bowler?'

'A bat, ma'am,' said Caleb, with respectful sorrow for my ignorance. 'Pretty good in the field as well,' he added grudgingly.

'If you enjoy family affairs like the regatta,' I told Percy, 'you will have plenty of them when we come out of Crop and the cricket starts in earnest. There is a match nearly every Saturday and Sunday.'

'Do you go?'

'Not if I can help it but Twice is as dotty about it as all the rest. Are you fond of watching games, Percy?'

'Not dotty about it but what I like is the family feeling, being there *with* a family and having a family feeling about Mr. Candlesham's boat because Bruce was in it and other families being interested in other boats.'

'By the way, was Bruce at the dance?'

'Yes. He and I danced once and then I saw him with a lot of other men talking about guess-what?'

'Sugar milling,' I said. 'Sugar men are crashing bores, I am afraid, especially the engineers.'

'I don't find it boring. I would like to know more about it. And there is something nice about people not just working for money but being sort of dotty about what they are doing. Well, I have to go over to Bachelors'. They had a proper whoop-up over there last night and it is in a real mess. Bob and Norman' – I could never remember which of these Christian names applied to Christie and which to Vickers – 'got bored with the dance too. They offered to bring me back to their party but I didn't want any more party. Joe Brown had been to the races and won a packet for all three of them and when he arrived at the Yacht Club they went and got a lot of beer and sandwiches from the Peak and came up here.'

'But you didn't go?'

'No. Oh, I see what you mean, my knowing about the mess. I sneaked out before five and went over there to make sure they were up. They asked me to because Norman threw their alarm clock on the floor the day before yesterday and they were afraid they would be late at the factory.'

'Young devils. You shouldn't bother with them, Percy.'

'I like to. I like looking after people. What I ought to have is a home and a bunch of babies.'

'Is that what you would like?'

'Yes. I think so. Yes. That is how I shall fetch up one day.' She stood with one foot on its toe, ready to be off.

'If you have time,' I said, 'look in at Mackie's place as well, will you? What with the regatta and the re-start, he has probably got no food in the house. If you are stuck, ask him here for lunch.'

'All right,' she said and went away, while I hoped vaguely that I had done something towards the smoothing of troubled waters. I spent the forenoon upstairs, coming down to have a cold drink on the veranda when Twice came home for lunch.

'Where is Percy?' he asked.

'Over at Bachelors' seeing to the clean-up. I gather they had a shindig there last night. How is Mackie?'

'Terrible. I haven't spoken to him. He is keeping out of my way.'

Percy's car now pulled up with a jerk at the bottom of the steps and she sprang out of it and on to the veranda. Some of her hair had come loose from its elastic band, making her look like a ruffled bird and she stamped one of her size-one sandals on the floor like an enraged sparrow.

'That Bruce Mackie!' she said. 'D'you know what *he* said? He said I made him—' She raised both fists above her head, yelled: 'Oh-oh-oh-oh!' ran upstairs and the door of her room shut with a bang.

'This has gone far enough,' Twice said and went to the telephone in the hall. 'Mackie? I want you over here at once. Not the factory, you clot, Guinea Corner!'

'Dear me,' I said when he came back. 'What a drama!'

'You keep out of this,' he told me shortly and now Mackie came up the steps looking, more than anything, like an all-in wrestler entering the ring. 'Percy!' Twice called from the hall. 'Come down here!' There was no sound from above unless a defiant silence can be called a sound. 'Percy!' There was still the silence. 'Mackie, go up there and get that girl!'

As Mackie crossed the hall towards the stairs, I began to feel that the drama was getting out of hand; as the altercation broke out up above, I put down my glass of lemonade and my cigarette but when Mackie arrived on the veranda with Percy under his left arm, her feet kicking behind him and her arms flailing helplessly in front, I felt an uprush as of hot champagne bubbles from my stomach to my head. I had not felt like this for years and although I could observe myself, I could not stop myself. I uncoiled my five feet nine inches from my chair, took a firm grip, thumbs upwards, on the edge of the wicker table that held the jug of lemonade, the tray of glasses and the ice bucket and said: 'You great hulking bullies! Can't you pick on something your own size?'

Until now, the emotionally charged field had been confined to Twice, Mackie and Percy, making them almost unconscious of my presence but suddenly the area of tension changed. It was now between Twice and me so that Mackie, as well as Percy under his arm, froze into immobile onlookers. Twice spun round and I saw his fingers curve tensely while I took a firmer grip on the table, ready to upturn it against him if he approached. 'I would like to see one of you carry *me* downstairs!' I challenged.

'Don't you push your luck,' said Twice and began to come on, warily, on the balls of his feet.

The table was just about to go when the voice of Sashie, like the cool drops of fountain spray on the vibrant air, said: 'God bless me liver and lights! What *can* be afoot?'

I lowered the nearer legs of the table to the floor, Twice straightened out of his aggressive crouch and Mackie quietly set Percy on her feet.

'Excuse *me*,' said Sashie politely, passing between Twice and me and on into the house. 'I only called to see Caleb for a moment,' and he disappeared along the passage to the pantry.

Suddenly, Percy became convulsed with laughter. Clinging to Mackie's arm, she hiccuped and spluttered and eventually managed to say: 'Bruce, I wish Madame could have seen Janet just now. Such a dear gentle person, Madame says. I wish she could have seen her!'

'Do you want me to lose my job?' Twice asked sternly and to me: 'Sit down. You should be ashamed of yourself. What came over you?'

'I know but I won't tell,' I said, picking up my drink. 'Why don't the rest of you try to find out what is the matter with you?'

'I felt a fool,' said Mackie. 'I hung about down at that dance till three in the morning and then I found out *she* had gone home hours ago.'

'But you didn't *say* about coming home!' Percy argued. 'How was I to know?'

Mackie pointed to Twice. '*He* said to take you home and—'

'—and he shouldn't have said anything of the sort,' I interrupted and turned to Twice. 'You ought to mind your own business,' I told him.

'You watch it,' he threatened me but to the others he

was apologetic. 'I am sorry,' he said, 'but that Regatta Dance gets pretty drunken and—' he could explain no further '—listen, let's have lunch.'

We went in, had lunch and the absurd episode was forgotten.

By this time, the masons had finished repairing the stone-work and roof of Sashie's house at Silver Beach and the carpenters and plumbers were about to move in. Twice, Percy and I formed a habit of driving down there on Sunday afternoons, taking a picnic tea with us and while Percy and Twice swam or pottered about on the beach which was literally silver, Sashie and I would sit around in the shade. The sea and sun turned Twice a darker and darker brown but Percy's pale skin took on no more than a faint apricot glow and I marvelled at the difference in pigmentation that could make Percy, so much fairer than myself, impervious to the sun while I blistered so painfully at the shortest exposure.

'They are born and boon companions, those two,' Sashie said one Sunday as we watched them strolling side by side along the beach.

'I know,' I agreed, 'so boon that they hardly ever talk to one another in the accepted sense. If Percy wants to talk about anything that is important to her, she comes to me. They simply accept one another in a comfortable sort of way.'

'And you don't mind?'

'I don't. There is no point. She is not taking anything that I could ever have had. Can you imagine Twice ever looking upon me as a daughter?'

'Even *my* imagination doesn't run to that, my sweet.'

I watched Percy pick up something from the water's edge and carry it to Twice, watched their two heads bend forward, examining her find. 'Sometimes, though,' I said, 'I feel a little anxious about Twice, in the future, you know. He is proprietary, possessive about his people. I think he tends to forget that he has no permanent lien on

Percy, that one day she will fly the coop but that is a bridge to be crossed when we come to it.'

The following Sunday, at Sashie's request, we included Caleb in the party and as soon as we got out of the car, Caleb looked about him and said: 'My, Mars Sashie, this is a sweet property!'

By 'sweet', Caleb meant what my father, George and Tom would have meant had they referred to a piece of land as 'fine' and what both words meant was that Silver Beach was fertile and had a good 'lie' to the weather.

The little property of some thirty acres lay at the end of a rough private road, on the plain between the Coastal Highway and the sea and it was true to its name, bounded on its north side by a long stretch of silver-sanded beach. The house, although much smaller than the great houses of the island, such as Paradise or Hope, was of the same period, of similar grey stone and of similar dignity as it had risen again from ruin under the direction of Sashie and it stood at the top of a slight slope of green grass that ran down to the sands. On either side and behind it, there was an overgrown garden with a few old trees for shade and a wall separated this from the groves of coconut palms which had once been its wealth, but these had been neglected for years and bore little fruit. Some of them were tall dead stumps that had had their mop-like heads of fronds lopped off by past hurricanes.

'You must get those rooted out,' I told Sashie. 'They look like decapitated bodies.'

'I agree, darling. Hideously depressing. But I think I shall have them all out, not only the decapitated ones. I feel no affinity with coconuts. They seem to me to be a very ill-proportioned, ill-designed growth but one doesn't want to create a dust bowl as in the Tennessee Valley, even on a minor scale. Caleb, what do you think?'

Caleb did not reply immediately. Instead, he fetched his cutlass from the car and while Percy and Twice went to the beach, Sashie and I followed him. He would pause, jab the sharp cutlass into the hard-baked turf, pick up a handful of earth and sift it through his fingers, move on fifty yards and go through the same procedure. Watching him, I was reminded of my grandfather, my father, George, Tom and all their acquaintance of my childhood, men who knew their land with a deep inner knowledge that came from the blood tie between them and their countryside.

'This is a coconut place, Mars Sashie,' he said at last. 'Coconuts and a few cattle, maybe.'

'Cattle? Those huge, hideous putty-coloured things with the humps on their shoulders and the dewlaps?' said Sashie, describing the Brahmin cattle of the island. 'Caleb, I should be terrified! And *must* I have those beastly tall coconuts?' he asked looking up at the boy who was about twice his own height and breadth. 'They make me feel so *small*, don't you see?'

'You make jokes, Mars Sashie,' Caleb told him, 'but you don't got to have these tall old-fashioned kind. You want the new bush sort like they call them. Them pretty, not much taller'n me and there is money in coconuts, Mars Sashie.' He looked round at the derelict palms and turned to me. 'What Mars Sashie needs ma'am is Sir Ian an' Big Sammy an' the Paradise rooter. Them and me and some of the boys from the Peak could clear this and plant over with bush coconuts in a coupla weeks.'

'I am sure that could be arranged, Sashie,' I said. 'Sir Ian likes nothing better than creating hell and destruction with Big Sammy and a rooter or a bulldozer. Shall I ask him to come down?'

'Only if Caleb is here to control him, darling. I cannot cope with Sir Ian effectively at any time and Sir Ian *and* a rooter, not to mention Big Sammy – no. Definitely no, unless Caleb comes and I can cower inside the house away from it all.'

'I should cower outside the house if I were you,' I told him, 'just in case they push it over by mistake. But Caleb will come too.'

'Have to be soon, Mars Sashie,' Caleb said. 'Have to

plant before the Crop rains, else wait till about November.'

'Let us begin at once, Caleb,' Sashie told him. 'I cannot have those headless skeletons round me until November. I should be found some morning hanging from one of them.'

'What about water, sah?' Caleb enquired next and he indicated a dry stream bed near where we stood. 'That ain't an all-the-year-round gully.'

By this he meant that the stream flowed, probably in spate, during the rains, filled with water from the higher ground inland, and then dried completely, as it was dry now, when the hot weather came.

'There is a spring, Caleb, over on the west boundary.'

Caleb looked where Sashie pointed and said: 'Don't see no sign of it, sah.'

'You can't see it from here. It is behind that clump of bush.'

'You sure, sah?' Caleb asked and set off for the boundary.

When we had fought our way through the tangled bush along a path cleared by Caleb's cutlass, the ground rose into a bank overgrown with dry grass. Out of this bank, stuck a length of pipe and from its mouth a dry stream bed led down to the beach but there was no water to be seen anywhere.

'Dear me,' said Sashie, 'where has the water gone? It was pouring out of that pipe, but *pouring* and the spring is marked on the title deed. How very peculiar and disobliging of it.'

'You saw the water, sah? When?' Caleb asked.

'About a year ago, when I first looked at the property.'

'We had the shake since then.' By this, Caleb meant the severe earthquake of 1956. 'The water done shifted.'

I knew that this lapse into the dialect of the island meant that the 'done shifting' of the water was, in Caleb's view, a serious matter and it became even more serious in my mind when Caleb walked away from us with a curious deliberation that prevented our following him.

'How very exasperating,' Sashie said, looking from the dry spout in the grass bank to Caleb's broad departing back.

'It is indeed,' I agreed. 'But, Sashie, aren't they going to bring a main along the Coastal Highway from the Bay? Only, it would cost a bit to get connected to that.'

'It is not the cost so much as the *time*, darling. That main will not be through for about a year and I did so want to turn into a hermit – but a hermit who could have a bath, don't you see – with the least possible delay. Let us go and take Twice out of the sea and ask *him*. Twice is always full of ideas.' But Twice had no ideas on this matter. He merely frowned and looked blank while I pondered, not for the first time and with something of panic fear, on the volcanic nature of the island, its underlying rock full of caverns, pockets and channels, which could shift and re-form in a new pattern in an earthquake, causing a water supply to drain away from one point and spring up in another. To me, there was something uncanny in this, as there was in the River Pedro that disappeared into one side of a hill and emerged out of the other side, as there was in the large lake near Pasture Plains which was there one month and not there the next.

'We could try a few bores if you like,' Twice said eventually. 'We have a small rig up at Paradise but I wouldn't have a clue where to start.'

Percy, discouraged and flattened like the rest of us, got up from the grass and wandered away round the house. As she went between the trees, she looked like some archaic creature of mythology, a nymph or a dryad, in her green swimsuit with the tail of hair dangling from her head.

'Bores!' said Sashie. 'It is one big bore. Oh, well, I shall just have to have water brought in by tanker until the main comes through' and he looked spitefully westward to where the dry spout protruded from the bank.

Sashie had a curious personal force that could carry others along with him and Twice and I, under the influence of this, looked westward too. Percy, bare-footed, was walking slowly along the top of the grass bank, her arms held out in front of her, while from the beach at the end of the bank, Caleb stood watching her. As we looked, she disappeared behind a tangle of bush, a green figure shading into more green so that I blinked, wondering if I had imagined that slow-moving slight figure. Without speaking, Twice, Sashie and I began to walk towards Caleb but just as we came within speaking distance, we heard Percy's voice, thin and flute-like from away behind the house. 'Ca-leb! Ca-leb!' Caleb walked towards the sound and we followed, to find Percy standing in a dry hollow among some boulders. In her hands she held a forked stick, a prong in each hand and as we looked the stem of the stick jerked upwards, dropped slowly down and jerked upwards again with a curious detached life of its own. Percy put the twig on the ground at her feet, put a stone on top of it to hold it in place and came over to us.

'It used to work on the moors at home, Twice,' she said, 'when we used to go up there from school. If you are going to try a bore anyway, you could try the first one there.' She pointed to the twig.

'You mean – you are a diviner?' I asked.

She smiled. 'My grandfather was, my father's father. And it worked on the moors, like I said.' She could not have been more mundane. 'Goodness, it's hot,' she said next. 'I am going back into the water' and she went away round the house while we all stared at her slim back.

Twice went to the place where the twig lay and looked down at it. 'What do you think, Sashie?'

'My dear Twice, there are times when one doesn't *think*!' said Sashie. 'How soon can that boring thing you spoke about come down from Paradise?'

'Any time.' Twice frowned, looking from the twig south-westerly and then around him in a long sweep. 'It is a different level, a different lie, it is as different as it can possibly be,' he said doubtfully.

'Twice, cease at once to be logical and scientific,' Sashie said. 'How much would you care to bet that there is no water there?'

'Five bob,' said Twice. 'If it is there, I'll pay with pleasure but I don't think I shall have to.'

'You lost your money, Chief,' Caleb grinned. 'Might as well pay right now.'

When we went back to the front of the house, Percy was sitting on a boulder at the edge of the water, her back to us, as she looked out to the far-off horizon and I had again the feeling of being in the presence of a creature who was only partly of the human world, who was in communication with mysterious forces that were beyond the reach of the rest of us. She did not come home with Caleb, Twice and me that evening, but stayed with Sashie to go back to dinner at the Peak and over our own meal I said: 'I wonder if you will find water at that spot Percy marked?'

'I doubt it.'

'But there are people who can find water like that, or there used to be, only I have always heard that they used a hazel twig. Percy had only a twig from some bush.'

'I have always thought that the hazel twig was the real mumbo-jumbo. Why hazel? I don't think a chemical analysis would show that hazel had any particular property to commend it.'

'Anyway, I hope there *is* water there,' I said. Twice was silent and I continued: 'You don't really hope so, do you?'

'Naturally, I would like Sashie to have spring water but—'

'Yes. But. You are a little scared but you won't admit it,' I told him.

'Scared isn't quite the right word,' he argued. 'I simply dislike the illogical. If there is water there, I want to know why Percy and a bit of bush cut off with Caleb's cutlass can detect it and the rest of us can't.'

176

'I am not sure about all this knowing,' I said. 'Maybe it is better just to accept some things.'

The next day, Monday, while I sat with Madame as usual, Twice, Sir Ian, Big Sammy and the drilling equipment went down to Silver Beach and when they came back I was acutely disappointed.

'We bored around until the place was like a colander,' Twice said. 'No water.'

'Maybe we didn't go deep enough,' Sir Ian ruminated. 'Still, can't go very deep on the coast like that. Liable to bring up salt water.'

When Twice and I went home and told Percy, she said: 'Queer. I felt sure it was there. Sorry, Twice.'

'Don't apologise to him,' I said. 'I think he is relieved more than anything. I am the one who is disappointed.'

It was about three evenings later that Sashie came dancing in while we were at dinner, in a wildly excited state which was very different from his normal aloof affectation. He looked more like a satyr than ever, a satyr fresh from some bacchanalian orgy. 'Twice, darling,' he cried on a high note in the doorway, 'you must come down to Silver Beach tomorrow and tell me how to control the flood. Percy's spring is gushing up out of the hole and water is rushing down the slope and into the cellars of the house!'

'Good God!' said Twice and glared almost angrily at Percy.

'I thought there was water there,' she said quietly.

'Hurray!' I bellowed at the pitch of my voice. 'Caleb!' The boy rushed in from the pantry. 'The spring at Silver Beach is working!'

'Miss Percy's spring, sah?' Caleb asked Sashie.

'That very one and no other,' said Sashie, leaning over to kiss me, then sitting down at the table with us where he leaned across, took Percy's hand and grinned mischievously at Twice before he said: 'Janet, darling, isn't this a triumph for all of us fairy folk?'

'Fairy folk be damned!' said Twice. 'I suppose with all those holes we drilled, we touched the water-table somewhere and it had to come up through *one* of them.'

'But it came up where *Percy* said,' I argued.

'That was where we went deepest,' he argued back.

For the rest of the evening, we argued to and fro in a good-humoured way about the mystery of the spring and even as he got into bed, Twice muttered: 'You and your fairy folk!'

'Fairies apart,' I said, 'you have to admit that the water is *there*. You have to accept it, Twice.'

'I am not good at accepting oddities. There is a logical explanation for that water rising at that point and I would like to know what it is, although I haven't got the time to excavate the whole of Silver Beach to find out.'

'That still wouldn't explain Percy and her twig of bush. I think you have to accept some things. There *are* miracles. There is one right here. Do you realise that a couple of years ago you could not, physically, have spent a day like Monday, drilling holes all over Silver Beach?'

'That is not in the same category. Two years ago, I was ill and now I am better.'

'Miraculously better,' I insisted.

'You are one bloody-minded female. Be quiet and come to bed.'

'I am not being bloody-minded, Twice. Your being better is inexplicable and mixed up with so many things, like my going home and writing to you about the children and Percy coming and I don't know how many more things. It is as complicated as the working of the water in all those channels in the rock under Silver Beach and no matter if you excavated for ever, you would never explain it completely. I wish you would stop wanting logic and reasons all the time and just accept. I do. I accept the miracles.'

'And I would not change you for all the world,' said

Twice diplomatically, his nose in the book he was trying to read.

'That's right. Shut me up with pretty speeches,' I told him, got into bed and was silent.

But I did not sleep. The discovery of the spring had stimulated me and I lay happily awake while I visualised the life-giving water bubbling up in that parched stony hollow, to flow down the slope towards the wall of Sashie's house. Twice fell asleep, his book collapsing face downwards on his chest as was usual. I removed the book and swung it out on to my bedside table and before I lay down again, I looked at him for several moments. Now, with his eyes closed, withdrawn into sleep, he was still Twice but yet not the Twice of his waking hours and I thought of his words: 'And I would not change you—' But he had changed me. He had begun the process of altering me in the moment I had first met him and that gradual unconscious process had been going on ever since, was still going on at this very moment.

The black velvet tropic dark pressed against the mosquito mesh of the windows, held in check there by the light of the electric lamp but beyond that barrier the darkness stretched away to an infinity that appeared changeless and yet held an illimitable possibility for change, where the galaxies moved and swayed in their unknowable rhythms. It was comforting and yet mysterious to know that inside this room where Twice and I lay in this pocket of artificial light, that cosmic ever-changing yet changeless pattern was repeated on an infinitely small scale for it was not the scale that was important, but the pattern.

I had complained from time to time of my seeming lack of an assured identity, of an established personality, of my malleability at the mercy of other personalities but on this night, for a brief moment, I saw clearly that my identity and this constant process of change were the same thing. My only assured identity or established personality was the ever-changing ever-increasing sum of my adjustments to the people around me and that the major force in making me what I was had been Twice. If I had never met him, I would have been a different person, perhaps better, perhaps worse and probably, I thought, the latter. And if, at this moment, by some cataclysm, I were deposited on a desert island alone and out of all contact with him and the people around me, I would disintegrate, as the galaxy in which the earth, the moon and the planets moved would fly apart if the sun were withdrawn from the sky.

Within three days, Sir Ian, Big Sammy and the rooter had razed the coconuts at Silver Beach to the ground, but the Crop rains that Caleb had mentioned did not come. The November rains were fairly dependable but the Crop rains could come at any time during May, June or even July, usually in the form of a sudden deluge that turned the roads about the estate into rivers. Caleb, good-humoured as he was, began to grow impatient like the cultivator that he was, with what he regarded as an important job being frustrated by the weather. The bush coconuts had been ordered from the Agricultural Department and were ready to be transferred to Silver Beach at any time but the sky remained far away, cloudless and steely blue while the weather became hotter day by day. Caleb did not even have his guitar-playing at the hotel to distract him now for that had ended before Easter when the wealthier tourists went home to Britain and the United States.

'My father always said that we would always be given seedtime and harvest,' I tried to cheer Caleb.

'Mars D. Sandison was right,' he replied, 'but seems that bush coconut seedtime is November this year.'

It was now that old Minna came across the grass from her laundry at the back of the house and I braced myself to deal with the latest trial that Providence had seen fit to lay upon her thin bent shoulders. Minna hardly spoke to me or to anyone other than to make a complaint but Caleb assured me that she was 'happy in her misery' and I had long since ceased to hear the doleful hymns that emanated constantly from the laundry.

'I beg ya, ma'am, to come and look upon this water,' she said. Caleb and I followed her to the laundry where, with a sad gesture, she indicated a sink full of what looked like liquid mud. I looked at Caleb.

'No, ma'am,' he said. 'Not me, ma'am.'

There had been a time when he had put some plants in one of Minna's spotless sinks which had led to his being forbidden to enter the laundry while Minna, for a whole week, sang without ceasing a hymn that began: 'Me gates is close' agin de sinner'. 'It comin' out de tap, ma'am,' said Minna, turning on a tap and causing the mud to flow before she turned her rheumy eyes upon me and said: 'Lawd Gawd, ain't me life sad an' hard 'nough widout wash de Chief's whites in dis?'

'Leave the washing for now, Minna,' I said. 'I shall speak to the Chief when he comes home for lunch.'

Minna raised her worn hands plaintively above her head. 'Leave de wash, she say!' She seemed to be address-ing the Almighty. 'Ain't me ever goin' to get done finish? Lawd Gawd, what me do me not can wash de Chief's whites?'

Caleb and I walked away, leaving Minna's desolation to take its course. Having accused the Almighty of his in-justice to her, as I explained to Percy, she would go on to pray for forgiveness for her presumption and then sing a few hymns of praise as a penance. I was little moved by the issue of mud from the laundry taps. It had hap-pened often enough before but usually after heavy rain when the Rio d'Oro was in spate. Our drinking water and the water for cooking was the catchment from the roofs of the house and outbuildings, stored in a tank in the back garden and boiled before being used but the water for the laundry, the bathrooms and garden standpipes came from the reservoir at the factory which was fed by the Rio d'Oro.

Halfway through lunch, I said: 'I don't suppose it matters, Twice, but in the laundry—'

'It matters all right,' he said grimly. 'You are getting silt?'

'Well, yes.'

'There is nothing but silt coming into the reservoir so nothing but silt can come out.' He looked at Percy. 'Sashie isn't the only one to have water trouble.'

'Trouble?' I said. He looked worried. The factory and the distillery consumed a vast amount of water. 'But nothing like this has ever happened before. The Rio d'Oro is spring-fed as well as catchment.'

'It is partly the weather but it is far more than that. I think there has been a general shift following the earthquake. The Great House lake is getting bigger, in spite of the drought. It is spreading out towards the bamboo grove. But the main factor is all that bloody tourism down on the Platinum Coast. Five new hotels went into operation last winter and they are all drawing their water basically from the Oro and the Pedro. Damn it, it should have been done last year but with the mess after the earthquake, there just wasn't time.'

'Time for what?'

'To enlarge the factory reservoir and put in a filter tower. If we can filter, we can cut down by re-using a lot of our water. I knew it had to come but I thought we might have got by this Crop.'

It was not until we were going to bed that night that the full far-reaching significance of the mud from the laundry tap was brought home to me.

'Darling,' Twice said, 'I can't go overseas this coming Out-of-Crop. We cabled the order for that filtration plant this afternoon. But if you want to go over to Jock's for a bit—'

I shook my head. 'I don't want to go over but I am sorry that you can't. I mean, what about Ireland, the boy—'

'I know.' He stared into the darkness beyond the window. 'But one had to decide, try to do the best thing. The youngsters—' he meant Mackie, Vickers and Christie '—had no leave at all last year. They gave up even their local leave after the earthquake and Christie's mother has been very ill so he must go this year. And Vickers might as well go too but Mackie refuses to go although I can't remember when he was home last. He may go after we get the new installation done but I can't walk out and leave him with it. He can't do that and my office bumph as well. But there is no reason why you shouldn't make a short trip.' He turned round to smile at me. 'I am pretty good on my own.'

'And Percy would keep house,' I said. 'I know. But I really don't want to go, Twice, if you don't mind. I was looking forward to your going to Ireland but otherwise – no.'

'I am pleased you don't want to really. I would much rather have you here.'

'Is it going to be a tremendous rush, all this work?' I asked and I could not help feeling anxious. 'Don't go and—'

'No. You are not to worry. There will be no rush and there will be no strain. What *would* be a strain would be to be in Ireland and wondering all the time how things were going. This is my job, after all. I want to be on the spot.'

Mud continued to issue from the taps in the laundry and bathrooms for three days, during which much of my time was given to preventing Minna from raiding the domestic tank for the laundry.

'Lawd Gawd, ain't I even not allowed to earn me livin' no more?' she asked of the brassy heavens but matters were eased by Sir Ian and Big Sammy filling a molasses tanker from the Great House lake and driving round the park, filling drums with water for the laundries of the various houses. Sir Ian was in his element. Here was 'somethin' doin' around the place an' sorry Missis Janet ye got a toad in that lot but he'd be handy for the slugs in the garden.'

'I have never seen a place like this,' said Percy, rescuing the toad from the drum and placing it under the hedge where it squatted, staring at Dram with an insulted baleful air. 'Anything can happen.'

'And frequently does,' I said. 'Sir Ian, would you and Sammy like a glass of beer?'

'Just the very thing,' he said coming on to the veranda while Percy carried a glass to Sammy behind the wheel of the tanker.

'Funny thing water,' Sir Ian remarked. 'Comes an' goes as it likes. Bloody-minded too. Too much where ye don't want it an' too little where ye do want it half the time. Ye know about these elements?' he asked me fiercely as if they were some threatening hostile tribe.

'Elements?'

'Ye learn them at school.'

Sir Ian's attitude to things learned at school, which comprised anything from the plays of Shakespeare to algebra and which, I was now discovering, included the elements, was ambivalent. He despised all such learning, on the one hand, as being utterly useless but he despised equally, on the other hand, all those who had not been subjected to the absorption of such learning. 'Earth, air, fire an' water,' he now barked at me, while Percy stood listening and bemused. 'Long ago, they believed there were four kinds o' people accordin' to what element there was most of in them. Somethin' in it, shouldn't wonder. Take Mother – fire, no question o' it. She is very put out about this drought, very. Well, can't sit here chattin' all day. Got to get a tanker-load for her rose-beds after this.' As he descended the steps, Sashie was making his way on foot round the tanker that was filling the drive. ''Mornin' Sashie me boy,' he said. 'What you doin' here?'

Sashie held up a gin bottle. 'I am bringing Janet a tiny drink of water from my spring, if you don't mind, sir,' he said coyly.

Sir Ian from the top of the steps looked down upon the

figure upon the gravel. 'When I think about it,' he said, 'maybe that element idea ain't the answer after all. There's some people you wouldn't know *what* was in them.'

'Sashie, you shouldn't tease him,' I said when the tanker had driven away.

'Nonsense, darling. He enjoys it' and this was true. In spite of Sashie's appearing to be everything that Sir Ian disapproved of, against his will almost, Sir Ian was fond of him. 'What element idea did he mention?' Sashie asked.

'Ye learn them at school!' I barked before explaining that our water shortage had sent Sir Ian's mind back about fifty years.

'I have always believed that people have affinities with the elements,' Sashie surprised me by saying. 'You are an earth person, darling. You have the nature of the earth and what grows in the earth. You are patient, slow-thinking, reliable. And you like the earth. You are always grubbing about in it.'

This had a curious ring of truth which fascinated me. 'And Percy?' I asked, looking at her as she stood on the lawn beside Dram in her habitual position, one foot on tiptoe. 'Air?'

'No. Water I should say.'

Percy could not hear us but she chose that moment to come on to the veranda and say: 'Now that the water has come, I am going over to the bungalows to get them started on the laundry.'

'Percy and her housekeeping,' I said when the little car had driven away. 'Water, you say? Oh, the divining, of course.'

'Water is a very strange element. In small quantity it can be made to take any shape and show no resistance but in its own nature it obeys its own mysterious laws, like the water at Silver Beach. Percy is in touch with those laws, darling. No doubt about it. That spring is gushing like crazy.'

'Yes. That was a very odd business. I liked it but it

made Twice furious. It still does if one mentions it.'

'Yes, it would. It *would* make the fire man furious. It is inimical to his very nature.'

'The fire man? You mean Twice and the element of fire?'

'But of course. Think of that factory, those turbine blades whirling, all that steam rushing through pipes, all those wheels going round, all that energy. And the fire of the wish to *know*. Trying to know is to reduce all the magic and beauty to ashes. But I don't think any of us will ever know how Percy knew that that water was there because she doesn't know herself how she knew. I think the magic will defeat us all in the end.' He blinked his dark lashes very rapidly a few times and his face became mischievous. 'Dear me, I feel very poetic this morning. I must have drunk too much of my spring water for breakfast. Darling, there are a few more bottles in the car. Have Caleb put them in your refrigerator.'

'You are very kind, Sashie, and I must say the domestic tank is getting very sludgy.'

'Is that lake at the Great House no use?'

'Not for drinking. It is brackish and then there is the fertiliser from the cane pieces, the effluent from the distillery and the toads. It grows pretty lilies though and the gawlens like it.'

'Those are the lilies you imported from the River Pedro up at Siloam?' he asked.

'Yes. They are a great success. It seems that I can dabble in the element of water as well as earth. By the way, having placed the rest of us, what is your own element?'

'I do not wish to be placed,' he said mock-huffily.

'I will tell you. It is the air that bloweth where it listeth.'

'Ah, that reminds me. Quite soon, I am off to London, darling, to have my furniture shipped to Silver Beach so if you want any shopping, you must let me know.'

'You could write to the warehouse and tell them to ship

it,' I said, 'but you can't stay away from those aeroplanes, can you?' When he had gone away, I went up to the back bedroom but there was only about half-an-hour of the forenoon left before Twice would be home for lunch. I stood looking down at my manuscript. Elements, I thought. In day to day life, we seemed to be a long way from the elemental things in ourselves. Several hours could be dissipated in attending to the water supply, a trip to Britain that might have been of great importance had been cancelled out of Twice's sense of duty and fairness to his juniors. The only element that had any bearing on our lives was that wind of circumstance and chance that blew where it listed.

On a Thursday morning late in June, I was cutting flowers in the garden when Caleb suddenly stopped work, stood upright and sniffed the air while he looked away to the hills on the south-east side of the Paradise valley.

'I think, ma'am,' he said, 'you should telephone Mars Sashie and tell him to get them coconuts down from the agricultural station to the property.'

I too looked at the hills and saw a tall pillar of cumulus cloud begin to climb over the horizon. 'The rains are coming, Caleb?'

'Yes, ma'am, an' soon an' heavy. There must be a blow out to sea.'

By the time Twice came home for lunch, it was obvious to all of us that we were on the edge of a blow and we did not need the radio to tell us that a hurricane had formed eighty miles off Hurricane Point, the eastern tip of the island.

'They say it is going to move north-westerly,' I said.

'Let us hope they are right,' said Twice. 'We humans are a shabby lot, Percy. If it goes north-west, the Bahamas will get it but we won't. Every man for himself.'

'How can they tell where it will go?' she asked.

'They can't predict it. They literally watch it from aircraft.'

'Hurricane is literally the wind blowing where it listeth,' I said. 'It can change direction in a matter of minutes.'

The hurricane atmosphere induces a mood of near-desperation, so that despite knowledge of the destructive fury, one begins to wish that it would break loose and reduce the tension of waiting. The air, which was deadly still, grew heavier and more humid by the moment, the sky became darker and nearer and all about the garden there was a lurid red-gold light that lay in pools and swathes that seemed to be generated not out of the sky but out of the earth itself. The voice of the weather announcer on the radio, speaking his latest news of the storm's movement between bursts of tinny recorded music, sounded puny and cowed as it came through the thick throbbing air and it was a relief when, about three in the afternoon, there was a long streak of lightning across the park, like a brilliant green whip-lash, followed by a crack of thunder that drowned the voice of the radio completely.

'Here she comes, ma'am,' said Caleb coming in through the french window and closing it behind him. 'Everything going to be all right, Miss Percy. The Chief and them all right at the factory too, ma'am. They got the crane boom lashed an' everything.'

'Good,' I said, pulling my damp shirt away from my chest. The whole house was battened down, the storm screens in place round the veranda, not an aperture left to admit a wind that, when it came, might lift the roof and carry it away like a dead leaf. I looked out between the window boards across the park with the swathes and pools of uncanny light on the sun-browned grass to the factory, where the tall smoke-stack looked punily defiant against the lowering sky. There was a second lurid flash of lightning that lit the whole landscape and left a deeper darkness when it passed, followed by a crash of thunder that might have been the earth itself exploding and Percy, close to me, whispered: 'You know – I am scared.'

'Better soon,' said Caleb and in the silence following

that crash, the eldritch voice of old Minna in the kitchen could be heard: 'An' dark is his paff on de wings ob de storm!'

'Do listen to Minna,' I said, taking Percy's hand. 'When I was a child, that hymn used to scare me blue until George and Tom told me that the Almighty had more sense than to go out in a thunderstorm. They said nobody went out in a thunderstorm except old Mrs. Miller from Achcraggan who hadn't the brains she was born with and—'

There was a sudden angry hiss that made my voice tail away, then a loud roar and through the window boards there was just time to see all the tall palms in the park bend over until they were like tensely drawn bows, their mop-heads of tossing fronds sweeping the grass, before the wind-driven deluge of rain enwrapped the house like a blinding blanket.

'Be all right now, ma'am,' said Caleb. 'I go upstairs an' make sure of the windows on the east side?'

'Yes, do that, Caleb,' I told him and to Percy: 'I am going to the kitchen to ask for some tea. Want to come?'

'No. I am all right. It is different now,' she said, listening to the roar of the wind and the hiss of the rain on the walls of the house.

On my way back through the hall, I picked up the telephone, wondering if it would work and heard the comforting voice of Twice from his office.

'You lot all right?' he asked.

'Yes, but the radio has gone out.'

'The aerial will be gone. Ours is still working here. The blow is changing course. She is turning north-easterly.'

'Do you all have to call them girls?' I asked. 'Come home soon.' The wind roared and the rain poured for twenty-four hours without respite. The park which had been burned brown lay under water and the line of the road to Bachelors' Bungalow was marked only by Vickers' water-logged old car which had given up in the flood when he was coming off night-shift.

'Well, I missed the earthquake,' Percy said, 'but I did get the hurricane.'

'Except that that wasn't hurricane,' Twice told her. 'It was only the edge of the blow proper. Caleb, Tony the Millman says we are in for about a week's rain on and off. What do you think?'

'Week or ten days, sah.'

'That clinches it,' Twice said. 'When in doubt, Percy, enquire of experience. We'll be blowing the whistle for the end of Crop at about seven this evening.'

'But why?' Percy asked. 'There is still cane to cut.'

'It will be water-logged. Besides, if the tractors go into the pieces, they will go down to the tops of their tracks.'

'What a shame,' Percy said to me when Twice had gone back to the factory, 'when Crop was going so well and everything.'

'I don't know,' I said. 'That factory is only a mechanical contrivance after all. I don't like a thing like that and the people connected with it to get too arrogant. I think they are the better of something to cut them down to size now and then.' I looked at the rain which was still heavy but thinning so that I could see the palms in the park now, upright again but their fronds still tossing wildly in the reduced wind. 'And it is an ill wind that blows no good,' I added. 'As soon as the rain goes over, we can all go down to Silver Beach and plant Sashie's coconuts.'

As the afternoon went on, the rain lessened and the wind continued to drop so that, once more, the sound of the factory could be heard. Shortly after four, the sound changed. The deep rumble of the crushing mills died out, indicating that the cane yard was empty, that the last sugar of the year was being processed through the plant and shortly before seven in the evening, the siren sent its scream through the dark.

Traditionally, all the men on the estate, such as Caleb, were allowed to have 'a blow at the whistle' at the end of Crop, while the women workers gathered with large tin bowls to be given the sugar which was scraped from various vessels prior to their cleaning. The siren was still screaming when Twice and Mackie dived from their cars through the rain on to the veranda. Percy was beside herself with excitement, threw herself at Twice who tossed her to Mackie and Mackie picked her up, swung her round and set her back on her feet.

'We have had a great Crop, Missis,' Twice said to me, his eyes brilliant as he waved a hand at Mackie. 'Pour out a glass of rum for my Chief, will you?'

PART THREE

'For never-resting time leads summer on
To hideous winter and confounds him there'
from a sonnet by SHAKESPEARE

WHEN nine days of rain were over, we celebrated the end of a record crop by planting Sashie's coconut walk. Even Mackie joined the weekend party which included Twice, Sir Ian, Caleb, Percy, myself and about a dozen of the garden boys from the Peak Hotel. I had offered to stay behind with Madame and Miss Poynter but Madame had decided against this.

'No, dear. You go along and see that they behave themselves and do nothing foolish. Gentlemen on their own tend to become very silly, especially at Cropover time and Maud and I have the racing to attend to.'

The garden boys, under Caleb as headman, made short work of the coconut planting while Sashie and I roasted a huge leg of pork in his new kitchen and Twice, Mackie and Percy lay in the shallow water on the beach.

'Mackie ought to have more sense,' I said. 'He burns.'

'Mackie is a tiny bit delirious with one thing and another, dear,' Sashie replied. 'The sweet smell of success – it is heady stuff, you know. When does he go on leave?'

'He isn't going. He and Twice have got this water filtration scheme under their skins and neither of them will leave Paradise until after it is carried through. Mackie might go home for a bit towards the end of the year, when they get the new scheme and the maintenance finished. Christie flew out this morning and Vickers goes at the end of the month. They have four months leave each because they had none at all last year.'

'Won't Twice be pretty short-staffed?'

'He says not. What can one do? I really think that he and Mackie are glad that Vickers and Christie will be out of the way. They are two good steady fellows but the mad enthusiasts are better on their own with the filtration lark. That is how they are regarding this Out-of-Crop – as a lark. The factory is in good shape after last year's major overhaul and here they are with a nice bit of filter-tower-building and pipe-laying to amuse themselves with. Sashie, do you ever feel that everybody is crazy except you?'

'All the time, darling, all the time. Let us go out and take a turn through my coconut walk. It is a walk, I understand, as opposed to a grove or plantation.'

Everything was fresh and green after the rains and what had been a dry stream bed a few weeks ago was now a noisy little torrent, tumbling between the sweeps of grass dotted with coconuts. Caleb and the boys, in their blue overalls, brilliant shirts and wide-brimmed straw hats sang as they planted the big brown nuts which had one or two green fronds about two feet high protruding from their tops.

'Plant one for luck for Mars Sashie, ma'am?' Caleb called to me and when he had dug the hole, I put the nut in and trod the moist earth firmly round it.

They were two light-hearted days. Sashie's piano had been brought down from Guinea Corner, his record-player brought from the Peak, Caleb had his guitar with him and when the early darkness came down, we all sat around while the boys sang the songs of their island. As the moon rose, flat and white, making a silver path across the water and the little waves lapped on the shore, it was difficult to recall the fury of the storm of so short ago and I told myself that I was foolish to try to recall it, that I should learn the island philosohpy of living in the moment.

On the Sunday evening, however, there came a few moments that made me glad of my retentive memory, a few moments that I was glad I would never forget. Sir Ian had gone home when it grew dark but the rest of us had stayed on late into the evening. Sashie was seated at his piano and I was sitting on the floor beside him. On the other side of the room was the semi-circle of boys, Caleb and his guitar in the centre and to one side, Twice with Percy on one side of him and Mackie on the other. The evening was coming to an end, the boys finishing their final glasses of beer before piling into the Peak station wagons that would take them home. There was no light except that from three candles in bottles on the piano and from the moon beyond the window. Sashie and Caleb had played songs from every country on the earth that evening, 'Waltzing Matilda', 'Linstead Market', French songs, German songs, Russian songs and, of course, a soulful rendering of 'Granny's Heilan' Hame' specially requested by Twice for my irritation.

In the drowsy end-of-the-day silence, Caleb began to pluck at the strings of his guitar and a melody began to form. It was the tune 'Crimond' to which, on one of Twice's records, a baritone and choir sang the metrical version of the twenty-third psalm, a tune that I had heard so often during my childhood in church at Achcraggan. Suddenly, Twice began to sing:

> 'The Lord's my Shepherd, I'll not want,
>   He makes me down to lie -
>   In pastures green; he leadeth me
>   The quiet waters by.'

The boys did not know either the tune or the words but

they were all naturally musical and after the first verse they joined in with an impromptu descant, their lighter voices interweaving in a background to the deeper voice of Twice. In my lifetime, I had heard that psalm sung hundreds of times but I had never heard anything like this and when I felt Sashie's hand on my shoulder, gripping hard, I knew that I was not the only one to be moved. This is one of those moments, I thought, to be remembered for ever.

There was a silence after the last note of the guitar had died away, broken by Twice who rose to his feet and said: 'Come along, you lot. The holidays are over. Old clothes and porridge tomorrow, Mackie.'

We all went out towards the cars and Sashie said to me in a low voice: 'Thank you for planting a coconut for me, darling. And I would thank Twice for blessing my house, only it would embarrass him so. Goodnight.'

'What was that you said about old clothes and porridge, Twice?' Percy asked from the back of the car, as if anxious to return to a more mundane level.

It was Mackie, sitting between her and me who explained: 'In former days, Scots had porridge for breakfast every day of the week except Sunday. On Sunday, they might have bacon or sausages and they wore their best clothes.'

'You don't know 'bout Scotland, Miss Percy?' Caleb asked, surprised, from his seat beside Twice.

'Not much,' Percy admitted.

'But she is learning,' Twice said and he and Caleb began to sing 'Loch Lomond' while the headlights of the car picked out the exotic shapes of the tropical vines and ferns on either side of the road.

The Out-of-Crop routine of nine till four each day now took over. We slept more soundly, for there was no longer the hovering menace of the intermittent screaming of the siren through the night, telling that the factory was in trouble. Twice and Mackie took to spending the forenoons at the factory and the afternoons in Twice's study where they worked on their plans for the filtration project and Percy did her housekeeping in the bungalows in the forenoons and was out and about with her sketchbook or with Madame at the Great House in the afternoons. Sir Ian at one end of the scale and Caleb at the other talked of nothing but cricket, with special reference to the villainous machinations of that lawless ne'er-do-well, Retreat.

'That lot got no conscience, ma'am,' Caleb informed me darkly and then became aggressive. 'This cricket tournament is between sugar estates, right? Then what business they got fieldin' Doctor Lawrie? *He* ain't sugar.'

'But Doctor Gurbat Singh plays for the Paradise team, Caleb,' I pointed out.

'That is not the same. Doctor Gurbat Singh is pure Paradise. He don't doctor nobody except Paradise people and got his clinic and his home right here on the estate. That Doctor Lawrie doctors all of Moonyon Town and my Uncle Abel as well as Retreat people and he got no business on that team.'

I did not attempt to argue further and Caleb went on: 'That Doctor Lawrie played for one o' them English universities once. I tell you, that lot got no conscience.'

On another day, I was upstairs busy in the back bedroom when Clorinda tapped at the door. 'Sir Ian downstairs, ma'am' and when I went down, Sir Ian was all a-bustle, marching up and down the veranda.

'D'ye know what these perishers up at Retreat are doin'? They got Mrs. Morgan's brother out here on holiday and they got him coachin' their team. He used to play for *Glamorgan*! It's a damn' scandal an' I rang up Macbeth an' told him so. Very unsportin' I said. Should be ashamed of himself, I said. Suppose you are goin' to play him on the team? I said, bein' sarcastic an' ye know what that perisher said? Well, he said, he's livin' here at Retreat.'

'My brother used to be quite a good cricketer,' I said, 'and he will be on holiday just now.'

'Would he come out here?' Sir Ian pounced.

'No,' I said.

The Out-of-Crop periods had always seen cricket in the ascendant but I had never known it to rise to such fever-pitch as this year. Everybody except Sashie and myself was smitten with it, even Madame and Miss Poynter. Every Saturday and Sunday, Twice, Mackie, Percy and Caleb climbed into the car with their picnic lunch and went off to the matches while Sir Ian's car pulled out loaded with himself, his chauffeur and as many factory hands as it could carry. In addition to this, four Paradise lorries were equipped with seats to carry a roaring crowd of supporters round the island and when a game was played on the Paradise ground, these lorries were used as stands by the wives of the workers.

'Are they all mad?' Sashie enquired of me. 'Or could there be some tiny thing the matter with you and me, darling?'

At times, I was a little ashamed of my lack of enthusiasm but the cricket left me a great deal of time to follow my own devices and alone in the bedroom upstairs I quickly forgot about it. Percy and Twice did their best to persuade me to go along to the matches with them, being a little guilty at leaving me behind, which put me in a slightly false position for I did not want to give my reason for being glad to be left behind.

'Don't worry about me,' I told them. 'If I don't go to the matches, I feel better about not doing anything about those awful Club teas.'

When a match was played at Paradise, lemonade, tea and sandwiches were provided not only for the teams but for any of the supporters who cared to partake of them and down my years on the estate I had done my share in the preparation of food for large numbers of people. It had always been a chore which, especially in the hotter weather, made me feel squeamish and the cricket teas this year had been weighing on my mind until I found them painlessly removed from my hands by Percy. She organised a small group comprising the nurse from the clinic, the typists from the factory office, raised a Teas Fund from Gurbat Singh who was treasurer of the Cricket Club and handled the whole affair in the Club House kitchen with great efficiency.

'That girl is a born plantation wife,' I said to Twice.

'More than one agree with you, including young Hugh Macbeth. We are all hoping she will get between him and his cricket, get his eye off the ball.'

'Vive le sport!' I commented and since the cricket coloured every aspect of life at that time and a Retreat man being a main and inimical aspect of cricket at that time, I thought that if I lived to see a marriage between Paradise and Retreat, I would have lived to see everything.

At the Great House, the cricket led to some asperity between Madame and Miss Poynter, because Madame wished to have all the cricket news read aloud to her as soon as the newspaper came in each day and Miss Poynter had the curious failing that as soon as she began to read, she fell asleep.

'A book or a newspaper is just like a sleeping-pill to me,' she said. 'I have always been like that.'

But, in truth, nearly every activity except eating and drinking was 'like a sleeping pill' to Miss Poynter. She ate enormously and drank a fair amount before lunch and before dinner but at most other times she could be found asleep in her chair beside Madame in the library, in a deck-chair in the garden or in a great, snoring fully-clothed heap on top of her bed. She could always be located at tea or drinks time by her snores which reverberated round the great empty house.

Thus, Percy's or my afternoon duty at the Great House nowadays was to read the cricket reports from the *Island Sun*. These reports from Monday till Friday I found ineffably boring for they all dealt with the two matches already reported by wireless at the week-end and despite the best efforts of the reporters to bring something fresh to their columns each day, the reports made me think of

Alexander the Great at the feast when he 'fought all his battles o'er again and thrice he slew the slain'. On a Wednesday afternoon towards the end of July, I was driven round to the Great House with a further two hours of cricket reading and discussion ahead of me, wishing that cricket had never been invented and grudging this time that I was being forced to waste. As I approached the door that led from the garden into the library, I could hear Madame's voice saying irritably: 'Are you asleep again, Maud? Janet is here. I heard the car. Do you hear me, Maud?' As I went into the room, Madame was sitting in her usual chair, facing the door and I could see Miss Poynter's fat elbow on the arm of a chair that had its back towards me.

'Good afternoon, Madame,' I said, passing Miss Poynter and taking the old lady's hand as I did every time I called for touch was important to her in her blindness. I then turned towards the other chair and felt a cold rigidity creep upward from my feet through all my muscles until my entire body was stiff.

'Is Maud here, Janet?' Madame was asking crossly. 'I did not hear her go out.'

Miss Poynter had gone out very silently and for good. Although I was forty-seven years old, I had not much experience of death. My mother had died when I was ten years old but my family had shielded me from that and down the years, distance had always stood between me and this immediacy but now it was in the room, close at hand, sudden and final. With an effort, I bent forward and took the left wrist in one hand, inserting the fingers of the other between the bracelets and the wrinkles of fat to find the spot where the pulse should be, but there was no movement and the flabby flesh had a curious unnatural weight.

'Janet, is something the matter?' came the voice of Madame, not afraid or nervous but impatient, rather, with the blindness that cut her off from full and immediate understanding.

'Miss Poynter is not well, Madame,' I said. 'I am going to call the doctor.'

'Ian is in his office at the factory. Telephone to him and come back here at once, please, Janet.'

I went to the room which was the Great House office and called Sir Ian. 'It is Miss Poynter, Sir Ian. I think she is dead.'

'Dead? Maud? She can't be. Just saw her at lunch.'

'Will you please call the doctor and come over to the house? I must go back to Madame.'

His voice changed. 'Yes, yes, me dear. You do that. We'll be right over.'

When I went back to the library, Madame, guided by her acute hearing, turned her face towards me as I came through the doorway. 'Janet, Maud is dead, isn't she?' she asked.

'I think so, Madame.'

'My poor Janet. What a shock for you. Come here, my dear, and sit by me until Ian comes.' She reached out and took my hand between her own, drawing me down into the chair beside her and at the same time drawing her own body indomitably erect. 'I ought to have known,' she said. 'If Maud was not talking, she was always snoring. I ought to have known. Poor Maud. Ah, that is Ian's car in the drive now.'

Sir Ian, Twice and Mackie seemed to tumble in from the garden and be suddenly arrested as they looked at the heavy body slumped in the large chintz-covered chair.

'She is gone all right,' Sir Ian said after a moment. 'Poor old Maud. Twice, take Mother an' your missis up to the drawin'-room, will you? Mackie, go outside an' bring Nurse an' Gurbat Singh in here when they arrive. No good upsettin' the servants an' startin' them howlin'.'

My legs felt weak as Twice and I, with Madame between us, went up the staircase to the big room on the first floor and as soon as we were seated, the old lady took command.

'Mr. Twice, you will find brandy and glasses in the cupboard in the corner. Be good enough to pour a drink for Janet. And then I think you should go back to the library, if you please. Ian may need your assistance.'

When he had done as she asked and had gone away, she said: 'Now drink your brandy and find a cigarette, dear. There should be some in the shagreen box on the table by the bookcase.' Obediently, I opened the box and was glad to find it full of cigarettes for had it not been, I knew that Madame would have had the servant responsible for the room summoned to her presence forthwith. Down the years, I had learned that Madame never allowed herself or her household to get out of control and the greater the crisis, the greater and more thorough was the determination with which she rose to meet it.

'Naturally, you are upset, my dear,' she said when I had lit the cigarette, 'and I am sorry that I was so silly. As I said, I ought to have known and have saved you that shock. But then, death is always unexpected, even when someone is very ill and one knows one must expect it. And Maud was not robust, you know. None of the Poynters were healthy in either mind or body although some of them lived to a great age, like Maud's grandmother but then, of course, she was not a Poynter by birth. She was one of the Pickerings of Castle Cardon. It is all very strange. Why I can remember when Maud was born, dear. She was only a few months older than Ian. Her mother *would* go out paying calls instead of remaining decently at home in *her* condition.'

The effect of Madame's reminiscences was to place Maud Poynter in the thick texture of the island's social history and to blunt the edges of the grim procedure that was in train in the room below. When Rob and Marion Maclean had been killed in the earthquake in the garden of this house the year before, Twice and I had been hurried from the scene by Doctor Gurbat Singh that Twice might be put to bed to combat the shock of what had happened and while I sat anxiously in his study-bedroom, watching for some unknown re- action, I had been harrowed by the haste and efficiency of a St. Jagoan funeral, the horrible details of the blocks of ice to be placed round the corpses, while the grave was dug, the coffins prepared, that the abandoned flesh might be put underground and away from the corrupting heat within twenty-four hours. It was grotesque and macabre that the life-giving sun should, at death, become a force of corruption that could rob two people of their final dignity, perhaps their only true dignity.

And now, while the procedure was followed through once more in the library below, Madame talked quietly of the social trivia of former times, blunting the edges of what had happened and was happening, making these things in some curious way acceptable. In a few hours, the worst was over. Miss Poynter's body lay on the ice-packed slab, the coffin at readiness on a table alongside. The island broadcasting service and the *Island Sun* had been notified of the death and the next day a representative of every European enterprise in the island would follow the white Paradise ambulance which would take the coffin to the Poynter private burial ground on the outskirts of the Peak Hotel grounds. Sir Ian was free to be with Madame and Twice and I returned to Guinea Corner, Mackie to his bungalow.

'Are you all right?' I asked Twice.

'Yes. I did nothing but the telephoning. What about you? You must have had a bad moment or two.'

'I am all right. Twice, Madame is remarkable, isn't she?'

He nodded his head. 'In the ordinary way, she is just a trivial, petty-minded, ill-educated old snob, but at a time like this there is something grand and monumental about her.'

'It is out of the triviality, the petty-mindedness and all the rest that the monument rises. Life itself, monumental as it is, is just an interwoven fabric of trivialities, pettiness, ill-thought-out ideas and snobberies. One doesn't live a life. One is caught in this web and dragged along by it through time, that is all.'

Suddenly, I began to cry, helplessly, almost angrily,

unable to understand what I was crying about, for old Maud Poynter had meant nothing to me. I had always thought of her as an ugly, rather malicious old woman and no more, but now I did not know what I thought of her or of myself or of anybody or of anything which was probably the reason for my helpless half-angry tears. Twice handed me his handkerchief and I mopped my face.

'Will you attend the funeral?' I asked, taking a grip on the next little strand of living.

'I suppose I must. White people's funerals are an established part of an estate manager's duties. I wish I didn't find them so embarrassing, all that scraggy singing of hymns and psalms at the graveside. Why do they have to do it? If they were natural singers like the negroes, it would be different. The singing at Mama Lou's funeral last year was magnificent.'

Mama Lou Lindsay had been the mother of Sister Flo who had nursed Twice through his illness.

'What time has been fixed for the funeral?' I asked.

'We leave the Great House at two o'clock.'

'Then I had better go round there with you and stay with Madame until you all get back.'

'The old lady is going to miss old Maud. Is there *any*-body else, do you think, that Sir Ian could persuade to come to the Great House?'

'I can't think of anyone.'

'Madame really has outlived her time.'

'Please don't say that, Twice. I don't like it. She may have outlived the rest of her generation but I believe there is some reason for it, something that makes her want to live on, something that she still has to do—'

Percy came quietly into the room. 'Is it true about Miss Poynter?' she asked. 'I was down town and I met Jimmie Crowther and he said he heard it on the wireless at the ice-cream parlour, so I came home at once.'

I noticed her use of the word 'home', her identification with us and with Paradise.

'Yes, Percy,' Twice said. 'When Janet went round to the house—'

'—she was sitting in a chair—dead,' I said when he paused.

'Janet, how awful! Is there anything I can do?'

'No, Percy. There is nothing that any of us can do. Twice will attend the funeral tomorrow and it will be all over.'

'And you will stay with Madame?' she asked. 'Would it help if I came with you? It might distract her a bit, do you think, perhaps?'

'That is very kind of you, Percy,' I said. 'Yes, do come. Madame will like it.'

The next morning, Twice went up to his office as usual but Percy did not leave the house. After he had gone, she and I sat on at the breakfast-table and she said: 'Janet, are you a religious person?'

'I don't think so. I am not religious in the orthodox churchgoing sense, although I went to church every Sunday from when I was about four until I was about sixteen. I suppose that some of what I heard then has stuck to me but I wouldn't call myself religious. No.'

'It must have been easier for people when they could believe that there was Heaven up above the sky.'

'Maybe. Yet I am not sure. Day-to-day living would have been much the same and death would have been just as awful – in the awe-inspiring sense, I mean – when it came.' I remembered my holiday in Scotland, during which my nephew Sandy Tom had been born. 'And birth would have been just as miraculous,' I added.

'I wish I understood better about it all. Somebody like Miss Poynter – she got born, she lived and now she is dead and it is all just nothing. Like my mother – she worked and worked and then she just died. It all seems so pointless.'

'I don't see it like that, Percy. I think that just by living we all accomplish something, contribute something. On the face of it, Miss Poynter was only a rather bad actress, perhaps, but somewhere along the line she must have helped somebody, have given somebody a little happiness. She helped Madame during these last months, after all, if only by being somebody to quarrel with. And your mother, she accomplished *you*, after all.'

'I was a sort of accident, I think,' Percy said ruefully. 'My mother was always striving for something that was just beyond her reach and she died before she got to it. She never got what she wanted, whatever it was.'

'Maybe what she really wanted was just the striving, although she may not have known it,' I said. 'One of the most difficult things to recognise is happiness. We want it but we don't know it when we have it. Probably the striving was your mother's happiness. I remember grousing to Sashie once about Life with a capital L and he pointed out that although I was grousing, I didn't seem very anxious to seek the quiet peace of the grave.'

'Sashie says some dreadful things. He was practically telling you to commit suicide.'

'He is very clear-sighted,' I said. 'And I don't think death is a purely physical thing like cancer, or a heart attack like Miss Poynter's or even old age. I think a time comes when people do seek the peace of the grave although they may not even be aware that they are doing it. All the time we don't seek it, we are happier than we realise, I think. Only, we are so busy thinking of all the things we haven't got that we don't think at all of what we have got.'

'I do try to count my blessings sometimes,' Percy said, 'especially since I have been here. Janet, this is the happiest time I have had since Gran died.'

'I am very glad and I hope that you will go on being happy here for a long time.'

'I have a feeling of being in the right place at the right time,' she said strangely and then changed direction in her sudden way.

'Janet, there are no gawlens at the lake. I was round early this morning and there isn't a single one.'

'You have been too busy with the cricket,' I told her. 'They are migrants. They would have gone about the end of June. They usually arrive just when we go into Crop and fly at Cropover.'

'I wonder why? I suppose they have their reasons,' she said and went out into the garden.

Left alone, my mind returned to Miss Poynter and from her to thoughts of George and Tom. For most of the time, those two had the character of a constant bulwark in my mind but now mortality seemed to surround their rock-like image like a hungry encroaching sea, for they were a lot older than the woman who had died.

I spent the forenoon weeding a rosebed in the garden, kneeling on the grass, my face close to the earth, my hands among it for, like this, the images of Tom and George in my mind became more concrete and their reality less far away.

Twice came home a little early and changed into his dark suit and black tie so that a sombre unfamiliarity lay over the lunch table and this became more marked when Sashie and Don Candlesham arrived, similarly dressed.

'We thought we would come up,' Don said, 'instead of just going to the burial ground. We thought Madame might like it.'

'She will. It was very thoughtful of you, Don,' I said, my eyes fixed on the cablegram that Sashie held in his hand.

'They stopped us as we passed the factory office, Twice,' he said, handing the envelope to Twice. 'Your secretary said it sounds corrupt but she has re-checked it with the cable office.' I felt cold as Twice slit the envelope open, read the message through and then began to laugh.

'Who is it from?' I managed to ask.

'Guess!' he said and read aloud: 'Please go Edinburgh

urgent send up complete outfit twins this time am very well but phlabber hyphen gasted.'

'That's from my friend Monica!' I said, my voice shrill with relief.

'No wonder the cable office thought its wires were crossed,' Don said.

'But why does she say please go Edinburgh?' Percy asked.

'That dates from the time of her first baby,' I explained. 'I was to be godmother and I said something pompous about going specially to Edinburgh to get an outfit for the baby. Say something silly and Monica remembers it for ever. Twins, just fancy!'

I went on talking compulsively, building a tomb of words over my fears of the forenoon and even during the funeral service at the Great House, I was thinking with what devoted care we construct our fears, our anxieties, our unhappiness. On the morning that Percy had shown the first sign of recovery, I had feared for Tom and George. Surely, after the death of Miss Poynter, the converse should have applied? Logically, I should have expected good news to counterbalance the bad but I had not and the fact that I had not made me deeply ashamed.

When the service was over and the cortège had left for the burial ground, Madame said: 'I shall miss poor dear Maud. She was a very irritating quarrelsome woman but I shall miss her none the less.' She now turned away from the dead towards the living and the young. 'It was nice of you to be present today, Percy, my dear. We have been seeing less of you lately but then you are very busy with the cricket teas and the housekeeping for the young engineers that Janet has been telling me about. I do not really approve of those young men living alone in that bungalow but what is one to do? They are not sufficiently established to marry. I must say, though, that the present ones are very steady sensible young men compared with some we have had in the past and Ian and I are delighted with Mr. Mackie, Janet. He took off a highly successful crop. Only, he ought to be married. In his position, he ought to have a hostess in his establishment instead of living like a hermit.' The disapproval left her face as she turned once more to Percy. 'I am so glad that you are enjoying your time here with us, my dear, and are you still finding suitable subjects for your sketching?'

Madame, by and large, did not approve of the arts or, rather, she did not approve of living artists who, she said, tended to be 'most peculiar'. After an artist had been dead for a length of time, like Shakespeare, he attained a certain respectability in Madame's mind, although much of his work might still be deemed improper and in questionable taste. Madame, for instance, found Cleopatra very ill-behaved and lascivious, especially for a queen, even although she had lived many centuries ago when the proprieties were held in less regard. Sketching, however, she regarded as a most suitable leisure occupation for a young lady.

Percy having assured her that she found no lack of subjects, Madame went on: 'A very pleasant pastime, my dear, but not a lifetime's occupation. Of course, I am old-fashioned. I like young ladies to marry and have homes and children.'

'I would like to have a home and children one day, Madame,' Percy told her.

'I am delighted to hear it and I hope that the day may not be too far away,' Madame said with satisfaction.

Fleetingly, I thought of Hugh Macbeth from Retreat and wondered if Madame's satisfaction would hold, should he be Percy's choice. I thought not for, the stigma of Retreat apart, Hugh was not what she called 'established', but another junior like the denizens of Bachelors' Bungalow. Madame, like most of her class and generation, had a nose for wealth; she knew that Percy was financially independent and was no doubt visualising for her some young man of similar means.

As I listened to them talk, I realised that Madame, with her views on marriage, was not as old-fashioned as she claimed to be, but contemporary with Percy. It was I, bridging the two generations between them, who was old-fashioned, for another cycle of time had completed itself and Percy was a member of the new generation who, like Madame, saw 'a home and babies' as her goal. When I had been Percy's age, I think I visualised marriage as a last resort more than anything, for did I not have the 'Flapper Vote' as it was called and a new freedom which women of former generations had never had? I had not been a 'career woman', as Percy's mother had been, because I had been gifted with neither the drive nor the acumen for financial success but I felt that I had had an approach to life similar to hers.

But Percy was a representative of the new wave that had come to my notice during my holiday in Scotland, the young people who married early, the boy not waiting to be 'established in life', the girl not waiting to collect a 'bottom drawer'.

When Madame had dealt with Percy's future to her satisfaction, she began to talk on her favourite subject, the past, describing to Percy the island and its society as they had been sixty years ago and while the girl listened, making a short comment or asking a question now and then, I had the sensation of being not part of the group in this room but of being an observer merely, not present here of my own will, even, but because, especially on this day of her old friend's funeral, Madame had to have company and I happened to be available.

Twice and Sir Ian returned just as Madame's butler brought in tea, Sir Ian stimulated as he always was by any event that gathered a few people together.

'A fine funeral, Mother,' he said, sitting down beside Madame. 'People turned out very well for old Maud. All the Retreat lot were waiting for us at the Bay – very neighbourly of them. Somebody there from every estate in the island and quite a few from the town. It was very decent o' Sashie an' young Candlesham to come right up here for the service, very decent indeed.'

'Very proper, Ian,' Madame corrected him. 'They bought the Peak property from Maud, after all.'

I thought of Monica and her love for words and of how she and I would probably have held a discussion on the curious link between the words 'proper' and 'property' in Madame's mind.

'—an' Sykes was there,' Sir Ian was continuing his account of all the people who had joined the funeral at the burial ground, 'drunk, of course. He's never sober. He'll die o' it one o' these days. Funny thing, when we were singin' the last hymn I was lookin' at him an' it came to me that people die o' the things they like best quite often – their weaknesses, if ye like, like Maud dyin' o' eatin' too much lunch yesterday. Always too fond o' her stomach, old Maud.'

'That will do, Ian,' said Madame sternly, indicating her liking for facts about funerals as opposed to philosophy about them, which was her attitude to most things.

The funeral, as Sashie harshly but truly said, had provided a twenty-four hour diversion from the cricket and before he left for London a few days later, I said: 'On the day of the funeral, Sir Ian said the Retreat people were neighbourly but now he is calling them those perishers again. Don't stay in London too long, Sashie. Remember my spiritual loneliness in this cricket-mad world.'

'Ought I to bring us back a little manual on the subject to lighten our ignorance?'

'No. Let us remain outcasts, burning our own little candles in our own little corners.'

There was less time to spend in my own little corner in the back bedroom now, however, for Madame required more of my time.

'When I took on this appointment,' Twice said, 'you

declared that you did not want to be involved and you are not involved. You don't *have* to spend half your life at the Great House.'

'I said I did not want to be involved with sugar politics and oil men from the States. I did not say that I did not want to be involved with life as I have to live it. My going to the Great House is nothing to do with your appointment, darling.'

'But I feel that I have landed you with it.'

'You have, in a way, I suppose. If I had never met you, I would never have met Madame but there it is. It has happened.'

Perhaps once a week, Twice salved his conscience with a speech such as this but I knew that behind it all he preferred to think of me sitting with Madame than to think of me pursuing my incomprehensible activities in the back bedroom.

Percy was very helpful. After she had attended to her bungalow duties, she would go round and read the newspaper to Madame who did not come downstairs until eleven and she would pay an afternoon visit or two during the week as well, on the understanding that I would free her for the cricket on Saturdays and Sundays. The young people from the Mission continued to come around the Great House too and now we arranged that they telephone me before their visits so that I need not attend unless it was necessary.

'But it won't do, ye know,' Sir Ian said. 'I appreciate what ye are doin' for Mother, me dear, but you got your own place to attend to. I got to get somebody to be with her.'

What I dreaded was that Madame might come to regard herself as a burden to the rest of us. I found myself in curious situation. I was not fond of Madame although, in some ways, I admired her and I did not dislike her, although I could be critical of her prejudices and her arrogance. She was more of a symbol or an institution than a personality in my mind, something that demanded a certain service from me in return for past benefits to Twice and myself and for another more obscure reason. It was as if my sacrifice of my time to the needs of Madame were an act of faith by which, somehow, George and Tom would be protected and cherished when they grew old, not in years for they were old in years now, but old in life also. Strong as was the call of my work upstairs each afternoon, the call of Madame was stronger and as has always been my way, I did the thing that called to me most strongly. When Twice made something of a parade of fulminating against Madame's grandson, Edward 'for larking around London and Paris' and against Sir Ian for asking me to do duty all day on a Sunday while he went to the cricket, I merely laughed out of a carefree certainty that Tom and George would be 'all right'.

It was now about the middle of August and Retreat, having come out of Crop at the same time as Paradise, was going through the cricket tournament like Attila, the Scourge of God. The Retreat Crop had been the annual calendar of disasters, with crisis after crisis, factory shut-down after shut-down but, as always, enough sugar had been milled to keep the estate from bankruptcy and the staff was now at large, scouring the island in battered old cars, beating one cricket team after another with a sort of remorseless nonchalance. They fascinated the supporters of other teams as a weasel fascinates rabbits, so that on any weekend that the Paradise team had no fixture, Twice, Sir Ian, Mackie, Percy and Caleb were irresistibly drawn along in the wake of the Retreat eleven. It was masochism of a kind, for Retreat invariably won and they would all come home in the depths of depression.

'It would fit them better,' Twice said with hideous smugness after watching them beat Happy Vale, 'if they gave less time to cricket and a bit more to cleaning up that junk-heap they call a factory.'

'That Retreat fellah that caught Ferguson of Happy Vale, ma'am,' Caleb complained to me in the garden the next morning, 'only caught him 'cause he stands six feet ten.'

'Who? Ferguson?'

Caleb looked at me sadly. 'No, ma'am, the Retreat fellah. With his arms as well, he is half-a-chain long. That ain't cricket – that's just size, ma'am.'

Twice, Caleb and indeed all the rest of the island kept hoping that by some miracle, some team would beat Retreat. That Paradise was also winning its way up the tournament did not seem to matter. But the ill-wishing brought no result. In spite of the brakes of the Retreat's spin-bowler's car failing one Saturday on the gorge road and precipitating car, bowler and four others of the team into the Rio d'Oro, they climbed unhurt up the precipice, a passing lorry gave them a lift and they arrived, sitting on top of a load of cabbages, in time to beat the team of Mahogany Grove.

The cricket did produce one concrete and beneficent result, however. On a Sunday when Retreat had no fixture and the supporters had watched Paradise win at Mount Ararat, Sir Ian came into the library of the Great House in the evening in high fettle. Having described the match in detail to Madame, he said: 'An' ye know who I met up at the Mount, Mother? Millie Spencer. She's retired. Stayin' with the Talbots at Green Springs. They came over to the match, brought her with them.'

'It is high time Millie Spencer retired, Ian,' Madame said. 'She must be nearly seventy. Nursing in hospitals in New York at her age, ridiculous!'

'Millie ain't anythin' like seventy, Mother, an' you know it. Millie's a goodish bit younger'n me. Nice little woman. Told the Talbots to bring her over to lunch on Wednesday. Thought you'd enjoy a chat with her.'

Madame changed her tune. 'Indeed I shall, Ian. That will be very pleasant.'

'Thought we might ask her here for a bit when she leaves the Talbots. She ain't settled anywhere. No home, as it were. Hasn't made up her mind whether to settle here or go back to the States.'

'We shall see, Ian,' Madame said warily, but Miss Spencer came to lunch on the following Wednesday and came to stay at the Great House the following week.

On the day that Miss Spencer was to arrive to release me from the forenoons at the Great House, there also arrived what I chose to regard as a good omen in the form of a letter from my niece Liz.

'Dear Aunt Janet, This is to tell of the Great Events of Sandy Tom's first birthday and his party which was me, Dunk and Gee, George and Tom, Granny, Roddy and Aunt Sheila, Fat Mary and Dad and Mum and Fly and Betsy were there in spirit although outside and Uncle Twice and you although in St. Jago. Dunk and Gee and I but it was mostly me wrote an Ode on the Birthday of Alexander Thomas and this is it:

Behold, Reachfar, the youngest of thy race,
Upon thy starboard quarter see his year-old face!'

'Hold it,' said Twice. 'Why starboard quarter, do you think?'

'Who am I to analyse the mind of a poet?' I asked. 'Actually, I should think it is simply a phrase that has caught her fancy.' I continued my reading while Twice and Percy gave me their fascinated attention: 'Goodness, I cannot write it all in this letter. It would make it too heavy.'

'She is darned right it would,' I interpolated and went on: 'He had a chocolate cake with glop in the middle and one candle and after tea when the boys and I were doing the Ode, the bees swarmed and went buzzing past the window and over the roof and out over the glebe and back again and settled under the hood of Sandy Tom's pram out in the garden. So we have two hives of bees now but the party came to a grinding halt because Tom and George got angry about the stinging wee boogers maybe that is not spelled properly Mum says there is no such word landing in Sandy Tom's pram. We meant to send you some cake like brides do but we ate it all but we thought of you when we were eating it. Best love to Uncle Twice from Elizabeth, Duncan, George, X Alexander Thomas (his mark).'

'I wish I could write a letter like that,' Percy said.

'Liz informed me when she was three years old that the Sandisons are a very reading and writing family,' Twice told her.

'Sandy Tom's mark is really his mark this time,' I said, looking at the heavy but wobbly cross. 'That awful Liz would have held his poor little fist.'

Sandy Tom suddenly took on for me the quality of a little yardstick, a small marker that put the vast stretch of my lifetime into perspective. He was one year old, we were all one year older, it was a year since I had first held him in my arms, two days old, in the room at the hospital. Where had that year gone? I looked at Twice and Percy, laughing as they chatted across the corner of the table. Time goes unmarked when people are happy.

Although it often seemed to me at this time that life contained nothing but cricket, this was not so. Sashie returned from his trip to London and arrived at Guinea Corner the following forenoon, just as I was coming down from the back bedroom.

'I am so glad you are back,' I greeted him. 'Stay for lunch.'

'Thank you, darling, if I shan't be in the way. I brought you a tiny gift.' He handed me a package. 'Don't open it now. Later.'

'All right.' I ran my fingers over the wrapping. 'A book? Thank you, Sashie.'

'Two books, one for fun and one for information.'

'Information? *Not* a handbook on cricket?'

'Certainly not. Don't be obscene. Is the fever as bad as ever?'

'Worse, but I don't mind as long as everybody is happy.' I brought him up to date on small events such as the arrival of Miss Spencer at the Great House until Percy came back, then Twice who brought Mackie with him. Twice was frowning as he poured lemonade and Mackie, as if trying to be helpful, said: 'The plans are complete and we'll get the shipment up from the Bay tomorrow, sir. We are just into September. There is plenty of time.'

'Yes, plenty of time,' Twice agreed in an abstracted fashion and went through to his study.

'What are you two building *now*?' Sashie enquired in a mock-irritable voice.

'It's this water filtration plant,' Mackie said and stood looking in the direction that Twice had gone until suddenly he reappeared.

'You know what?' he said explosively as if something had to be said now or never, 'I don't like this bloody plan we've got, Mackie.'

'Don't you like the plan, sir?'

'No, I don't. You have put a lot of work into it and I'm sorry but we've made a mistake.' He strode along to the east end of the veranda and pointed to the factory. 'Look at that complex. It looks right and it *is* right. It looks good from every side and if a thing looks good it usually is good. Now—' he looked wildly around him, saw Percy's sketchbook and a thick black crayon on a table, seized them and drew a sketch of the outline of the factory in a few seconds '—we are going to have this filter tower sticking up *there*—' the crayon-point hit the paper. 'It's wrong. It should be *here*' and he drew in the tower on the other side of the smoke-stack. The finished sketch made the outline of the factory look more like a ship than ever.

'But the reservoir, sir—'

'The *old* reservoir. We'll build a new one and use the old one as a settling pond before re-filtering.' He threw the crayon on to the table. 'If we are careful, we needn't go much over our original estimate. Sir Ian will fall in all right. Come on.' He was making for the study.

'You fall in for lunch, Twice Alexander,' I said.

He blinked at me, coming back from the distance. 'Yes, in a minute. I just want to give Mackie a sketch I made last night.'

'Ten minutes at the most,' I said.

'Yes,' said Percy, 'or your lunch will be ruined too, Bruce.'

Sashie went to the table and looked down at the sketch. 'Percy, darling,' he said, 'here you have the skeleton of a work of art.' He moved his small hands palm downwards in the air above the rough sketch with a smooth sweeping gesture. 'That is drawn from the inside outwards, with knowledge and with love.' He held the block up in front of me. 'Twice is more of an artist than he knows,' he said.

'Then don't tell him,' I said. 'He would never forgive you.'

'He would think you were potty,' Percy said and she seemed to indicate that she would agree with Twice before she picked up the block and went upstairs.

'When does your furniture arrive?' I asked Sashie now.

'Already at sea, I hope, my sweet. Ten days, a fortnight? And then, if you like, you and I shall have fun. While they all go to cricket, we shall turn Silver Beach into a gentleman's residence, shall we?'

'I'd like that, Sashie.'

He went away immediately after lunch and Twice could not get back to the factory quickly enough to set about the measuring for the new drawings for the re-siting of the filter tower.

'What I like is how Twice makes up his mind,' Percy said. 'I don't like this bloody plan we've got, Mackie,' she mimicked. 'All that work they have done, all these plans they have drawn and he throws them in the dustbin just like that.'

'I don't see that as so very admirable,' I said. 'It would

have been better if he had had his idea *before* they had drawn a complete set of plans.'

'It must have been quite hard to make up his mind to scrap them though.'

'I don't think so. To go on with the original ones would have been what he calls painting them red and making them do.'

I explained the origin of this phrase to her, whereupon she said: 'It is quite easy to paint a thing red and make it do. If it had been me, I'd have gone on with the first plans, probably. Would you like me to go round to Madame this afternoon?'

'I should be very glad if there is nothing else you want to do.'

'Not a thing,' she said. 'I'll go up and put on a dress. It is queer about Madame. You feel she would *know* if you had the cheek to visit her wearing shorts.'

When she had gone, I went to the back bedroom and opened the package that Sashie had given me. It contained a new novel and a thickish volume that bore the title: 'Writers' Index 1957'. It was an alphabetical list of publishers, literary agents, magazines and periodicals, that gave information about all who were interested in marketing the written word. I put it into a drawer of the table and picked up my pen.

By the end of September, not only were the new filter plans completed but much of the piping had been laid and the tower itself was rising above the roofs of the lower factory buildings, reminiscent of the bridge of a ship. The tower was of open steel-work and looked pleasantly airy compared with the black solidity of the smokestack.

And the cricket fever was raging as high as ever but I suffered less from it now for, with Miss Spencer at the Great House, I was free to spend Saturdays and Sundays at Silver Beach with Sashie and Twice, with Percy, Mackie and Caleb who seemed to constitute our family, would come too if there was no cricket match.

Sashie brought Liza, the old seamstress from the hotel along with him at weekends, together with her sewing-machine and gradually curtains went up at the windows. I had never seen in any private house furniture more beautiful than the eighteenth-century pieces that Sashie had brought out from London and as we arranged room after room, the house became ever more gracious and ever, in a curious way, more typical of its owner. It had the effect of scaring Mackie, who was more comfortable among the wicker and canvas of the veranda and Percy said that she thought it a 'bit effeminate' and was a little put out that Twice did not agree with her. She seemed to have difficulty in accepting the breadth of his shoulders and his humour alongside his eye for design. Mackie was more of whole cloth and his attitude was easier for her to understand. Caleb, of course, was interested only in the out-of-doors and with the help of some of the boys from the Peak, the walled garden adjacent to the house was coming under his control. The coconut walk was now established, and more and more young green fronds rising from the grass each week and in the far corner where the old spring had been, the jungly bush had been rooted out and what I called a 'Caleb Corner' was developing.

We had a similar place at Guinea Corner, a trial ground, where Caleb planted bread-fruit trees, avocado pear trees, varieties of citrus and bananas, cho-cho vines, anything he could acquire on his trips to his home at Missy Rosie's or on his visits to his Uncle Abel. Any plant that thrived in the Caleb Corner was in time and season transferred to a chosen spot in the main garden. It was in this way that the Guinea Corner garden had developed in its fertile variety and Caleb was now setting Sashie's garden on a similar course. He also began to develop a vegetable garden on either side of the stream which had been dry at the time that Percy found the spring but where now water burbled over the stones. At this time of year, there was rain on the heights of the Sierra Grande and the little watercourse was bringing Sashie his share of it. As Caleb had said, Silver Beach was a sweet property that seemed to be endowed with the best the island could give.

'What have we here, Caleb?' Sashie asked as he watched him sow seed in the fine alluvial tilth by the stream.

'Trying some lettuces and some carrots, sah. There is good money in lettuces and carrots.'

'The thing I admire so much in Caleb,' Sashie said as we walked away, 'is that he is such a professional.'

'A professional? The good money touch, you mean? I should have thought that the last thing you wanted to do with this place is to make money out of it.'

'The good money is only Caleb's way of putting it. Lettuces and carrots are high on the market here because they are difficult to grow well but Caleb doesn't go for an easier crop that will sell for less. My definition of the true professional is the man who is like David in the Old Testament when he danced before the Lord with all his might. Caleb gardens with all his might. I do so dislike the dilettante who does a little at this, fiddles about with that and has no might to put into anything.' I was amused, although I tried not to show it, for Sashie, as he presented himself to the world was everyman's conception of the dilettante. He did a little at music, fiddled about with oil painting and was now spending a great deal of time and money on an experiment in interior decoration.

'I rather admire the dilettante type myself,' I said. 'By the way, how is your collection of island songs going? I am out of touch since your piano came down here.'

'I sold the collection of Working Songs when I was in London,' he astonished me by saying. 'Well, sold is not the right word. I signed a contract for their publication. Quite soon, I hope to give Caleb a little something for his bankbook.'

'Sashie, you simply cannot help making money, can you?'

'I am a pro, like Caleb, my sweet.'

'You saw money in those songs from the start?'

'Not exactly. I wrote them down in the first place because I liked them and wanted to write them down. But not being the dilettante type, darling, just to write the songs down was not enough. I see no point in doing a lot of work and then hiding it under a bushel. I had to put what I had done to the test and the test in a money society is to try to sell your work for money.'

'Are you saying that nothing is worth doing unless you can get money for it?'

'Not precisely. What I do say is that nothing is a contribution to a money society unless one can get money for it and I see myself as a contributing type, if that is not too uppish of me. By next year, I hope that Caleb and I will be able to contribute our collection of Religious Songs.'

'For a suitable sum, of course?'

'But naturally, my sweet. We are professionals and not too cowardly to put our work on test in the market-place.'

'A very high-falutin way of saying that you like to make money,' I said irritably.

'You must remember that it all begins with our liking for the songs. If we did not like them enough to work on them without hope of reward, like casting bread upon the waters, I am convinced that nobody would pay us money for them. Paradoxical, isn't it?'

'Nonsensical would be a better word,' I told him but I felt a curious mental discomfort and dissatisfaction that set me to brooding darkly in a corner of the veranda with my needlework when I was alone at Guinea Corner.

I was fairly sure that Sashie talked to me more than he did to any other person I knew and that he revealed more of himself to me than he did to others, but, at the same time, I never knew where I stood in relation to him. And something in what he had said that day haunted me, striking a peculiar sort of echo, almost a note of accusation. The conversation had taken place casually enough, arising as it had out of Caleb's lettuces and carrots and yet in retrospect it did not seem casual but to have a double-edged significance. Perhaps, I told myself, the biblical expressions that Sashie had used, sounding echoes of many sermons heard at church when I was a child, had given what he had said a false importance. David danced before the Lord with all his might. Hiding it under a bushel. The market-place. Bread upon the waters. I have a fairly good aural memory and I went over what had been said many times and at last I sat facing, as if they stood before me modelled in concrete, the words: '—not too cowardly to put our work on test in the market-place'.

Guiltily I recognised that the linen cupboard upstairs might in one sense be called a bushel, for there were four parcels of manuscript on its shelves now. Were they there because I was a coward? Was I a mere fiddler-about with pen and paper? This last was not true. My might was nothing much, perhaps, but I had written with all the might I had and as my father had often said, one cannot do better than one's best. Was I a coward then? Yes, I was. I was afraid to be told that it was bad. I stood up in my corner, threw aside the needlework, strode forward as if breaking through those concrete words that had formed in front of me and went upstairs. Neither Sashie de Marnay nor anyone else was going to call me a coward. I fetched my typewriter, took it to the back bedroom and turned two sheets of paper with a sheet of carbon between into the roller. Then I took a parcel at random from the shelf of the linen cupboard and began to turn manuscript that was legible only to myself into typescript that some distant unknown in some market-place could read. I found this preparation to cast bread upon the waters a very pleasant occupation.

About mid-October, there came a cricket match which, all the sportsmen hoped, would knock Retreat out of the tournament for good. This was their fixture against Pasture Plains, an estate at the other end of the island which, along with Retreat and Paradise made up the big three of the cricket world. Paradise was still in the tournament, of course, but this to the sportsmen was of no account. Nobody cared any longer which teams played the final as long as Retreat was not one of them.

Caleb, who had been out with his friends on the Saturday night before the match, cheered everybody on the Sunday morning with a rumour that Crockett, the Retreat bowler and deadly fielder who, arms included, was half-a-chain long, had fallen in the factory during the week and dislocated his shoulder.

'Which shoulder?' Sir Ian asked, making sure.

'The left one, sah.'

'By Jove, that ought to do it!' said Sir Ian. 'Come along. Time we were off.'

I spent the day at Silver Beach and when I came home in the evening, I knew as soon as I got out of Sashie's car that the worst had happened for Sir Ian, Twice, Percy and Mackie were lying flaccid in chairs on the veranda while Caleb was watering the garden, the hose drooping from his hand as if shedding tears.

'Who won?' I asked of the heavy silence.

'Bah!' said Sir Ian disgustedly.

'In spite of Crockett's dislocated shoulder?' I enquired, showing intelligent and sympathetic interest with my way of it.

'Dislocated nothing,' Sir Ian barked at me. 'He was there large as life an' twice as ugly. Wasn't him that fell. Some labourer or another. People who start these rumours should be shot.'

The next day, while we worked in the garden, Caleb gave me a gloomy blow by blow description of the match from which I gathered that the several boundaries scored by Retreat were not cricket at all but 'just brute force ma'am an' no style', that all the wickets taken by Crockett were not cricket either but had fallen to his immoral cunning and that the same Crockett caught Pasture Plains' best batsman because 'His arm, ma'am, it about as long as the crane boom an' his hand about the size of a cane sling'. Indeed, according to Caleb, Crockett being more of a gorilla than a 'nat'ral human man' should not be allowed to play cricket at all. Finally, in a voice that tried to be scornful but succeeded in being envious, Caleb said: '*And* they brought the lemonade on to the field in a cart, ma'am.'

'In a cart, Caleb?'

'Yes ma'am, a proper cute little soft-drinks cart with wheels an' everything.'

At lunch, I said to Twice: 'It seems that for Caleb the final insult of yesterday's débâcle at Retreat was that they brought the lemonade on to the field in a hand-cart.'

'So they did,' he agreed, 'and I wish you had seen it – an old wooden box on a perambulator chassis. One of the wheels fell off when they were taking it back to the pavilion. Macbeth should be damn' well ashamed of himself, letting a thing like that out of his workshops. But it was typical of the whole place. They use their transport yard as a car park and we could hardly get into it for old tractor tyres and junk.'

I thought of the transport yard at Paradise with its regimented rows of tractors, trailers and trucks, each one parked on its own numbered spot and said: 'Still, they had the idea of the hand-cart instead of a lot of people rushing about with jugs.'

'Not much point in having an idea if its wheels fall off and break half the glasses. But Macbeth is the grand high master of the pent-it-ridd-an-mak-it-dae-school,' Twice said.

Several matches remained to be played but they had no urgency or interest for the spectators. The defeat of Pasture Plains had made inevitable the Paradise-Retreat final that everybody, throughout the season, had tried so hard not to expect.

'Anyway,' said Caleb, 'the final will be on *our* ground this year an' not on that carved-up old cane piece o' theirs up at Retreat.' I should have mentioned earlier that the Retreat cricket ground was recognised by one and all as so unsporting that it played for its own side.

The cricket now died down to comparative calm but only the calm which preceded the storm that would break out over the final at about mid-December and Mackie, instead of spending sporting Saturdays and Sundays, put on overtime shifts at the weekends and pressed on with the water filtration plant, while Twice sat on the veranda at home with his small drawing-board on his knees. 'Having altered the shape of the entire factory, what are you getting up to *now*?' Sashie enquired one Saturday forenoon.

Twice laughed. 'The mighty fall, Sashie,' he said. 'I am designing a lemonade barrow.'

I dropped my needlework. 'Twice Alexander, you can't be serious!'

'I was never more serious in my life. Sir Ian wants a lemonade barrow for the Final. Have you any of those cheap mass-produced tumblers in the house like the ones round at the Club?'

'In the bathrooms. Why?'

'Fetch me one and save me from getting out from under all this clobber, will you?'

'What for? There are glasses here for the drinks.'

He sighed. 'I want to measure it, you ass.'

I fetched the tumbler and handed it to him while Sashie stared in amazement.

'You don't understand, Sashie,' I said. 'You are too old and grown-up. This lemonade barrow has to be the lemonade barrow to end all lemonade barrows. Retreat has a lemonade barrow so Paradise has to have one too and a bigger, better, fancier one, so there! *Our* lemonade barrow is better than your lemonade barrow, yah, yah, hay! Ach, Twice, it is too too childish!'

He had measured the tumbler and he now set it

aside. 'Remember the morning we went into Crop?' he asked.

'Yes. Why?'

'You made me change my stocking because there was a small hole in the heel. You said it was your contribution.' He rolled his pencil between his fingers and pointed it at the drawing on the board. 'This is Sir Ian's and my contribution.'

'I see,' I said.

'And say nicely that you are sorry,' Sashie said to me in his old nannie's voice.

'Actually, I am sorry. I am very sorry I was bitchy about it, Twice.'

'Think nothing of it. You can be bitchy to me any time.'

'Only I shouldn't go too far if I were you, darling,' Sashie told me mischievously before going out to the back of the house to see Caleb.

The cooler weather had come now, bringing with it the wealthy tourists of the winter season and Caleb and his guitar were once again on duty at the hotel. Quite frequently, now too, Caleb went home to Silver Beach with Sashie on Saturday nights so that, on Sundays, he could inspect the cultivation and he and Sashie could work at their collection of religious songs. They were an odd-looking pair but they were genuine friends. About the middle of October, the water filtration plant was complete and ready for test.

'There isn't much point,' I said. 'The water is pretty clean just now.'

'We are going to couple up just the same,' Twice told me, 'and hope that Minna will have no complaints when the November rains bring the silt down.'

'You don't know Minna. She will find something to complain about. It didn't take you and Mackie long to knock that thing together though,' I complimented him.

'It was mostly Mackie. He goes like all hell when he

gets his teeth into a thing. And he will get a bit of leave now after all. He can go home for December if he wants to. The place is in good shape.'

'December on Clydeside – g-r-r-r- Still, it is time he saw his people, especially his mother.'

When the filtration plant had passed its test, Mackie celebrated by stopping the weekend working and suggested that they should all attend a cricket match being played somewhere that Saturday. It was a minor match and Twice said: 'Not for me, thanks. It is too long a trek.'

'I have to be at the Peak by eight o'clock, sah,' said Caleb, disappointed.

'I could drop you there on the way back,' Mackie said and he, Percy and Caleb set off.

Twice and I had gone in to lunch when the telephone rang and I answered it.

'Mrs. Alexander? Hugh Macbeth here. Is Percy there?'

'No,' I said, was about to add that she had gone to the match and thought the better of it. 'She went out.'

'Oh. I am at Maxie's.' This was a snack bar in St. Jago Bay. 'She was to meet me at one. It's all right. She'll turn up.' Oh confident youth, I thought, replacing the receiver and to Twice at the table I said: 'That little brat has stood Hugh Macbeth up. He is waiting for her at Maxie's.'

'She must have forgotten,' Twice said.

Oh charitable father, I thought, if you knew young women like I know young women but I said nothing aloud.

The next forenoon, Sunday, when Twice had gone to pay a call on Madame, I said to Percy: 'Hugh Macbeth rang at lunchtime yesterday.'

'Oh, Hugh,' she said, as if he were a distant memory from long, long ago although I knew she had been out dancing with him only two evenings before.

'He said you were to meet him at Maxie's.'

'I rang Retreat before we left. There was no reply.

There's no harm done,' she said and went out into the garden.

Like 'that lot up at Retreat' I thought, young women have no conscience and dismissing the matter from my mind I went upstairs and rattled away on my typewriter until lunchtime.

Twice and I were drinking the usual lemonade when Mackie's car came up the drive. Mackie often had a glass of beer with us on Sundays before lunch and now Percy came downstairs to complete the party.

'Hello, Mackie. Beer?' I said.

'There is something I want to say first, Missis Janet.' He turned from me to look at Twice and I noticed that Mackie was suddenly 'the same only different'. He was as long and bony and gangling as ever, yet subtly different. Suddenly, he put his right arm round Percy so that she dangled in the air, head to the front, feet to the back. 'This is my baggage, sir,' he said, 'and we want to get married.'

I had never seen such joy on Twice's face since the morning long ago when I had told him that I was pregnant with the child that never came to birth. His lower lip trembled, his eyes filled and his knuckles showed white as he gripped the arms of his chair in his effort to control himself. I stepped between him and the young people, hiding him as I faced them and said: 'I don't think I have ever been more pleased about anything in my whole life.'

'Nor me neither, forbye and besides,' Twice said in the idiom of our friend Tom as he got up and came forward.

Mackie set Percy on her feet and looked down at the top of her head as if she were something that he had made with his own hands and was inordinately pleased with, while Percy looked at Twice and me with a shy expectancy, as if she were meeting us for the first time and hoped that we would like her.

While we chattered and laughed, I found myself thinking that there was, indeed, in a relationship much of what was showing in Percy and Mackie now. Mackie had indeed induced a change in Percy by making her over to conform to some image in his own mind and Percy had altered Mackie by convincing him that what had been a dream image was a reality. This subtle mutation of personality seemed to be an integral part of the complex relationship which we call love. The loved one subconsciously tries to become the person the lover desires and the separate identities of each go into abeyance to some extent but, at the same time, an extension rather than a diminution of the individual personalities is achieved.

Madame, of course, was delighted at the engagement and seemed suddenly to shed about ten years of her age, to become once more the dominant old woman I had met when I first came to the island. 'We must have a dinner party in celebration, Janet,' she said. 'I have been saying that I cannot cope with large numbers but that is just laziness. I should like to give the party here. We have been getting into more and more of a rut recently and it is not good for the servants to lay the table for three night after night. They will get so that they cannot lay it except for three. Now, we shall have the young people of the Health Mission and the estate staff of course. Fetch paper from the office, dear, and let us make a list.'

The list, by the time Madame had finished with it, contained over fifty names and at this point I had speech with Sir Ian.

'I think a formal dinner of this size is too much for Madame,' I said, 'and these youngsters have probably never been to a formal party in their lives. Their idea of a party is a few bottles of beer and coke, some sandwiches and a record-player. Don't you think you could talk Madame into a buffet lunch like the thing we had at Guinea Corner after I came back from Scotland?'

'I can try. I suppose you are right. The youngsters certainly enjoyed that day at your place.'

'And it would be all over by four or five o'clock.'

'Yes. I'll see what I can do, me dear.'

At first, Madame was displeased but was brought round by Sir Ian's argument that it was necessary to move with the times. We did not dare to use the more cogent argument that her household staff, the youngest of whom was over fifty, were no longer capable of mounting the entertainments that had been given at the Great House in the past.

'Very well,' she said in the end. 'The young people must have what they enjoy. It is their party, after all. Cold food and salads, you say? How very dull but very well.'

In the end, Sashie and some of his staff drove up to the back door of the Great House early in the morning before Madame was downstairs and unloaded the food for the party into the cold room.

When it took place, the party had a dual character for it was not only a celebration party but a farewell party for the Health Mission who had completed their work and were to leave the island at the end of November. Originally, it had been intended that they should spend only a year in St. Jago but the aftermath of the earthquake had caused delays in the early stages and their tour had been extended by three months.

'You will find it rough landing in Liverpool in December,' I said to Mary Crockford.

'After this, I won't stay in Liverpool for long. I like this mission work,' she told me. 'I'll join one for India or Africa or somewhere.'

The world lay before them, within their reach in a way it had never been when I was young.

'Lucky thing,' I said, 'flying about all over the place.'

'Selina and I are going to sail back to England,' she said. 'We are booked on a banana boat. We have never sailed before and flying is so boring.'

I remembered the pioneering days of Colonel Lindbergh and Amy Johnson, the flights that were my generation's idea of high adventure and marvelled at how short was the time it took for high adventure to become merely boring.

'We are going to miss you all,' I said, feeling that I was old and being left behind in more than one way by this new generation.

'Percy will still be here,' Mary said. 'It is terrific that she should have found a place where she fits. She has always been a sort of loner, even when she was at school. Even then she was a here-today-and-gone-tomorrow sort of person, as if she felt she didn't really belong anywhere, as if she were always searching for something she couldn't find.'

'She seems to have found it in Mackie – Bruce, I mean,' I said. 'And he is the happiest of fellows.'

'Queer how things happen. I hadn't seen Percy for ages before that day I met her down in the Bay. I hadn't seen her since school. Selina and I were just saying last night that when we brought her here to Paradise, we had no idea we were bringing her here for good. They will go on living in the house Bruce is in now, won't they?'

'Yes,' I said, visualising the house.

'School Bungalow' as it used to be known stood well back from the park on a little loop of road that served only itself. It had been so placed to ensure that the children of the Compound in those earlier days could not run out of the gate into the danger of the old cane carts which were drawn by teams of six oxen, far more difficult to control than modern tractors. Seeing the house in my mind, I suddenly thought: 'It is a bungalow with cushions of blue flowers in the rockery' which was true for School Bungalow was surrounded by low clumps of plumbago, growing wild among outcrops of stone, for neither of the Yates were gardeners. Their yard boy mowed the grass and grew a few vegetables at the back of the house and that was all.

I do not believe that people can ever go back and perhaps this accounted for my uneasy moment as I looked across the room at Percy and thought of her parentage.

Her father, I felt, would have been content with the bungalow, the blue flowers and the 'bunch of babies' that Percy had spoken of with reference to herself but, for her mother, this way of life had been written off in the words 'that awful bungalow'. Percy, as I had come to know her, seemed to display an evenly balanced mixture of inherited traits. She said that physically she resembled her father but she showed much of the acumen in her money affairs that must have been characteristic of her mother. She had inherited the gift for drawing from her father but since the time when she had decided that the docks were 'silly and boring', as her mother might have dismissed some unpractical activity, she was using her sketch-book and pencil less. The question rose in my mind. Were the bungalow, the blue flowers, even the bunch of babies what Percy wanted? I shook my shoulders, shedding the question and the doubt.

'Selina is madly pleased with herself,' Mary was saying. 'She says that but for us Percy would never have met Bruce but I am not so sure.'

'Neither am I but I am sure of one thing. It did not *begin* with you and Selina. But for the earthquake, you people would never have come to Olympus at all.'

Mary giggled. 'The Teeth and Feet Lot,' she said. 'We all call ourselves that now.'

Christie had returned from leave in the middle of October, Vickers had then gone on leave and would be back early in January but the factory was now ready to go into Crop and Mackie decided that he and Percy would fly home to Scotland in the first days of December and be married from his home there.

'It will be a bit of a whirlwind,' he said, 'but my mother will like it.'

'It needn't be such a whirlwind,' Twice told him. 'Christie and Brown and I can take this place into Crop if need be.'

'Twice won't really push the wrong button and blow the factory up, Mackie,' I said.

'It isn't that. It is just that I feel I ought to be here and Percy doesn't mind, do you?'

'Not me,' said Percy. 'I like it here.'

She suddenly seemed to be older, more sedate, used her sketchbook now to write down curtain measurements and make notes about her new home. Sir Ian had made her free of the cellars at the Great House with their hoard of furniture and she spent a lot of time there, labelling pieces that she would like to have. She was quietly and thoughtfully happy as she made her plans and from her and Mackie at the centre, the happiness radiated to the rest of us, making of the November rain season, which was usually a dreary fretful time, a sort of halcyon summer when all was fair and good.

Mary and Selina were to sail on the day before Percy and Mackie were to fly to Scotland and Percy went down to St. Jago Bay to see them off. As she left after breakfast, I felt transported back in time to her early days with us when visits to the docks occupied most of her spare time. She had changed a great deal since then, was no longer the swallow poised for flight. I watched her drive away and then went up to the back bedroom.

I had now completed the typewriting of my manuscript and had the some two hundred pages bound into a folder and with grim, now-or-never decision, I took out of the drawer the book that Sashie had brought to me from London. Opening it at the pages that listed literary agents, I took a hairpin out of my hair, straightened it, shut my eyes and stabbed it down on the book. 'Bush & Co. Ltd.,' said the hairpin, 'and address in London, W.C.2. Mm-mm-mm. Interested in work by new writers. Established 1910.'

'You will do,' I said aloud to Messrs. Bush. 'You have an earthy name, I am a new writer and you are the same age as I am.' I wrote a short letter informing them that I would be interested to have their views on this manuscript by Janet Sandison, that I was enclosing a cheque for one pound to cover its return postage, that all correspondence concerning it should be addressed to me and that I was theirs faithfully, Janet E. S. Alexander. I then wrapped manuscript, letter and cheque into a brown paper parcel, heaved a great sigh of relief and hoped that Sashie would call that forenoon as he had said he might. He did and I gave him the parcel, asked him to mail it for me in St. Jago Bay.

'A pleasure, darling,' he said. 'Registered airmail?'

'Certainly not,' I said. 'Are you mad? It is nothing urgent or important. Send it by ordinary surface.'

This caper, as George and Tom would call it, had already cost me a pound and that was plenty.

'Just as you say, my sweet,' he agreed with his sidelong mischievous glance. 'You are all alone this morning?'

'Percy has gone down to see Selina and Mary off. Twice and Mackie are down town too, at the Sugar Shippers' meeting.'

'A whole long day on your own then?'

'I have the Great House in the afternoon. People are never satisfied. Madame used to complain that Miss Poynter always fell asleep instead of talking to her and she is now complaining that Miss Spencer never stops talking.'

Sir Ian joined Madame, Miss Spencer and me for tea, after which his chauffeur drove me home. When we turned into the drive, Percy's car was sitting at the front door. When I went into the house, I heard her come out of her room up above but when she appeared on the staircase, I felt a cold leaden heave in the pit of my stomach. She was wearing the navy slacks and white shirt that she had worn for the regatta and over them a light white coat that billowed behind her like wings or the sails of a ship as she ran downstairs. And now I noticed the two suitcases in the corner of the hall. She came to rest at the foot of the stairs, as a bird comes momentarily to rest and said: 'Janet, I've seen him! He was at the rail of the *Niobe* as she left port!'

'And Niobe all tears,' I heard the echo in my mind from some poem read long ago.

'Who?' I asked. 'Who did you see?'

'Peter. The *Niobe* is cruising. She is calling at Port-of-Spain for a few hours and then going to Montevideo. I have been to the Line office. I am going straight to Montevideo. I have to be at the airport at six.'

As Sashie had said, I am a slow thinker except when I am angry and I was not angry now but filled with a desolation that seemed to fog my understanding, to clog my speech when I felt that there was so much I must say.

'But Percy, you can't do this!' I protested but, as she stood there, poised for flight, it was obvious that she could and the words died on the air. 'What about Mackie – Bruce? What—'

'I can't help it,' she said ruthlessly.

'But Percy,' I turned into the drawing-room and she followed me. 'Percy, this young man, Peter, you saw him only once and that was nearly two years ago. Anything could have happened since then. He could be married—'

'If he is I have to know.'

I sat down, lit a cigarettte, tried for cold hard reasoning. 'He may not even remember you or have any interest in you. You said yourself that he was all mixed up in your mind with your mother's illness and death. You may not have made anything like such an impression on him.'

'I have to know,' she repeated.

'Percy, this is rather a terrible thing you are doing to Bruce and to *Twice* too, Percy.'

'I know but I can't help it. Please, Janet, try to understand. I can't marry Bruce now anyway, not after seeing Peter again. I don't understand now how I ever thought I could marry Bruce. And if I don't go now, I shall lose Peter all over again.'

'But Percy,' I argued brutally, 'Peter is not yours to lose. He may not want to have anything to do with you.'

'I have to know,' came the four words again like the distant but persistent call of a bird.

'And when you get to Montevideo, what will you do? Walk up to him on the wharf and say: Remember me?' I asked bitterly.

She nodded her head, the pony-tail with its blue ribbon bobbing. 'Something like that,' she agreed. 'Janet, everything you have said makes sense but I have been through it all before again and again. When I used to go down to the docks, watching every ship, looking for him, I used to tell myself all these things you are saying. I even made myself believe them and stopped going to the docks. But now that I have seen him again, I don't believe them any more. I have to go and find him.'

New knowledge flowed upon me. 'You came out here to the island because of him in the first place?'

'Yes. He said that night that he wanted to transfer to a line that sailed to the Caribbean and South America.'

I had a slumping feeling of defeat, a desolate sense that her going was inevitable, like the swallows leaving Reach-far in September or the gawlens leaving the Great House lake at the end of June. She and they were moving in obedience to an instinctive law that had no basis in reason or logic and while she spoke of her gratitude to Twice and me, while she promised to write, while she told me how happy she had been with us and how sad at what she now had to do, I accepted that all the bonds of custom and affection could not hold someone who heard the call that she was hearing.

'I sent Caleb over to the house with a letter for Bruce,' she said. 'I am not good at letters but I did my best and I have left a letter upstairs for Twice. There are a few odds and ends of clothes on my bed that may do for Minna's grandchildren. And my car. I shall leave it in the Peak park and give the keys to the attendant. Please sell it and divide the money between Cookie and Caleb and Clorinda and Minna. You won't get much for it. It was second-hand when I bought it and it is only running because of Bruce.' She frowned, the glasses slipped and were replaced by the small straight forefinger. 'I am sorry about

Bruce but I can't help it. And it is better for him, this way.'

She went out to the hall and picked up a suitcase in each hand. She then stood on tiptoe and kissed me on the cheek. As she turned away, the air moved lightly as if a bird had flown past and she was gone.

Over an hour later, when Twice came home, I still had not collected myself but was sitting in a corner of the veranda, feeling stunned and giddy.

'What's up?' he asked at once.

'Mackie isn't with you?'

He jerked his head in the direction of the bungalow with the blue flowers. 'I dropped him at his house. Why?'

'Twice, Percy is gone.'

'Percy?' His face sharpened, his eyes became too hard and bright. 'Gone? What d'you mean gone? Where to?'

'Montevideo.'

'Montevideo? You must be mad!' he almost shouted.

'She left this for you.' I picked up the letter which I had brought downstairs and handed it to him. As if the white rectangle of paper carried more conviction than the spoken word, he dropped into a chair beside mine and looked with searching eyes into the darkness of the park. After a moment, he slit the envelope, took out the single sheet it contained, read it and handed it to me.

'Dear Twice, I am sorry to go away so suddenly and without saying goodbye but I have to do it because it is my only chance. I am sorry about everything but I cannot help it. Janet will explain and I hope to see you both again before too long. Thank you for being so kind to me. I shall never forget. Love, Persey.'

The first thought to come into my mind on reading the banal little note was that, in all the time she had been with us, I had known so little of her that I had even misspelled her nickname in my mind.

238

'What does she mean about you explaining?' Twice asked, then his voice became angry as he added: 'Did you and she quarrel?'

'No,' I said, wishing that we had indeed quarrelled, that the reason for her going might be in some way connected with him or myself, for the most desolating thing was that, compared with the young man she had seen at the rail of the *Niobe*, neither Twice, myself, Mackie nor anyone had the slightest importance for Percy. 'No,' I repeated. 'There was no quarrel with anybody.'

'Mackie? He seemed all right all day.'

We both looked across the park at the lights of the bungalow. 'She sent a letter over to him,' I said. 'He is probably reading it now and feeling a lot worse than we are.'

'You mean that she has thrown him over altogether?'

'Yes. I am afraid so.'

'But she can't do that!' he said loudly, banging the arm of his chair with his fist.

'Twice, there is simply no point in getting angry. She can and she has.'

He tried to be calm, succeeded in becoming cold, 'What is this explanation you can make?' he asked harshly. 'Hadn't you better set about it?'

'About a year past last April,' I began, 'she went to a party back in Liverpool—'

I told the story as exactly as I could and he listened to me with open disbelief at first which changed, later, to an astonished bleak sadness.

'She was really talking to me about her mother,' I said. 'Remember I told you at the time what a shock her mother's death must have been to her? And naturally, I was thinking about her mother too. I didn't think that this young man had any importance but she admitted today that she came out here to the islands because of him.'

The conversation between us went on through dinner which we ate with little interest and on into the evening, punctuated by long pauses during which we tried to assimilate what had happened.

'I feel cheated, hurt,' Twice said at one point. 'Is that childish? I simply never imagined that she would do this or anything like it to us.'

'I don't think young people realise how important they become to older people,' I said. 'They don't mean to be hurtful. I hurt my father many times but it was largely because I didn't realise how much he cared for me. And you cared for Percy, Twice, more than I did, I think.'

His teeth showed, gripping his lower lip. 'I certainly never thought she would do anything like this,' he repeated.

'One knows so little about people. I always thought of her as P-e-r-c-y. Did you know it was P-e-r-s-e-y?'

He rose from the table. 'Yes. I knew. It was short for Persephone, her father's nickname for her.'

There was a long silence, while I thought that, during these months, Twice and I had known in Percy two different people. He had known that he was calling her by the pet-name that her father had given her, with its associative link with the young spring goddess and she had arrived in his life at the precise time when the long slow recovery of his health was complete, when he was able to emerge fully into the world again after what looked, now, like a long winter of hibernation.

On the veranda again, we stood looking over at the lights of Mackie's bungalow.

'I wonder if I ought to go over there?' Twice said and then: 'Why in hell did she ever get engaged to Mackie?' he exploded angrily. 'If she had such a fixation on this other bloke, why get mixed up with Mackie? Especially a deep hell-and-high-water bloke like Mackie?'

'Twice, do sit down and try to look at this more calmly,' I said. 'We have been through something like this before with Dee Andrews and Roddy Maclean. People don't live in separate little pockets. They are influenced by the people around them. You and I kept Percy almost constantly in the company of Mackie. It is difficult to pinpoint where anything begins but I shouldn't be surprised if the Percy-Mackie thing was triggered off by you and me right here on this veranda, that day after Hugh Macbeth brought her home from the Yacht Club dance. Then there was Madame going on about how all young ladies ought to marry and about how Chief Engineers should have hostesses for their establishments and Heaven knows what else. These Percy-Mackie things don't take place in a void. No happening does. They are accidents of time and place and circumstance—'

'And how do you describe a happening like a young woman tearing off to Montevideo after a fellow she met once in a pub? If there isn't something of a happening in a void in that, I am the planet Neptune.'

'Twice, I know that in our convention it is an outlandish thing but the female does pursue the male. You have always said that I hunted you down and it is true. I did. But think of that old record of George Formby "I'm leaning on a lamp-post" that Percy was always playing – that and "I cover the waterfront".'

'What the hell have old records to do with it?'

'In modern terms, Percy was here in the West Indies, covering the waterfront, leaning on a lamp-post, at the corner of the street, waiting for her young man to come by. It is only the same old thing in modern terms, that's all.'

'I never heard such rubbish in my life.'

'And he came by,' I continued persistently. 'We had influenced her into not covering the waterfront or leaning on her lamp-post but the young man came by and in spite of all our influence she was there when he came.'

Twice was not even listening to me, too hurt and stupefied, it seemed on the surface, to see any sort of reason in what had happened but there was another under-the-surface factor which worried me more than his hurt and stupefaction.

Near-mortal illness and the recovery from it had caused

a change in his character which had been in abeyance for a year but which was showing again now. This was a curious distortion of the will. His recovery had been brought about as much by his will to live as by medical means and it was as if this will, having discovered its power, had become manic. He would accept no comfort or reason about what had happened, I felt now because, wilfully, he believed that by non-acceptance he could alter the turn of events. He was countering my every argument with a determined 'no' and in a wider sense he seemed to me to be throwing a defiant 'I *will* not!' in the face of life which made me feel a cold fear creeping through my flesh as I sat looking at the sullen heavy droop of his face and body.

'I wonder if I ought to go over there?' he repeated, looking again at the lights across the park. I made no reply and he answered himself: 'There is no point. All the talk in the world won't alter it' but he seemed to be implying: 'I won't talk about it but I won't accept it either.'

His face suddenly took on a mask of indifference which made him look strange, for he was not given to being indifferent about any subject. 'I don't understand what has happened,' he said coldly, 'but I don't suppose that matters.'

'To understand it, one would have to remember exactly what it felt like to be young and that is very difficult,' I said. 'We cannot see or feel like Percy any more.'

'I don't see that feeling comes into it very much,' he said and there was a defiant bitterness in this. 'Whatever feeling Percy had, it is not for us—' he looked towards Mackie's house '—or anybody,' he ended.

We were still sitting there, dropping disjointed remarks into the silence, when Mackie drove in and came up the steps. He was drunk, but in a cold controlled fashion and he seemed to see us and to speak to us from a great distance.

'You know what has happened, of course?' he asked

without preamble. 'I came over to say that I am leaving for Scotland tomorrow as planned. I don't want to disappoint my mother. Goodbye.'

He turned away and went down the steps while Twice got up to follow him. 'Mackie, listen—'

As if he did not hear and perhaps he did not, Mackie got into his car and drove away.

'Doesn't want to disappoint his mother,' Twice repeated quietly. 'Maybe—'

'Yes, Twice?'

'Nothing,' he said and turned away. 'There is no point in all this. We might as well go up to bed.'

I took a long time to go to sleep, not because of Percy or Mackie but because there was a sinister sound in the room that I had not heard for a long time. Twice was having difficulty in breathing. I felt that it would be true to say in cliché form that we had been 'stabbed to the heart' by what had happened but now the phrase was literally and terrifyingly true. Twice's heart had been affected by this sudden stress. A few hours had wiped out some of the long years of recovery.

In the days that followed, it was both exasperating and sad for me that everyone talked unendingly about Percy's flight, except Twice who might have gained some comfort if he could have brought himself to talk about it but he could not or would not. I tried in every way I could devise to rationalise for him what had happened, pointing out on the one hand how thoughtless and reckless we ourselves had been at her age and on the other how difficult it was for us to understand a financially independent young woman like Percy who had no responsibilities or family ties. The mention of family ties was a mistake that caused Twice's face to shrink and then to harden. Indeed, it was difficult to mention the subject at all without falling into error and I soon gave up my efforts although I was aware that his mind was given to little else.

In the meantime, Sir Ian, Madame and Miss Spencer

also thought of nothing else and they had no hesitation in making their thoughts heard. Twice was eluding Sir Ian among the covered ways, corners and galleries of the factory but it was less easy for me to elude him and we went over the same ground again and again. All I had told them was that Percy had decided that she did not want to marry Mackie and that she had gone to South America.

'After all,' was my refrain, 'girls do change their minds. She came out here originally as part of a travel tour and South America is quite logical as the next stage.'

I felt that there was no point in complicating the issue further by any mention of the young man, Peter. Madame was disappointed at the breaking of the engagement, irritated that Paradise had given the veranda gossips of the island a talking-point but she would have been outraged at the idea of a young woman pursuing round the ports of the world a young man whose name, even, she did not know. I was, in spite of myself, slightly outraged at this on my own part, felt that Percy's behaviour was absurd and ridiculous and I did not want to make it public.

With Sashie, it was a different matter. I told him the truth and then said: 'Twice is making himself ill, Sashie. It has hurt him dreadfully and he can't bring it into the open. Do you think you could make him see that he mustn't let it matter so much?'

'Darling, I can try but I don't think I shall get very far. Twice is not given to words. And if it does matter to him, he can't make it stop, you know. He became much too fond of her. It would have been better if he had fallen in love with her in the silly way that some men of his age do with young girls, but instead of that he came to love her as a daughter. That goes much deeper than any sexual thing. Sex?' He shrugged his shoulders. 'Tout lasse, tout casse, tout passe because in sexual love there is always an element of antagonism. But in the attachment that Twice formed for Percy, he allowed her to become part of himself and that is something that re-

mains. No man can be antagonistic to something in himself. The prophet who said that if one's right eye offended one, one should pluck it out was asking far too much of humankind.'

It is said that a common sorrow draws people together but Percy's going did not have this effect on Twice and me. On the contrary, the event drove itself between us like a wedge, bringing out all the basic differences between our two natures. Twice, by far more passionate, affectionate and by far less critically observant of people than I was and with the parental side of his nature which was not present in myself, had become emotionally involved with Percy and also with Mackie in a way that I could never have done. Twice, always accepted as more rational and logical than I was, could bring neither reason nor logic to bear on this situation and became angry, hurt or cynical when I tried to do so. And in the background there was always that stone-wall force of 'I *will* not'.

And the deteriorating health, which he would not admit, was a powerful factor. His reaction to his original illness had been a withdrawal into himself, a voluntary imprisonment within his own mind from which it had taken him nearly two years to break free and the withdrawal was repeating itself now. The more ill he became, the further he receded from myself.

But the difference between us that emerged most clearly of all was something that had been a matter of amusement and sometimes of exasperation between us down our years together. Twice had always been able to put the past behind him as I had never been able to do and he had often accused me of 'carrying forward all sorts of impedimenta' in my mind, but now a situation had arisen which he seemed to be unable to accept and put behind him because he had not carried forward in his mind the 'impedimenta' that would help him to accept it. He could no longer recall, as I could, the sense of driving immediacy that had sent Percy to Montevideo, the same drive that, many years ago, had caused Twice himself to marry Dinah and then leave her, as Percy had left Mackie, the same drive that had caused me to 'run away' with Twice, outraging the conventions of my family.

Desperately, as he withdrew further and further into himself, when Sashie failed to reach him, I even tried to draw this analogy between Percy and himself.

'It doesn't help to bring that up,' he responded coldly. 'It only points the fact that I, as well as Percy, had no decent scruples. Or maybe you are right to remind me that I have no right to criticise.'

'Twice, I think you are behaving really badly about this.'

'I am trying not to behave about it, as you call it, at all. Can't you let it alone?'

It is difficult to let alone something that is ever-present, that hangs over the day-to-day like a miasma, distorting the most ordinary meanings, giving undue significance to objects, even, like the closed door of what had been Percy's bedroom. I tried again on a different tack.

'Twice, I don't think we should wait till we go home next summer before we try to do something about the boy. Our adjutant in the Air Force was a solicitor from Glasgow. He was a nice bloke, a few years older than we are. I have his address in the Unit Club members' list. Shall I write to him?'

'No.'

'Will you write then?'

'No.'

'Why not?'

'I can't at the moment. I'll think about it. You see, I feel – God almighty, what have I got to give to the boy, to give to anybody? What right have I – Janet, let it alone. Please let it alone.'

I even made the plea that seemed to me almost like blackmail.

'Twice, you are not well. Your asthma is getting worse. Do you know how you are worrying me?'

'I am all right.' He was stonily defiant. 'I may have

got a slight cold but there is nothing to worry about. I am all right, I tell you.'

In this way, the first two weeks of December passed and Madame spoke a little less of Percy and her sudden flight and more of the 'festive season' which, from my point of view, loomed ahead like a leaden cloud. I remembered the quietly happy family party of the year before while my mind acted like a trapped squirrel as I wondered how Christmas Day was to be made bearable this year.

The cricket final between Paradise and Retreat had been fixed at the Paradise ground on the Saturday before Christmas and as the day came nearer, I reproached myself for my boredom and even irritation when the fever had been at its height. Now, in the silence of the days, I would have been grateful to have the table at meals and the veranda in the evenings dominated by talk of cricket or by talk on any subject, yet I avoided the garden and Caleb's enthusiasm, for it was too strongly in contrast to the lack of interest shown by Twice. I was doubtful if he would even attend the match for, once the nine till four routine of the working day was over, he lapsed into lassitude, a book which he did not read held between his hands. Since Percy had gone, I had shortened my afternoon visits to the Great House and was being driven back to Guinea Corner at four o'clock to have tea with Twice. On the Friday afternoon before the match, I came home as usual, Clorinda brought the tea-tray as usual but Twice did not arrive. As the minutes ticked past, I became more and more anxious and at five o'clock I had just asked Caleb to go up to the factory when the car turned into the drive. Slowly, Twice got out and slowly came up the few steps on to the veranda. His eyes were glittering with a cold unnatural blue light, the bones of his skull were showing through the skin, his white shirt and shorts were filthy and clinging with sweat to his body. But his eyes were the most frightening of all, for around them, were pale rings of clean skin, standing out against the black dust that covered the rest of his face. With my reason, I knew that he had been wearing welding goggles but reason was away beyond the horizon at that moment. I sprang out of my chair and the tea things jerked and rattled.

'Twice, what have you been doing?'

'Building a lemonade barrow.' His breath was coming in short gasps, the pulse under his jaw throbbing hard, fluttering, then giving another jerking throb.

'A lemonade barrow?' I heard myself say, high and shrill.

'Christie handed it over to the apprentices.' He reached out and put his hand for support on the doorpost of the house. 'They made a Paddy's hash of it. Couldn't let it be seen on the Paradise ground. Had to make a new one. Must have a bath.' Unsteadily, he went into the hall, paused for a moment looking at the stairs, then walked past them along the back hall towards the ground-floor bathroom. I pushed open the door of the study and propelled him towards the surgical bed which was covered with a sheet, pushed him down to sit on it.

'Dirty,' he said. 'Need a bath.'

'I'll sponge you here.'

'No.'

'Please, Twice.'

He became bored. 'All right.'

I unbuttoned the shirt, stripped it off and threw it on the floor, threw the rest of his clothing after it, then kneeled down to unlace his shoes.

'Get up,' he panted. 'I'll do it.'

I ignored him, unlaced the shoes, peeled off the knee-length ribbed stockings. His insteps, ankles and legs were grossly swollen, the skin showing the indentations of the shoe laces, even the marks of the fine cotton ribbing of the stockings. 'Oh, Twice,' I said, 'that you should have done this for a lemonade barrow!'

The moment the ugly reproachful words were out of my mouth, I regretted them. Standing now, I looked down at the infinite sadness of his face, found it unbearable and turned away to fetch water and towels.

When I had sponged him, I telephoned Doctor Mark Lindsay who had brought him through his original illness. At that time, I had been terribly afraid but now I was beyond fear and lost in a desolate hopelessness. At that other time, Doctor Mark had alleviated the fear but this time he did nothing to dispel the hopelessness. His examination was short and silent. The sedative was administered and he led me out of the study to the veranda.

'I shall send up two nurses,' he said.

'Yes. Yes. Anything.'

There was nothing more to be said. He knew and I knew that there were no weapons to fight the bleak indifference that had taken hold of Twice. It was dark now and the lights of his car, as he drove away, looked weak and puny in the blackness of the night.

I sat on, huddled in a corner of the veranda. The nurses arrived and took charge with quiet efficiency. Sir Ian came, spoke in whispers and then went away. Then Caleb came to me and said: 'Minna sends these, ma'am, the things from the Chief's pockets.' He put the few things on the table beside me, the wallet with the driving licence and a few bank notes, the bunch of keys. There was a piece of white paper, badly stained with sweat, which must have been in the breast pocket of the shirt. I opened it out and read the words: 'Dear Sir, Sir Ian will have told you that I have resigned from Paradise. I am very sorry and will never forget working with you or all you have done for me but after what has happened I do not feel that I can come back. I have asked Sir Ian to take into account leave due to me as notice of the termination of my contract—' There was more but I did not read it. This was the blow that had called forth the violent physical protest, the blow that had caused Twice to put up a fight against circumstance, a fight which was too much for his physical resources. But the protest was only the culmination of many things that had gone before. Where had it all begun? Where did anything begin? Beginnings could never be traced but endings were distinct and clear.

Paradise beat Retreat and won the cricket tournament and Christmas and New Year came and went but Guinea Corner lay unheeding in its pool of silence. There was a postcard from Montevideo: 'He was on relief and left the ship at Trinidad but I know his name now. Leaving for London tomorrow. Love to you and Twice. P.' I could not bear to tell Twice about this. There was a letter from Liz: 'Dear Aunt Janet, This is to thank you and Uncle Twice for our Christmas money and to tell you about our plans—' I tried to read this letter to him, also the one from George and Tom but his effort to be even mildly interested was an obvious failure, for which he wore a mild air of apology. His reactions and responses were few and all were mild, gleaming momentarily like a watery moon through the clouds of his morbid indifference.

The household adapted itself to a routine that revolved round the tilted surgical bed in the study. I had my little sessions in there by the bedside, a forenoon visit when the post came, an afternoon visit at tea-time, a goodnight visit at bed-time. In between, Twice lay on his back, neat, tidy, either asleep under sedation or half awake, his face expressing nothing but that dreadful indifference. When I was not beside the bed, I wandered round the house, attending automatically to the housekeeping and to the needs of the nurses but I too was weighed down by indifference, indifference towards all the visitors and enquirers, indifference even towards people I loved like Sashie and Sir Ian.

On the first Tuesday of the New Year, Paradise went into Crop under the chiefship of two temporary engineers engaged by Edward Dulac, who had flown out from London with them. Edward himself took over the paper work in Twice's office at the factory but even Crop, the heartbeat of Paradise, was muffled and lost in the cloud of nothingness that lay over Guinea Corner. One forenoon, out of an uprush of sheer desperation, I said: 'Twice, I believe that Mackie will come back.'

His eyes changed. I held my breath. I had broken the barrier. Then 'No,' he said. 'I didn't go back after I walked out on Dinah's father.'

I felt as if I had been thrown to the ground but I gathered my forces and tried again. 'Mackie cared for you more than you ever cared for Dinah's father.'

'No,' he said, turned his head away from me and closed his eyes as if in ineffable boredom.

On a forenoon about the middle of January, I carried the mail to the study. It was an 'overseas letter' day and there was one from my family, in reply to my letter which had told them of Twice's illness. I read only parts of it aloud to him but he did not evince even a polite show of interest, so I put it aside and automatically slit open the other envelope that lay on my lap. I had reached the stage of wondering why I bothered him and myself with this daily farce. Why couldn't I accept – Accept what? With a shudder, I clenched my teeth and tried to concentrate on the sheet of paper that I had unfolded. 'Dear Mrs. Alexander, We have today discovered that by an oversight the manuscript by Janet Sandison which you sent to us was not acknowledged on receipt. We apologise for this but we are happy to inform you that we have shown this work to Messrs. Canterbury, Arden & Co. Ltd. who have today informed us that they are interested to publish it. We are shortly to meet them to discuss terms of contract—'

A cold paralysis seemed to grip me. Here, within my grasp, was something that I had wanted for years, the realisation of a long-cherished dream but I knew no joy, only an icy fear. I clenched my fists above the sheet of paper as I fought for calm but it seemed that some vibration from my mind broke through to Twice, for he turned his head languidly on the pillow and looked at me with a faint shadow of a question in his eyes. I knew a gleam of hope. Perhaps this extraordinary thing would break through the indifference, perhaps it would even make him angry.

'Twice,' I swallowed, trying to steady my voice, 'don't be angry. All these years I have been sitting around, I have written a novel and people in London want to publish it.'

'Novel? Publish it?' His eyes opened wide and they stared at me, bright blue, distant, as if I were some creature he had never seen before and I felt a stab of agonising loneliness. He looked away from me now and round the room, then back at my face again as if he were looking, astonished, at things that were no longer part of the world that he knew, of a world that he no longer wanted to know. And now the astonishment faded from the eyes. The veil of indifference was creeping back as he smiled with faint wryness, let his heavy eyelids with the crescents of black lashes fall over his eyes and said: 'Some people build lemonade barrows. Some people write books.' That was the last moment of communication between Twice and me, that moment when he seemed to point out our isolation in separate worlds, to point out that fundamentally every human being stands enshrouded in his own loneliness.

He died twelve days later. He died late in the evening, on a Saturday, I remember.

Sashie had come up that afternoon and he and I sat upstairs in the back bedroom while Sir Ian and Edward made the arrangements that had to be made. It is possible to be materially capable, even efficient, while the animation of the mind is suspended. I was aware of nothing except guilt. As if trapped in a circular cage, my mind went round and round and over and over the things I should never have done. When given the opportunity to use my influence, I should never have agreed to his taking charge of Paradise, knowing as I did that it would call forth his manic drive towards perfectionism. I should never have asked Percy to stay. I should never have let the matter of his son be lost among the daily trivia. I should never have grabbed at every opportunity to retire to the back bedroom where we were now sitting instead of guarding his health by watching him. I should never have allowed him to rush about to meetings and cricket matches. I should never— The word 'never' recurred and recurred, like the tolling of a bell, but in spite of it time moved on and life with it, demanding that things should be done.

I remember dictating the cablegram to be sent to my brother and I remember interviewing the minister who was to conduct the funeral service at three on the Sunday afternoon.

'The important thing,' I told him, 'is that there should be no singing.'

The minister was a middle-aged man and he looked at me with a mixture of astonishment, disapproval and obstinacy which made me feel guilt at outraging his conventions but none the less I turned to Sashie and said: 'He was always embarrassed by what he called the scraggy singing.'

'There will be no singing at the service,' Sashie told the minister and he did not express astonishment, disapproval, obstinacy or anything any more. His face seemed to fade away momentarily, like the face of the Cheshire Cat.

'Janet,' Sashie said, 'tell us how you would like the service to be conducted.'

'If they would just read the Lord's Prayer, then the metrical version of the twenty-third psalm, then commit the body – that is all.'

It was about ten o'clock on the Sunday morning when the minister went away and I apologised to him for causing this extra duty on his busy day of the week. That was another manifestation of the guilt that lay over everything I touched. Sashie took him downstairs and came back again.

'Darling,' he said, 'you must come downstairs now. Madame Dulac is down below.'

'Madame?'

The first thing I felt was guilt, guilt that we should be the cause of bringing this old lady out of her own house for the first time in years. But then I was aware of a pride in her fortitude that seemed to breed fortitude in myself. When I went down, she was standing in the hall between Sir Ian and Edward, tiny, indomitable, dignified, a black lace scarf over her white hair, immaculate white gloves on her hands.

'Madame—' I said.

'My dear Janet,' I had never before heard her voice quiver, had never before seen tears in her eyes, 'you will never know how gladly I would have gone in his stead.'

It was now that I began to cry. I cried for a long time and when I looked up, Mackie was standing in front of my chair, looking down at me with his big dark eyes.

'Missis Janet, I came back—'

All I could do was to shake my head from side to side and say: 'Sashie, please will you re-arrange the pall-bearers? Mackie must be beside Caleb.'

'Mr. Sashie,' said Madame, 'be good enough to conduct Janet upstairs and when everything is over, please bring her to me at the Great House.'

I was longing now for everything to be over. There had been too much in too little time but at last I was sitting between Sashie and Sir Ian in Sir Ian's car, a little way behind the white ambulance which was going to the burial ground on the other side of the Great House, near the lake.

I stood at the end of the deep grave that was lined with ferns and sprays of flowers and there were flowers in pools and swathes round my feet that reminded me of the lurid light of the hurricane. The minister spoke the prayer but as he began to read the psalm, there came a single note from Caleb's guitar which struck him to an astonished silence. Standing in his place beside Mackie, Caleb began

254

to sing and the huge concourse of factory and field workers who stood packed inside the burial ground and in thick ranks in the park beyond its walls joined him.

> 'The Lord's my Shepherd, I'll not want,
> He makes me down to lie,
> In pastures green; He leadeth me
> The quiet waters by.'

As the voices rose towards the faraway sky, the gawlens, who had returned in the course of their mysterious wanderings to the Great House lake, rose and sailed snowy white above the trees. They reminded me of a time of happiness, when there had been with us my friend Percy, the swallow.